W9-BAF-235

WIDOW'S WREATH

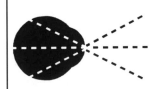

This Large Print Book carries the
Seal of Approval of N.A.V.H.

A MARTHA'S VINEYARD MYSTERY

WIDOW'S WREATH

CYNTHIA RIGGS

THORNDIKE PRESS
A part of Gale, a Cengage Company

Farmington Hills, Mich • San Francisco • New York • Waterville, Maine
Meriden, Conn • Mason, Ohio • Chicago

Copyright © 2018 by Cynthia Riggs.
Thorndike Press, a part of Gale, a Cengage Company.

Thorndike Press® Large Print Mystery.
The text of this Large Print edition is unabridged.
Other aspects of the book may vary from the original edition.
Set in 16 pt. Plantin.

LIBRARY OF CONGRESS CIP DATA ON FILE.
CATALOGUING IN PUBLICATION FOR THIS BOOK
IS AVAILABLE FROM THE LIBRARY OF CONGRESS

ISBN-13: 978-1-4328-6351-7 (hardcover)

Published in 2019 by arrangement with The Quick Brown Fox & Company LLC.

Printed in Mexico
1 2 3 4 5 6 7 23 22 21 20 19

A12007 272746

For
Dionis Coffin Riggs,
Poet
1898–1997

CHAPTER ONE

Victoria Trumbull stood at the entry door, watching a tall, bearded young man in denim shorts, boots, and stained T-shirt emerge from the cellar, walking sideways up the narrow stone steps. The bulkhead doors were open, and the young man was brushing cobwebs from his bearded face and dark hair, unreeling what looked like miles of white electrical wire from a spool. Presumably, he had plugged the other end into the overhead electrical outlet at the foot of the cellar steps.

"Does that take care of your electrical needs?" Victoria, at ninety-two, still thought in terms of candlelight for weddings.

The young man looked up and grinned. "No ma'am. We need four separate circuits."

"What in the world for?"

"Heaters, sound system, fryers, lights, cookers — you know — all that."

"Fryers?" asked Victoria, puzzled. "Sound

systems?"

He stepped over the sill onto the grass, freshly cut on this beautiful May day. The lilacs, in full bloom, perfumed the air, and below the heavily blossomed branches, tall stalks of delicate white flowers swayed in the light breeze.

"Don't want to put too much of a load on your electrical circuits. They look pretty old." He headed toward the west pasture, leaving a trail of white wire behind him, like crumbs marking his return path.

Victoria, shaking her head in bemusement, made her way back into the kitchen, where her granddaughter, Elizabeth, was making sandwiches and chatting with Penny, the bride.

Penny, a twenty-five-year-old blond with almost white hair and a golden, even tan, though it was only mid-May, was sitting in one of the kitchen chairs. She stood up, with the squeak of bare flesh separating from the painted chair. "Thank you soooo much, Cousin Victoria. What a great wedding present, having our reception here."

Victoria tried to look pleasant. "I imagined cake, lemonade, and white wine. I didn't realize you needed four electrical circuits."

"You're so charmingly old fashioned!" Penny clasped her hands under her chin.

"That's what I love about you, Cousin Victoria." She was almost as tall as Victoria and was wearing a skimpy white halter that showed off shoulders and collarbones. Below the halter, Victoria noticed a navel stoppered with what looked like a large diamond. She tried to look away modestly, but couldn't help seeing the ragged cutoff jeans that barely covered what was necessary. The bride was barefoot. "Rocco is so thrilled that we're getting married on Martha's Vineyard. He wants us to do it up right. And Cousin Victoria" — she held out her arms, and Victoria plopped down into the chair at the head of the table to avoid the hug she saw coming — "Cousin Victoria, this will be a wedding to beat all the weddings that have ever taken place on this Island."

Victoria thought of the crates of orchids that had been flown in from Hawaii for one wedding, of the white doves that had been released at the Gay Head Lighthouse for another. She wrapped her arms around herself to control a shudder.

Penny did a sort of pirouette on tiptoe, her hands holding her hair out in a fan. "They're coming with the tents this afternoon."

"Tents," said Victoria. "More than one?"

9

"There's always something," said Elizabeth. "Besides, Cousin Penny is a compulsive shopper.

"Um . . . Mrs. Trumbull?" The electrician knocked on the side of the kitchen door. Watery sunlight made its way into the entry, turning the old bottles Victoria had perched on top of the window sashes to muted shades of emerald, ruby, and gold.

"Can I help you?" she asked. "By the way, what's your name?"

"Mark," he replied. "Mark Johnson." He stepped up into the kitchen. "Mind if I take down that dummy? It's in the way of one of the lines I need to run."

"Dummy?" Victoria, puzzled, eased herself up from her seat at the kitchen table. "What dummy?"

"Left over from Halloween, I guess. Unless you had a treasure hunt or something."

Victoria shook her head. "I have no idea what you're talking about."

Mark heaved a sigh and shifted from one booted foot to the other. "I got to run a wire across the ceiling in the cellar, Mrs. Trumbull. It's in the way." He lifted both hands, palms up. "I'll take it down if you don't mind."

"I suppose I'd better take a look," said Victoria.

Mark followed her out of the entry and across the patch of bright grass to the cellar. The fog bank to the west was rolling in and had already hidden the view of the town center in the distance.

The bulkhead doors were open, and the smell of old brick, stone, and dry earth wafted up from the cellar.

Victoria let Mark go down the narrow stone steps first, and she followed, carefully bracing her hand against the cold stone walls. At the foot of the steps, she waited a few moments, standing next to Mark until her eyes adjusted to the gloom. She'd always loved this cellar, with its uneven brick floor, stone walls, and racks of clean jars for pickles and jelly. At one time, Jonathan, her husband, had tried to grow mushrooms down here. The cellar was too dry, and the mushroom bed was still here, still full of dried manure.

Mark, next to her, said, "Great place for Halloween. Pretty spooky with all those cobwebs. You got some busy spiders."

By now Victoria's eyes had adjusted to the gloom, and she didn't hear him. She saw what hung from the heavy beams. The object, draped in a cloth, swung gently in the air they'd stirred up. Her first thought had been, like Mark's, that it was a dummy, and what was it doing here?

Her second thought was one she would prefer to dismiss: that it looked very much like a body, hung by the neck, its sheet-wrapped head lolling to one side. She stepped around the boxes of old bottles and across the bricks to where it swung from a dirty nylon rope, completely covered — head, shoulders, body, even feet.

"Unh," said Mark, who'd apparently realized at the same time as Victoria what they were looking at. "Mrs. Trumbull?"

Victoria glanced around at him. "Do you have your cell phone?"

He started to pull it out of his pocket and dropped it.

"Oh shit." He glanced at her. "Pardon me." He bent down, picked up his phone, and brushed it off.

"If it's not broken, see if you can reach 911," said Victoria. "Tell them there's a body in my cellar."

CHAPTER TWO

About the same time the electrician was punching 911 into his cell phone, the bartender at the Tidal Rip, a weary-looking woman in her forties with sparse black hair, and a nametag that read "Toni" approached the four young men sitting at the bar. "You guys old enough to drink?" She wiped her hands on the towel tucked into the belt of her slacks. "Need to see picture IDs. All of you."

"It's been years since I was carded," said the lanky young man at the end of the row. He pushed a lock of dark hair out of his eyes.

"Heard that before," said the bartender, waiting. "Kind of early to start celebrating whatever."

"Never too early," said a boyish guy with red hair.

One by one they hauled out wallets and slapped driver's licenses onto the bar. She gathered them up and started to leave.

There was a mutter of protest.

"Hey, where you going?" asked the lanky guy. He got up from his bar stool.

She sighed and turned back. "Making copies. Got a problem with that?"

He folded his arms across his chest and frowned. "Yeah. I got a problem." The frown emphasized a thin white scar that ran down the left side of his face from his hairline to his mouth, giving him a sort of sinister look. "Never seen that before."

"Well, now you have. You want something to drink, or you want your licenses back right now?"

"Forget it, Cosimo," said the man at the other end of the row, the only one who hadn't protested. "Sorry about these juveniles, ma'am. Do what you have to do." He smiled at her, showing fine white teeth and intense black eyes. His chin had a haze of dark beard.

She sorted through the licenses checking each one carefully, then looked up. "You Rocco?"

"The same. We'll all have whatever single malt scotch you got. Straight up. I'm paying."

"You want lunch to go with the booze?"

"Why not?" said Rocco. "Couple of large

pizzas with everything" — he squinted at her nametag — "Toni."

"No anchovies," said the redhead. "I hate anchovies."

"That okay, Rocco?" asked Toni.

"Whatever." He waved a hand in dismissal.

She turned away from the bar and was gone for several minutes. When she returned, she was carrying empty whiskey glasses, which she set down, one in front of each of the four men. "Pizza will be out in ten minutes." She retrieved their licenses from a pocket and dealt them out to their owners. She glanced from the redhead next to Cosimo to the photo on his card. "Just made it, didn't you, Red? Happy birthday. That what you're celebrating?"

"Nope." Red pointed his thumb at Rocco. "He's getting married."

"That right? Local girl?"

"Kinda sorta," Red began, but Rocco interrupted.

"My fiancée is Victoria Trumbull's cousin Penelope Arbuthnot." He stumbled over her last name.

"Know her pretty well, don'tcha?"

Rocco flushed.

The bartender reached down a bottle from a high shelf, opened it, and poured

17

golden liquid into the four glasses.

"Rocco here is one lucky dude," said a pudgy guy with rosy cheeks and short blond hair sitting on Red's left. He held up his glass.

"Hear, hear, Elmer," said Red holding up his own glass. "To Rocco and what's-her-name. Martha's Vineyard, playground of the rich and famous."

"Victoria Trumbull may be famous," said the bartender, "but she sure as hell ain't rich."

"The bride has enough to live on, right, Rocco? Tents, caterers, florists." Elmer rubbed a thumb and finger together.

Rocco, flush fading, scowled at him. "Watch it," he said.

Elmer ran a finger around the inside of his black turtleneck collar. "Warm in here, isn't it."

"Live music," said Red. "Awesome."

"You haven't seen many Vineyard weddings, then." She swiped a damp cloth over the bar. "So when's the date, Rocco?"

"This Saturday." Rocco turned in his seat and put a hand on the back of the empty barstool next to him. "Anybody seen Dominic? He's supposed to be here by now. Doing his usual fuckup, I suppose."

Cosimo had seated himself again at the

far end of the group of barstools. "He flying in?"

The bartender dropped her cloth into the sink beneath the bar with a splash. "No flights came in this afternoon. Fog."

"Fog?" asked Red. "I don't see any fog."

"You will. It's out there. Moving in."

Rocco said, "Dominic won't fly. He'd be on one of the afternoon boats."

"I suppose the boats aren't running either," said Cosimo, picking up his glass and taking a swig. He brushed the stray strand of hair off his forehead again.

"Fog won't stop the ferries," said Toni. "Wind does."

"Don't worry — he's Rocco's best man. He wouldn't miss his brother's funeral." Elmer punched Red on the shoulder and chortled. "Oh, excuse me, Rocco, I meant *wedding.*"

"Funny," said Rocco. "Very, very funny. I should've known better than to ask my asshole brother to be best man."

"Who else would agree to the job?" said Cosimo.

"Think you're funny, don't you," said Rocco. "Well, you're not."

The state police responded to the 911 call. By the time Victoria reached the top of the

19

cellar steps, the cruiser had pulled to a stop, with Sergeant John Smalley driving and Trooper Tim Adams riding shotgun.

Smalley swiveled out of his seat. He was a tall, handsome man with thinning hair, a former football player, and Victoria was glad to see him.

"What's this about a body?" asked Smalley.

Victoria, out of breath, gestured toward the cellar. "You'd better see for yourself, John. We didn't disturb anything."

Victoria Trumbull was an official deputy in the West Tisbury police force. This had come about after she had backed her car into the Meals on Wheels van, doing considerable damage. Chief Mary Kathleen (Casey) O'Neill had confiscated her driver's license. Seeing Victoria's distress, the chief offered to give the elderly woman a ride any time she needed one, and Victoria, of course, climbed into the shotgun seat and became a much welcome source of information, advice, and common sense in police inquiries. Casey, acknowledging Victoria's worth, named her a deputy and presented her with a police hat. Gold lettering stitched across the front read "West Tisbury Police Deputy." Victoria carried the hat with her wherever she went.

Smalley climbed down the steps and emerged a few minutes later, wiping a cobweb from his forehead. "I've contacted Doc Jeffers, this week's medical examiner. He'll be here shortly. I'll be calling the forensics people to get here as soon as possible."

"I thought it was a dummy. It was pretty realistic." Mark moved off to one side. "Looks like I don't work on the electricity for the reception for a while."

"They won't be having a reception here for a while," replied Smalley.

Earlier in the morning, before all this commotion happened, Victoria had dug up Jerusalem artichokes from the west end of the vegetable garden. They had not yet started to sprout and were full of all the good energy that would go into making ten-foot-tall sunflower plants. That good energy meant delicious eating. The Island's Wampanoags had made the "sun roots" a staple part of their diets long before the European settlers discovered them.

Later that afternoon, while she was scrubbing earth off a knobby tuber, Sergeant Smalley knocked on the side of the open door and strode into the kitchen.

Doc Jeffers, the medical examiner, had

declared the victim officially dead. An autopsy would determine time and actual cause of death. Toby, the undertaker, would then take the body in his hearse to the funeral home, where it would await identification.

Victoria looked up from her work. "Hello, John. Have you been able to identify the person yet?"

"No one seems to know the victim's identity." Smalley took a bandana handkerchief out of his pocket and wiped his forehead. "Fog's gotten pretty thick. Almost a drizzle." He put his handkerchief back into his pocket. "Hate to ask you this, Mrs. Trumbull, but wondered if you might . . . ?" He glanced at her.

"I'll be glad to help in any way I can." Victoria dropped the tuber back into the bowl of water, tore a paper towel off the holder over the sink, and dried her hands. "Is he — or she — still in the cellar?"

"No, ma'am. We've taken him out. It's a male. The cellar's so dry, the body . . . decomposition hasn't . . ." He glanced at her and didn't finish.

"I know," said Victoria, thinking of the failed mushroom farm. She started toward the door.

"Getting chilly out there," said Smalley.

"You might want a sweater."

"Yes, of course." Victoria slipped on the tan cardigan she'd earlier draped over the back of one of the kitchen chairs, and followed Smalley outside.

The fog bank that had loomed on the horizon most of the day had closed in. Tendrils of mist swirled around the tall cedars in the west pasture and drifted around the stalks of bridal wreath in bloom below the lilacs.

Trooper Tim was standing guard over the body, covered now with the cloth that had been draped around it while it dangled from the cellar beam. Tim's hair was pearled with droplets of fog — even his eyebrows had beads of moisture. He was wearing a short-sleeved uniform shirt and was shivering.

He bent down and uncovered the victim's head when Victoria approached. "They wanted you to have a look before they took him away, Mrs. T. See if by any chance you might know him."

The victim had dark, curly hair and had probably been quite handsome, but not now. His wrinkled face was an ugly purplish-gray. His tongue and eyes protruded.

Sergeant Smalley stood behind Victoria. "Doc Jeffers figures him to be anywhere from twenty-five to thirty-five years of age, in pretty good shape except for scars on the lower half of his body, possibly the result of an automobile accident." He glanced at Victoria, who was studying the victim. "Dead for some time, several days at least."

Victoria shook her head. "I've never seen him before."

"We left the rope in place, pending the autopsy."

"I understand whoever does the autopsy will determine what killed him, whether it was hanging or something else." She looked up at Smalley, who was several inches taller than she. "I wonder if he was a wedding guest."

"You mentioned a reception. Who's getting married?"

"Penny Arbuthnot, a young cousin of mine. Her wedding is this Saturday, and she's invited several hundred guests to the reception. She planned to have it here."

"She'll have to postpone the reception." Smalley took a notebook from his shirt pocket. "If the victim is related to the wedding, every guest could potentially be a person of interest. Can you get me a copy of her guest list?"

"Of course."

"I can't believe it, Cousin Victoria!" Penny,

the bride, had been upstairs in her room when Victoria called to her to come downstairs. She too had been asked if she could identify the body and, like Victoria, had never seen him before. "It's gross, that thing under the sheet. Why ask me? I don't know who he is." She seated herself with a plop on the gray painted chair in Victoria's kitchen. "They can't postpone the reception. It's all paid for. It cost me a fortune."

Tears started to flow, followed by sobs. Victoria tore another paper towel off the rack and handed it to her.

"Thank you," Penny mumbled.

"The tents haven't arrived yet. I'm sure you can cancel their delivery," said Victoria.

"I don't know why they demand that we postpone the reception. *I* didn't put the body there." Penny choked back another sob and dabbed at her eyes, careful not to smear the eyeliner. "What a mean thing for someone to do, to leave a body in your cellar."

"Indeed," said Victoria.

"What are my guests going to think?"

"You don't need to postpone the wedding, just the reception."

"The only reason for the wedding is the reception," said Penny, glancing up, her large eyes magnified by tears. "That's the point of the whole thing."

"I'm sure we can find another place for your reception." Victoria turned back to the sink and the Jerusalem artichokes yet to be scrubbed. She picked up the vegetable brush. "The police need a copy of your guest list, Penny. Would you see that they have it? You said you'd invited two hundred?"

Penny nodded. "Most of them are already here. Staying at a fancy hotel in Edgartown. And a lot more are coming. It's not until Saturday. That's three days from now." She let out another long sob.

"The police need your guest list," Victoria said again.

"I suppose they think one of my guests killed this unknown man." Penny choked back another sob. "That's so embarrassing."

"The victim may be one of your guests."

Penny shook her head. "I never saw him before," she said again.

"One of your fiancé's friends, perhaps someone you've never met."

Penny shook her head, and her pale hair swirled around her shoulders. A few strands stuck to her wet face. She brushed them away. "Rocco thinks I'm as rich as he is. I mean, Martha's Vineyard, our family home, family roots. But you know, Cousin Victoria . . ."

"Yes, I certainly do," said Victoria, turning back to the sink.

"His family has money. Bufano Industries. I mean a *lot* of money. I need to impress them." Despite the care she'd taken in dabbing at her eyes, the eyeliner had smeared, leaving black streaks on her face. "I spent every cent I had. I maxed out my credit cards. I borrowed money from my friends." She held the paper towel against her eyes. "What am I going to do? How could someone do this to me!"

Victoria continued to scrub the knobby vegetables in her sink. "One of the costs of murder, I'm afraid."

CHAPTER THREE

Mark, the electrician, was standing by his truck, with wisps of fog swirling about him, when Penny stormed out of Victoria's kitchen, her hair streaming behind her. Her tanned legs were especially fetching in the misty dim light.

"Sorry about your reception," he said as she flew past him to her car, parked near his truck.

"You're not half as sorry as I am. I've had to pay for all this."

"Yeah, well I can't get my equipment out of the cellar." Mark studied Penny, from her streaky face to the glass diamond in her naval, to her bare legs and high-heeled sandals. "Aren't you cold?"

She glared at him.

He shrugged. "I'm supposed to wire four more wedding receptions for Saturday and another two for Sunday." He scowled at her. "I gotta make a living. Unlike some people."

"Oh, tough!" sputtered Penny. She continued to her car. She flung open the car door, paused for an instant, drew her hands up to her face, and screamed.

Stretched across the front seat, head lolling facedown on the passenger side, was a young man. When she opened the door, his legs, which were bent at the knees, straightened, and his feet, clad in boat shoes, no socks, flopped down, smacking her on her bare thighs.

Mark had been about to step up into his truck. He swiveled around, saw what appeared to be a dead body, reached into his pocket for his cell phone, and punched in 911.

Penny stood, eyes wide, hands up to her face, further smearing the eyeliner, which already made her cheeks appear cadaverous.

The young man in the car moved.

Penny screamed again and backed away.

Mark raced toward her, his phone at his ear.

Victoria, hearing the screams, abandoned her vegetable brush and made her way, as quickly as she could, out the door and down the steps.

As she approached, Mark looked up from his phone. "Yeah, Mrs. Trumbull. I know the 911 drill."

The young man in Penny's car moved again.

He groaned.

He rubbed his eyes.

He braced an arm against the dashboard and pried himself up in a series of jerks to a semi-sitting position. He focused his eyes unsteadily on Penny.

Penny stumbled backward until she fetched up against a tree. She slid down into a sitting position, her back against the trunk.

The man mumbled, "Who're you?"

His breath and clothing reeked of liquor.

"Where in hell am I?" He dropped onto his back and slung an arm across his face.

Victoria moved as quickly as she could, stopping just short of the car. "What is going on?"

Penny stared at the man in the car. Her hands had dropped by her sides.

Mark said into his phone, "Sorry. Everything's okay after all."

"Who is that man?" Victoria asked Penny.

Penny shook her head.

Mark stepped away and said into his phone, "Sorry. Looks like he's not dead."

The man snored.

Victoria wiped her hands on a dish towel she'd grabbed when she heard the scream.

"Penny, do you know who that man is?"

Penny nodded and muttered something.

"What did you say? Speak up!"

"Dominic." Penny glanced up at Victoria. "Rocco's brother."

Mark folded the phone and put it back into his pocket.

"Your fiancé's brother? What is he doing here in your car?" asked Victoria.

Mark went over to Penny's car. Dominic's lower legs hung down from the driver's seat, his feet almost touching the ground. The rest of his body was slumped like a sack of onions across the driver's and passenger's seats.

"Better get this guy out into the fresh air before he messes up your car."

Dominic was a bulky man. Mark grabbed one of his arms and tried to wrestle him into a sort of fireman's carry, but he was a dead weight.

Dominic mumbled, "Don't like this."

Mark half-dragged, half-carried him over to a grassy spot under the Norway maples and lowered him to the ground.

"He's going to get soaking wet and chilled lying there," said Victoria. "Call your fiancé, Penny, and get him here right away. We need help getting his brother into the house.

Then get a blanket from the upstairs closet to cover him."

At the Tidal Rip, Rocco slapped three hundred-dollar bills onto the bar and stood.

Toni shoved one of the bills back at him along with a fifty and change.

"Keep it." Rocco stretched and yawned.

"You leaving me a hundred-and-fifty dollar tip?" For once, the bartender was nonplussed.

"Why not? I'm marrying a rich bitch."

"I'm not so sure about that 'rich' part, but thanks."

"You're welcome."

She scooped up the money, reached up, and tucked it into her bra.

Rocco turned to the three still sitting. "C'mon, you guys. We got to find Dominic. Dry him out before the wedding." He headed toward the door, muttering, "A drunk best man. Just what I need to impress the rich bitch's family."

"Un momento," said Red, holding up his half-full glass. "This is my first legal drink since my birthday."

"It's your third," corrected Elmer.

"Bring it with you," said Rocco. "I paid for the glass."

"No open containers," said the bartender.

"Watch out for the Oak Bluffs cops."

"Leave it, Red. There's more where that came from." Rocco turned on his heels and walked out, not looking back. "We gotta find Dominic before he gets me into some kind of trouble."

Red took a long swallow of his scotch, drained the glass, wiped his mouth on his sleeve, and trailed out after the others, carrying the empty glass.

"So, Rocco, where are we going to look for Dominic?" asked Elmer, his chubby cheeks pinker than when they had entered the bar.

Rocco didn't answer.

Cosimo, striding leisurely next to Elmer, said, "He's going to check all the bars in town."

"Oh," said Elmer, huffing slightly as he tried to keep up.

Including the Tidal Rip, there were five bars on Circuit Avenue, and the young men went into each of them.

Rocco led. Cosimo followed with Elmer close behind him, and Red trailed far behind, carrying his glass.

In the first establishment, the bartender was sitting on a stool, working on a cross-word puzzle. He slid his glasses down his nose and looked up when the four came in.

"Was a guy who looked like me in here today?" asked Rocco.

"Hasn't been a soul in here all day." The bartender waved a hand around the empty room and shoved his glasses back into place. "Try again in a couple of hours. Place'll be flying." He returned to his puzzle.

Same response in the other bars: Come back later.

Fog had closed in, a chilly fog that cut through their light clothing.

"That's it," said Rocco. "I've had it with Dominic. Drink himself to death, for all I care. I'm going back to my hotel. I'll drive you to the ferry terminal first so Red can pick up his gear, then drop you guys off where you're staying."

He'd parked his BMW, nose in, in front of a stationery store that had a gigantic yellow pencil with a red eraser and a sharpened point suspended over its door. The four got into the car, Cosimo in front next to Rocco, and Elmer and Red in back.

Rocco draped both hands high on the steering wheel and leaned over it. "I gotta tell you, I'm fed up with him."

"Any other bars on the Island?" asked Cosimo.

"Edgartown," said Rocco.

They were discussing where next to look

34

for Dominic when Rocco's phone barked out. He pulled it out of his pocket, flipped it open, and looked at the screen. "Yo, Penny, what's up?" He scowled. "Can't understand what you're saying. Reception sucks . . . no, not the wedding reception . . . I still can't understand what you're saying . . . Okay, I'll be there in twenty minutes." He snapped the phone shut and started up the engine.

"What was that all about?" asked Elmer.

"Dominic is at Penny's cousin's. Drunk, as usual. I gotta get there now. Sober him up in time for the wedding."

"You don't need us tagging along," said Cosimo. "I can walk to the hotel I'm staying at." He opened the door, slid out, and slammed the door shut behind him. He leaned over and spoke to the two in the back seat. "C'mon. Time to leave."

By now, the fog had thickened and was almost a fine drizzle. Cosimo turned up his collar.

Red leaned over Elmer. "Where you staying, Coz?" he said, his voice slurred.

"Hotel on the Harbor. Couple blocks from here. Hurry up. I'm getting soaked."

Red had slumped against Elmer's shoulder. Elmer pushed him back. "Red," he said. "Hey, Red. Wake up."

"I'm awake."

"Where are you staying, Red?"

"I dunno," said Red.

"You have a reservation somewhere?"

Red shook his head.

"C'mon, you guys," said Rocco, tapping his fingers on the wheel.

"Where'd you say your luggage is, Red?" asked Cosimo.

"Locker at the ferry." Red giggled.

Rocco stopped tapping his fingers and slammed his hands on the wheel. "You guys getting out or are you coming with me? Make it snappy, will you?"

"Okay, okay," said Red, reaching for the door handle to let himself out.

"Watch it," said Elmer. "Car's pulling in next to you."

"O-kay," said Red. "I'll jusht get out your side then."

Cosimo said, "You have my cell number, Rocco?"

"Yes, of course I have your cell number. Get them out of here, will you?"

Elmer helped Red slide across the back seat, and the three stood on the sidewalk in the misty drizzle. Rocco backed out of the space and headed up Circuit Avenue.

The others watched his car get swallowed up in the fog.

Red said, "I'm getting wet."

"I got news for you," said Cosimo. "We all are. Where are you staying, Elmer?"

"Same place as you, Coz. Hotel on the Harbor." Elmer turned to Red. "You got enough to pay for a room there?"

"I got at least three hunnerd bucks." Red tugged his wallet out of his back pocket and dropped it.

Elmer bent down and picked it up. "You got a credit card?"

"Prob'ly."

"Let's get moving," said Cosimo. "Pick up Red's luggage from the ferry terminal, then get him a room where we're staying. He needs to sleep it off." He headed toward the harbor. "If they don't have a room available, he can bunk with you."

"Thanks, but no thanks. I'm not babysitting him." Elmer was puffing out misty breaths. "How about we slow down a bit?"

"Taxi!" shouted Red to the vacant street.

"Get moving. It's only about three blocks to the ferry terminal and another couple to the hotel.

Red was still holding his empty glass. "I'm getting cold."

Later that afternoon, Sarah Germaine was in her usual seat on the front porch of Alley's General Store, under the sign that read "Cans of Peas." Condensation from the fog was dripping off the roof. She had just come from Aquinnah, where she worked at the Wampanoag Tribal Headquarters. Today Sarah was wearing a gray sweatshirt that read "Two Braves Hauling" in orange letters. Joe, the plumber, was at his usual place, leaning against one of the posts that held up the porch roof. Lincoln had parked his truck, almost hidden in the dense fog, and was stepping up onto the porch.

"Afternoon, everybody." Linc had come from his landscaping job and smelled faintly of manure. "Nice day."

Sarah sniffed. "Smells like someone's putting in a garden. Kind of late in the season, isn't it?"

"Never too late," said Linc. "I just put a load of manure on Manny Acosta's strawberries."

"I put cream on mine," said Joe.

"Ha-ha. Very funny," said Sarah. "Not." She wrinkled her nose.

Joe took a knife out of one pocket and his Red Man out of another and carved off a chunk that he stuck in his cheek. "So, Linc. What's happening?"

"Nothing much," answered Linc, their usual greeting. He established himself in his

38

place, leaning against one of the two doors that led into the store.

"Well, not to change the subject," said Sarah, "but have either of you heard anything more about Mrs. Trumbull's body?"

Joe chortled. "Last I heard, Mrs. Trumbull's body was seen at the Post Office."

"You're so comical, Joe," said Sarah. "Have they identified him yet?"

Joe and Lincoln looked at each other and shrugged. "Not that we've heard," said Linc. "I heard Doc Jeffers thinks the guy was dead before he was strung up."

"Is that right?" said Joe. "What killed him?"

"Wire around his neck."

"Yuck," said Sarah, a hand at her own throat. "Why'd they hang him in Mrs. Trumbull's cellar?"

"Good question," said Linc.

"As a warning," said Joe.

"Like, 'You're next'?" said Sarah.

"Something like that."

"That seems sort of unnecessary," said Sarah. "I mean, once he's dead, you've said it all."

"Maybe the killer thought the victim was the groom. So when it turned out it was the wrong person, he didn't want to waste the opportunity and strung him up as a warning."

"This raises a whole lot of questions," said Sarah. "How did they know about Mrs. Trumbull's cellar? I mean, we all know Mrs. T. and her house pretty well, but have either of you been in her cellar?"

Both Joe and Lincoln shook their heads.

"I sure haven't," Sarah continued. "I know where the bulkhead doors are, but I don't, or didn't until now, know whether the cellar was just a crawl space or full of plumbing and electrical stuff or what. I mean, before you cart a body down there, you'd have to be pretty sure you could hang it up, right?"

"Good point," said Linc.

"I mean, that's a lot of trouble, carting a dead body down into a cellar and hanging it up."

"Dead weight," agreed Joe.

"Furthermore," said Sarah, ignoring him, "once you kill someone, the body starts to, you know . . ."

"In other words," said Joe, "you better work fast if you're going to use a corpse to send a message to someone."

"We know now her cellar is dry, unlike some cellars I know," said Sarah. "The killer must have known that beforehand too. Otherwise . . ."

"Yeah, yeah," said Joe. "No need to get graphic."

"So where was the guy killed? And how come he knew so much about Victoria Trumbull's cellar?"

Joe leaned over, spit tobacco juice off to one side, and wiped his mouth on his shirt-sleeve.

"That's really disgusting, you know?" said Sarah.

"Nothing but weeds down there. Good bug killer."

Linc looked at his watch. "It's getting late, you guys. Whose turn is it to buy the soda pop?"

Victoria returned to the kitchen and was putting the cleaned Jerusalem artichokes in the refrigerator, when a car pulled up into the drive, appearing through the fog like a ghostly vehicle.

She went to the door.

She had never met Penny's fiancé, but immediately recognized the tall, dark, handsome young man with the stubble of a beard, who unfolded himself from a low-slung, bright blue BMW. He looked very much like a slimmer version of the man who was lying under the tree, snoring out breathy fumes.

41

"You must be Mrs. Trumbull," said Rocco, walking up the steps toward her. "I'd recognize you anywhere. I've heard so much about you." He held out a hand, which she took. "I'm Rocco. I look forward to becoming part of your fine family."

"Come in," said Victoria, leading the way.

"I understand my brother paid you an unexpected visit." Rocco wiped droplets of moisture from his hair. "We are imposing upon you, and I am so sorry."

"He's lying outside on the ground, and we need to get him inside before he gets thoroughly soaked."

"Where outside?"

"Under one of the maple trees at the end of the drive. We laid a blanket over him, but I'm sure it and he are both wet by now."

"I can find him, Mrs. Trumbull. No need for you to get soaked too."

"Thank you, but I'd better go with you," said Victoria.

"Then please allow me." He picked up her sweater and held it for her. Victoria slipped it on, and they walked out into the soupy fog. Condensation dripped from the branches overhead. In the distance a foghorn moaned.

Mark was in his truck with the radio on. An electric blue sign on the side of the truck read "Mark Your Favorite Electrician." He turned off the radio, got out of the truck, and introduced himself. "Mark Johnson. You the groom?" He held out his hand.

"Rocco Bufano." He shook Mark's hand. "Nice to meet one of the workers putting this show together."

"I don't know about that," said Mark.

They shook hands. Rocco said, "Where's that brother of mine?"

"Over there." Mark pointed to a huge tree just beyond where he'd parked. "On the other side of the bride's car."

Penny was sitting in her car with the door open, the heater on. "Darling!" she cried, slipping out of the car. "Thank god you got here." She grasped Rocco's hand.

Victoria said, "We need to get Dominic into the house, where it's dry and warm."

"I'll help you move him," said Mark.

Rocco was examining Penny, her short raggedy shorts and the fake diamond in her navel. "Don't you think you should get some clothes on?"

"I didn't have time to change, darling. So much is happening and so, so . . ." She wrapped her arms around herself.

"Why is Dominic here?"

"I have no idea." Penny was shivering. "He was in my car. Lying across the front seat.

43

When I opened the door, I thought he was dead."

A few feet farther on, Dominic lay on his back, a blanket draped over him, snoring. Victoria waited nearby. Droplets of mist beaded her white hair. She took a used napkin out of her pocket and blotted her nose.

Rocco leaned over his brother. "Drunk, as usual," he muttered.

Dominic groaned, smacked his lips, snorted, and went back to snoring.

Rocco straightened up and looked from Penny to Victoria to Mark. "Surely he didn't drive in that condition?"

"Somebody must have left him in my car," said Penny. "People have been coming in and out of the drive all day. It's been awful."

"We need to get him inside," said Victoria.

"Let's go, Rocco, my man," said Mark.

"Your call was breaking up, Penny," said Rocco. "I heard you say something about a body." He gestured at his prostrate brother. "I assume you meant him." He took a handkerchief out of his pants pocket and wiped his hands.

"I tried to reach you all afternoon, darling."

"You can talk later," said Victoria. "You

need to get him inside."

"Come on, Rocco," said Mark. "Take his left arm, I'll take the right."

They hoisted Dominic to his feet and half-carried him to the house. Victoria led them to the downstairs bedroom. Rocco took off his brother's damp jacket, trousers, and shoes, and Victoria draped the wet clothing over the screen in front of the unlit fire.

"There's a slop jar in the attic, Rocco," she said. "Get it and put it on the floor near Dominic. He'll need it when he wakes up."

Rocco left and returned a short time later. His black shirt was festooned with lacy spider webs, and the ancient chamber pot was full of long-dead spiders and fly carcasses.

"Rinse it out in the bathroom," said Victoria.

After Dominic was settled, Mark left, and the others gathered in the kitchen. Victoria sat at the kitchen table. "We could all use a cup of tea."

"Please, stay seated, Mrs. Trumbull," said Rocco. "I can handle the tea making if you'll tell me where everything is."

Penny stood near the east door, combing her fingers through her long, pale hair. She had scrubbed her face in the downstairs bathroom while the others were taking care of Dominic, and had changed into jeans and a sweatshirt. There were still smudges of mascara that she'd missed. She no longer looked cadaverous — more like a street urchin with a dirty face.

Rocco filled the teakettle and set it on the stove. "Penny, my dear, since Dominic's body isn't the one you were referring to, whose body *were* you referring to?"

Penny stopped combing her hair. "The most awful thing happened, darling. We have to cancel the reception."

"The body?" asked Rocco.

"Early this afternoon, right after lunch, we found a body in my cellar," said Victoria. "The police ordered Penny to postpone the reception until the body is identified."

"I'm not sure I understand," said Rocco. "Was this an accident of some kind?"

"A nasty person hung him, darling," said Penny. "And I've already paid the caterers and the tent rental people and —"

"You're saying he was killed?"

"The electrician found him and thought it was a Halloween dummy or something from a scavenger hunt."

"Who is the victim?" asked Rocco. "Someone you know, Mrs. Trumbull?"

"He hasn't been identified as yet," said

Victoria. "I didn't recognize him, certainly."

"Well." Rocco leaned against the sink. "I don't know what to say. Or think. This is disturbing news."

"I was asked to look at the body," said Victoria. "It was difficult to tell much about him. He was a young man, probably about your age, with dark hair."

"Where is the body now?" asked Rocco.

"At the funeral home," said Victoria. "It wasn't possible to tell how long he's been dead, or even how long he'd been in my cellar. Because my cellar is dry, decomposition was slowed up."

"How long has it been since someone was last in the cellar?"

Victoria thought for a moment. "Probably the last person to go down there before today was my granddaughter Elizabeth when she put away the lawn chairs in early November."

"So the body might have been there for months?" asked Rocco.

"Probably no more than a few days, at most. There'll be an autopsy, of course, and I'm sure it will determine time of death."

The kettle whistled and Rocco went silently about the process of brewing the tea.

"It's all so unfair," said Penny.

"I'm sure you can cancel the caterers as

well as the tents," said Victoria. She turned to Rocco, who was pouring water into the teapot. "Where are you staying, Rocco?"

"In Edgartown. At the Turkey Cove Inn."

"Such an elegant hotel," said Victoria. "When I was a child, occasionally on a Sunday my grandfather would hitch our horse, Dolly, and take us to Edgartown to dine at the inn." She smiled. "I loved to sit on the big rocking chairs on the wide porch."

"They still have those porch rockers." Rocco poured out cups of tea, and Penny passed them around. "Anything in it?"

"Milk in mine," said Victoria. "There's a lemon in the icebox."

Rocco poured a dollop of milk into her tea, and she stirred it. "I must have been six or seven years old. I can remember I had to sit up straight to see the lighthouse because the railing was in the way."

"Children still do just that," said Rocco. "You'll see them sit up or stand to see the lighthouse." He took his wallet out of his back pocket and drew out a business card. "If you need me for anything, call me any time, Mrs. Trumbull. Don't use the number at the inn. Use my cell number, the one on my card. Any time, day or night."

The phone in the cookroom, a tiny room

off the kitchen, rang. Victoria got up to answer.

"That was Sergeant Smalley," she said when she returned. "He wants to talk to you, Rocco. He'll be here shortly."

"Sergeant Smalley?" asked Rocco.

"He's with the state police. He hoped you might be able to identify the victim."

"Of course," said Rocco. "I'll help in any way I can." He looked down at his shirt, the black silk patterned with attic dust and cobwebs.

Victoria dampened a dishtowel and gave it to him. "The cobwebs wipe off easily."

Rocco accepted the towel and went into the bathroom. By the time he came out, Sergeant Smalley had arrived. Victoria introduced him to Rocco and they shook hands.

"I know Penny, of course. Known her since she was a bratty seven-year-old."

Penny gave him a coquettish smile. "Who, me? Bratty?"

"Congratulations to you both, Penny, Rocco. Sorry to foul up your reception, but this, as you know, is murder. And, it's just possible the victim was one of your wedding guests." Smalley turned to Rocco. "I'd like your help in possibly identifying him. That would simplify things."

Rocco brushed the front of his damp shirt and looked up at Smalley. Rocco was tall, but Smalley was even taller. "I'll certainly be glad to help," he said. "Where is the body?"

"At the funeral home," said Smalley. "It may take us some time."

"No problem," said Rocco.

CHAPTER FOUR

While Sergeant Smalley was escorting Rocco to the funeral home on Martha's Vineyard, Zoe Harrington, the head of a small company in downtown New York that specialized in printing poetry books, was discussing the work of one of her poets.

"Ms. Harrington, you have a call on line two."

"Who is it, Bev?" Zoe had asked not to be interrupted.

"It's a Dottore Leonardo Caruso, ma'am. He said it's personal and urgent. He said very urgent." *Dottore* was Leonardo Caruso's title, an honorific signifying that he commanded great respect.

Zoe turned to her poet. "I'm so sorry, Laverne. I'll have to take this call."

"Shall I step out?"

"I don't think there's any need to, thank you. Shouldn't be more than a minute or two." She hit the blinking light for line two.

"Zoe Harrington here, Dottore Caruso. How may I help you?"

"Dottore Caruso!" murmured Laverne. "Caruso Shipping!"

"Zoe, my dear, have you heard that Rocco Bufano is to be married this Saturday?"

"This Saturday? I thought she planned their big wedding for September. We're just about to print the invitations."

"He's not marrying Bianca, my dear. He's marrying a woman named Penny Arbuthnot, whose cousin is Victoria Trumbull, the poet."

"I–I . . . I'm dumbfounded. I don't know what to say."

Laverne got up quietly and tiptoed out of the office.

Zoe asked, "How did this come about, do you know? Who is this Penny Arbuthnot? What does Bianca have to say about this?"

"Firstly," said Dottore Caruso, "Bianca hasn't heard, at least as far as I know. I believe we would all know if she had."

"True," said Zoe. "Her voice carries a long way. But who is Penny Arbuthnot?"

"Let me answer this way. As you know, Rocco has no money. My cousin, Rocco's father, has disowned him. As you may not know, Rocco has run up some sizeable debts. His creditors are anxious. Ms. Arbuthnot's cousin, Victoria Trumbull, lives on Martha's Vineyard."

"Playground of the rich and famous. I see." Zoe turned to look out her window. "I don't think everyone who lives on Martha's Vineyard is rich. Especially not poets, but I think I'm beginning to understand. Rocco smells money."

"Ms. Penny Arbuthnot appears to be Rocco's way out of his financial trouble."

Zoe's office was on the sixth floor of the old shirt factory. From there, she could look uptown and see the tall office building that Caruso Shipping owned and from which Dottore Caruso was probably calling.

"I knew you'd understand," continued Dottore Caruso. "There's a further consideration. My daughter, Lily, is missing, as is her cousin Angelo. I believe Angelo is your special friend, am I right?"

"Oh, my," said Zoe. "The complications are frightening. And I have an uncomfortable feeling you are about to ask me a favor."

"True," said Dottore Caruso. "I believe Angelo has gone to Martha's Vineyard, and it's likely Lily has somehow managed to go with him."

"Since I owe you more favors than I can count for all the things you have done for me, the answer is yes. Whatever I can do to help." She turned back to her desk. "What is it that you wish me to do, Dottore?"

Victoria Trumbull returned to the kitchen, leaving a snoring Dominic tucked into bed with clean sheets around him, the chamber pot by the side of the bed.

Rocco and Sergeant Smalley had gone to the funeral home, and Penny was upstairs.

While Victoria was clearing away the tea things, someone knocked on the kitchen door.

"Hello, anybody home? Mrs. Trumbull?" A woman's voice. High, young, and sounding worried.

"Come in," said Victoria.

The young woman at the door was about Penny's age, slender, almost anorexic, with spiky magenta and blue hair, and glasses with enormous black frames. The girl hugged her upper arms as though she was cold, and she probably was. The fog had settled in, here to stay.

"Yes?" asked Victoria.

"I know you must be busy with this, you know, wedding and everything." The girl paused and Victoria waited. "But we have, like, an emergency and I hope you can help?"

"Oh?" said Victoria, not liking what she

was hearing.

"My cousin got out of a truck, and you know how foggy it is, and he slipped on the mud and, like, sprained his ankle."

"Is he a wedding guest?"

"He's Rocco's and my cousin. His name is Angelo."

Victoria sighed. "Where did this happen?"

"Right at the end of your drive."

"Where is Angelo now?"

"He's coming this way."

"I can't help him," said Victoria. "You'll need to take him to the hospital."

"Well, he thought, you know . . ." The young woman paused.

"I know what?" asked Victoria, thrusting her hands into the pockets of her gray corduroy pants.

"Well, hospitals are bad."

"What is it that you expect of me?" Victoria asked, more sharply than usual. The young woman clearly didn't have her wits about her.

"We thought if we could stay here for a few days, you know."

"A few days!" Victoria was aghast.

"For the wedding and all. He took a branch from that little tree at the end of the drive. It's his crutch."

"Are you here for the wedding?"

"We're Rocco's cousins, Angelo and me."

"What is your name?" asked Victoria.

"Lily Caruso. You can call me Lily."

"You'd better come in, Lily."

A young man was making a painful-seeming way up the drive. Victoria held the door open for him. The branch he'd broken off and was using as a crutch was from the golden chain tree she'd been trying to nurse back to health after last winter's storm.

"Is his truck still at the end of the drive, Lily?" Victoria spoke through tight lips.

Lily shook her head. "We hitchhiked. We rode in a white truck. He couldn't get a ferry reservation for his car."

It was only a short walk to the Steamship Authority terminal, but Cosimo, Elmer, and Red were uncomfortably damp by the time they got there. Red fumbled for his locker key and found it in an inside pocket. Elmer took it from him, checked the number, found the right locker, and opened it. Red's luggage consisted of a backpack.

"This it?" asked Cosimo. "No other luggage?"

"Travel light," said Red. "My motto."

"This is a Martha's Vineyard wedding," said Cosimo. "You're expected to dress for the occasion."

"I heard people get married on the beach on Martha's Vineyard," said Red. "Barefoot." He giggled. "They got nude beaches on Martha's Vineyard. Don't need clothes for a Martha's Vineyard wedding."

"Not this wedding," said Cosimo.

Elmer handed the backpack to Red. "Well, here you are."

Red slung it over one shoulder.

"Hotel's only a couple blocks from here," said Cosimo. "Once we check in, I'm taking a long, hot shower and then I've got some work I have to do. You two are on your own."

"I'm doing the same," said Elmer. "Red, you're on your own."

"No problem." Red stumbled off the curb. A horn honked. Brakes squealed.

"Watch it!" someone shouted.

Cosimo pulled Red back onto the sidewalk. He and Elmer exchanged glances.

"We're stuck with him until he sobers up," said Cosimo.

Elmer's cheeks were puffy and pink from exertion, and he was sweating. "I don't have time for this."

"You think I do? C'mon, let's get to the hotel. The weather isn't improving."

They left the ferry terminal behind, one on either side of Red. They passed a red painted building with the words "Flying

Horses" emblazoned on the side in white paint.

"I'm flying!" said Red. "Get me a horse!"

"Shut up," said Cosimo.

"I heard it's the oldest carousel in the country," said Elmer.

"I'm hungry," said Red. "We can eat at the Flying Horses. I could eat a horse."

"Have you registered yet, Elmer?" asked Cosimo. "I checked in before we hit the Tidal Rip."

Elmer nodded.

They crossed Circuit Avenue and hurried on. The harbor was on their right.

"We're close to the hotel now," said Cosimo. "I'm going up to my room. You go ahead and register, Red. How about we meet in the lobby around six or so. That'll give us a couple of hours."

Red looked confused.

"You okay with that?" asked Elmer. "Just give them your credit card. I'm pretty sure they have an available room."

"I can't use my credit card," said Red.

"Why not?"

"It's maxed out. Rocco's paying."

"Rocco's paying expenses for me too, but not until after the wedding," said Elmer.

"Jeezus, Red," said Cosimo. "Why in hell did you come to this damned wedding?"

"Rocco invited me. He's paying."

They reached the large, sprawling hotel, a gray-shingled building built in the 1800s. They went up the steps and into the lobby. An ancient, threadbare oriental carpet covered much of the wood floor. The floor not covered by the carpet had been painted gray. The paint had worn off, leaving a path where there'd been heavy traffic.

"He'll have to share your room, Elmer," said Cosimo.

"Look here, Coz, I've got my own business I have to tend to. I don't want him breathing over my shoulder."

Cosimo studied Red. "Tell you what," he said to Elmer. "Take him up to your room. He needs to sleep it off. When he sobers up, we can take it from there. I'll meet you in the lobby around six."

"Are we planning to dine together?" asked Elmer.

"Up to you. I don't much feel like eating alone tonight."

"Me either," said Elmer. "It's a date."

"I don't want to stay here," said Red.

"Tough," snapped Elmer. "I don't want you staying here either."

The funeral home was a twenty-minute drive from Victoria's house. As the afternoon wore on into evening, the fog thickened. Eddies of mist streamed off to either side of them.

Smalley and Rocco were silent during the drive. Smalley turned onto the Edgartown Vineyard Haven Road, passed the high school, and turned right into the funeral home's parking lot.

Toby, the undertaker, met them at the top of the loading dock at the back of the building. He was a stout man wearing a lab coat over black trousers and a white shirt, open at the neck.

They went up the concrete steps to the platform, and Toby held out his hand. Smalley and he shook.

"Thanks for staying here so late," said Smalley.

"Of course," said Toby. "Not often we have an individual who needs a name."

"This is Rocco Bufano here," said Smalley, introducing him.

"Mr. Bufano. Glad to meet you," said Toby.

"He's marrying one of Victoria Trumbull's cousins on Saturday," said Smalley. "Then this happened."

"Terribly sorry, Mr. Bufano. Most unfortunate." Toby smoothed his hand across the front of his lab coat, unclipped a pen from the breast pocket, took it out, looked at it, then put it back.

"Well," said Rocco, "Whatever I can do to help."

"The sooner we can identify him, the sooner you can go ahead with your plans." Smalley stood with his feet slightly apart, his hands in his trousers pockets.

Toby pressed a button on the side of the building, and the steel door lifted with a clang of metal plates, moving up and out of the way. A gust of icy air met them. They stepped into a cold, brightly lighted austere room with cement block walls and concrete floor. A stainless steel table was in the center of the room. Under the table a metal grill covered a drain. On the table a white sheet covered a form.

Toby said, "Most people find it difficult, Mr. Bufano, looking at a deceased person they might know. Will you be all right?"

"Yes, of course," Rocco said with assurance.

"He's been dead a number of days, but in a dry environment."

"I can handle it."

Smalley clasped his hands behind his back. He glanced from Toby to Rocco, then nodded at the form under the sheet. "You're sure you're okay with this?"

"If you need to sit down," said Toby, "I can bring over a chair."

"No problem. I've seen plenty of dead bodies before."

Toby shrugged and slowly drew back the sheet.

The man's face was gray. His tongue protruded. His opaque eyes were dotted with black specks of blood.

Rocco drew in his breath sharply and staggered back.

Smalley held out an arm to steady him. "You know him?"

"No," said Rocco. "No. No." He shook his head. "I don't know him."

Smalley looked at him carefully. "I assumed from your reaction that you recognized him."

"I'm . . ." Rocco started and stopped. "I'm not used to . . ." He paused. "It's a shock, that's all." His face had paled.

"You'd better sit, Mr. Bufano," said Toby, pushing the metal chair across the concrete floor with an awful scraping sound.

"No!" said Rocco.

"A dead body looks quite different from the way it looked in life," said Smalley. "Are you quite sure you don't recognize him?"

"I need to get out of here," said Rocco.

Toby reached for a bottle on a table near

the entrance. "Take a sniff of this, Mr. Bufano. Brace you up."

Rocco held up both hands. "No. I don't need that. I need to get out of here."

Smalley and Toby exchanged glances. Toby shrugged.

Once outside, Rocco stumbled down the steps leading from the loading platform. Behind them, the steel door ratcheted shut and settled with a final clank.

Smalley and Rocco walked to the cruiser, almost hidden in the soupy fog. They said nothing until they reached it. They both sat, Smalley in the driver's seat, Rocco in the passenger's. Smalley adjusted the rearview mirror, which didn't need adjusting, and cleared his throat. He settled himself in his seat. He turned the key and the dashboard lights went on, but he didn't start the engine. "Quite a shock for you."

Rocco glanced over at him.

"We'll identify the corpse sooner or later," said Smalley.

"I don't know what you mean." Rocco stared straight ahead. There was a brief glimpse of trees behind the mortuary before the fog closed in again. Sounds from the nearby Vineyard Haven Road were muffled.

"You know exactly what I'm talking about." Smalley sat with both hands high on the steering wheel. He still hadn't started the engine.

Rocco said nothing.

"It's going to be one hell of a lot harder on you if we have to go to the trouble and expense of checking dental records and getting a DNA analysis." Smalley glanced over at him.

"Please!" said Rocco. "Stop!"

"I know you know the victim, and I don't intend to give you time to call your old man or whoever else you plan to call. We'll sit here for a minute or two."

"You can't do that," said Rocco. "You can't hold me."

"I'm not holding you," said Smalley. "We're having a chat. I'm giving you some fatherly advice that you don't have to take. But I suspect you know the consequences if you don't take that advice."

"I need to think." Rocco looked at his hands clasped tightly in his lap. His knuckles shone whitely in the light from the dashboard.

"This is a murder investigation," said Smalley. "You don't want to be held as a person of interest, your wedding coming up and all." He glanced again at Rocco, who seemed to have shrunk into the seat. "We can book you on suspicion and hold you in the county jail for twenty-four hours without charging you, you know. Possibly ninety-six hours, since this is murder. You can call your old man from there."

Rocco opened the passenger side door and started to get out.

"I wouldn't do that if I were you," said Smalley. "Where do you plan to run to?"

Rocco shook his head.

"Where are you staying?"

"I booked a suite at the Turkey Cove Inn."

"Not exactly cheap," said Smalley.

"Yeah, well," said Rocco. He shifted his legs back into the police cruiser and slammed the door shut.

Smalley took out his notebook. "What's your room number?"

Rocco sighed. "I canceled."

Smalley slapped his notebook against his hand. "Where are you staying, if I may ask?"

"I swear to God. I don't know him," said Rocco, thrusting his hands up in a dramatic gesture. "I swear on my mother's grave."

"I didn't know you'd lost your mother." Smalley glanced at him. "My condolences."

"What?" Rocco's face, illuminated by the dashboard lights, was blank. "My mother hasn't passed. . . ."

"Forget it," said Smalley. "I asked you where you're staying."

"I haven't booked a new place yet."

Smalley started the engine. "It's getting along toward supper time. My treat. A great French chef at the jail."

"You're not taking me to jail, are you?"

"I'm inviting you to dinner, that's all."

"Not at the jail."

"Okay. We'll get something at the Dairy Queen and eat in the cruiser."

They drove in silence. As they reached the outskirts of Edgartown, the fog thinned. Smalley parked behind the Dairy Queen, and they went in and ordered: burger for Rocco, chicken wrap for Smalley.

"Thanks," said Rocco.

"On the town," said Smalley.

"About the body," said Smalley after they returned to the cruiser with their food. "You recognized him. Who was he?"

"I don't know, I tell you. I don't know."

Light was fading, so Smalley turned on the dashboard lights. They unwrapped their food,

"Why the reaction when you saw him?" Smalley's face, illuminated by the lights, was sharply chiseled into an expression of sheer, pure exasperation.

"It's a long story," said Rocco.

"We've got time." Smalley pulled away the paper from his chicken wrap and took a bite. "Let's have it."

"He's been stalking me."

"What?!" exclaimed Smalley.

"For a couple months. Six weeks, maybe."

"Stalking you. Why?"

"How am I supposed to know?"

"I don't know how you're supposed to know," said Smalley. "Why was he stalking you?"

"I owe somebody some money."

"The stalker? You killed him, maybe?"

"No, no!" said Rocco. "No. Of course not. The guy I owe money to must have set him up to bug me."

"You didn't kill him?"

"I don't even know who he is!" Rocco's voice rose. "I'm losing my appetite."

"Calm down," said Smalley. "Anything more you want to tell me about how the body got into Mrs. Trumbull's cellar?"

Rocco took a deep breath, set his uneaten burger on the divider, and leaned forward. "I think I'm going to be sick."

"I'll open the window," said Smalley. "Go on."

"The guy looks like me. A lot. Looked, that is."

"And?" said Smalley.

"They killed him off."

"Who did?" asked Smalley

"The guy I owe money. A message."

"Cough up the money or you're next?"

"I don't have the money," said Rocco. "I can't pay."

"About the dead guy," said Smalley. "They killed him simply as a warning to you?"

"Oh, God!" Rocco bent forward, his forehead touching his knees.

"You must owe one hell of a lot."

"I swore I'd pay once I got married."

Smalley turned and stared at the picture of dejection sitting next to him, reeking of fear. "Once you got married? To Victoria Trumbull's third cousin once removed? Penny what's-her-name? You have to be shitting me."

"She's got money. The wedding. Tents. All-day raw bar, DJs . . ."

Smalley started the engine. "Oh man. Are you in deep doo-doo. Cousin Penny doesn't have a pot to pee in."

CHAPTER FIVE

While Rocco was at the Dairy Queen with Sergeant Smalley, Victoria was left to address the problem of his cousins, Angelo and Lily.

"Can you negotiate the stairs?" she asked Angelo.

He shook his head and emitted a pitiful groan. His hair, the same glossy black as Rocco's, curled around his face in an angelic way that Victoria found irritating.

"I'm going to call for the ambulance," she said. "They can take much better care of you than I can."

"Like I told you, Mrs. Trumbull, Angelo says hospitals are bad," said Lily. "It's okay, Mrs. Trumbull. His ankle will be okay in, like, a couple of days." Lily pushed her heavy-framed glasses back into place with her index finger. "We can sleep on your floor. I can bring a mattress down from upstairs?" Lily was small, almost a half-foot shorter than Victoria.

Victoria felt a strong surge of irritation. "I don't like —"

Lily interrupted her. "I'm strong, Mrs. Trumbull, really. Yoga, you know." She flexed her arms. "I can carry the mattress down."

"I don't want —"

"We can set it down, like, in the dining room? We'll try not to be in your way."

"I don't . . ." Victoria stopped. She knew when she was beaten. She took in a deep breath and let it out slowly. "Put it on the library floor. It won't be in my way there."

Angelo, who'd said nothing until now, smiled broadly. Lifting himself out of Victoria's chair with the help of the broken-off golden chain tree branch, he murmured, *"Grazie! Molte grazie!"*

In a penthouse apartment on the seventh floor of the old shirt factory in downtown New York, Giovanni Bufano, Rocco's father, was about to make a phone call he didn't want to make. Windows on two sides looked out over the city. To the north he could see the tall buildings of midtown Manhattan, where Bufano Towers was located. Almost adjacent to Bufano Towers was the Caruso Shipping Building, owned by his cousin,

Leonardo.

Years ago, when he'd only been a boy, he had sworn to buy the shirt factory, and he had. It took him until he was almost sixty, but he bought it and paid several millions for it, far more than it was worth. During its lifetime it had gone from shirt factory to electronics manufactory, to storage building, and had been partially destroyed by fire.

The shell of the building had been a dark warren of small cubicles, blackened wood floors, narrow windows with rusted steel bars keeping intruders out and workers in, and filthy ceilings lined with cracked iron pipes and dangling wires and rusting metal tubes.

After he bought it, he transformed it. Floor-to-ceiling windows let in light. The wood floors had been sanded, scraped, and varnished until they looked like polished amber. The glass dome in the ceiling let in more light from a roof garden above. A bookcase covered an entire third wall. Behind the full kitchen, where a fourth wall might have been, were his sleeping quarters.

It was a simple layout and that simplicity, on the top floor alone, had cost him more than a million dollars. The lower floors he'd converted into offices and high-rent apartments.

This building, this former shirt factory, was where his great-grandmother had worked, from the time she was twelve until she married his great-grandfather, stitching buttons onto shirts in semidarkness. Twelve hours a day, six days a week. He had sworn he would buy this factory building where she'd worked, turn it into a monument to her and others like her, and he had. He'd named it The Shirt Factory, and it was a prime address.

He was seated on a couch, his feet up on an ottoman. He lived alone. He brewed himself a cup of espresso and was sipping it while he waited for his call to go through to his cousin Leonardo. He and Leonardo shared the same great-great-grandparents.

The call was about Rocco, one of his two sons. And it had to do with Leonardo's daughter, Lily.

At six o'clock, about the same time Rocco's father was waiting to speak to his cousin Leonardo, Cosimo and Elmer met in the lobby of their hotel.

"Red not joining us?" asked Cosimo.

"He's out like a light."

"Just as well. It's early for supper, but I'm ready."

"Me too," said Elmer.

The dining room was at the front of the hotel, with windows facing onto a wide porch. Beyond it the harbor was shrouded in fog. The dining room itself was fairly small, with only a dozen or so tables. Only one was occupied by three middle-aged women, who were talking quietly over drinks.

A young man in white shirt and blue tie printed with seagulls greeted them. "Charles" was printed on his nametag. "Table by the window, sir?"

"Fine," said Cosimo.

The young man seated them and gave them menus. "Can I get you something to drink?"

"Vodka martini with two olives," said Cosimo.

"Whiskey sour," said Elmer.

"It'll be only a minute," said Charles. "We're not exactly busy tonight."

"I noticed," said Cosimo.

"You here on vacation?"

"Yeah," said Cosimo, picking up his menu.

"Here for a wedding," said Elmer. "Looking forward to that drink."

"Coming right up." Charles left them and went over to the table with the three women.

"Thought you drank scotch," said Elmer. "Single malt scotch. You switch to vodka?"

73

"I'm footing my own bill tonight."

"Understood," said Elmer. "Rocco was sure throwing money around earlier. A hundred-dollar tip at the bar? Who's he trying to impress?"

"Hundred-and-*fifty*-dollar tip," Cosimo corrected. "Wants it to get around the Island that he's got money to burn. Big spender. Worthy of this rich Martha's Vineyard girl he's marrying."

"Where'd he get the money he's throwing around?"

"Pawned something he stole from his old man, most likely."

"She's going to have a surprise when she wakes up." Elmer looked around the room, then opened his menu and studied it. "Not that great a selection."

"Better than another walk in the rain," said Cosimo.

Charles returned, set their drinks in front of them, and left.

"I guess he got the hint," said Elmer.

Cosimo lifted his martini and sipped. "Didn't mean to stick you with Red." He set the glass down. "I had something I had to do and needed to concentrate."

"Yeah well, I did too, you know," said Elmer. "I take it you're not too fond of Rocco."

"For me, the wedding is just an excuse to be here."

"Same with me," said Elmer. "You ever been to Martha's Vineyard before?"

"Once, couple years back. You get Red settled all right?"

"He lay down on one of the beds and went out like a light," said Elmer. "You get any of your work done?"

"Enough." Cosimo picked out one of the olives from his martini.

"Business related?"

Cosimo chewed the olive. "Personal business."

Elmer shrugged. "Didn't mean to pry."

They were silent for a few moments.

"Any idea why he invited Red to this wedding of his?" asked Elmer.

Cosimo smiled. "Rocco doesn't share his thoughts with me."

"He's only a kid. Doesn't seem like a good fit."

Cosimo shrugged.

Elmer took the orange slice from the side of his glass, squeezed it into his drink, and stirred. "His wedding sure came up in a hurry. I don't know anyone here except Rocco, and I don't know him that well. How do you fit into this? You're an Esposito, right?"

"Right," said Cosimo.

"Are you related to him?"

"His stepbrother. My mother married his old man."

"Yeah? Bufano Industries?"

"The same. Marriage only lasted ten years." Cosimo picked up his martini. "The old man was a real pain in the ass." He took another sip. "My brother and I couldn't stand Rocco. Bastard can be sickeningly sweet when he wants something. 'Such a gentleman. So polite. Lovely manners.' All bullshit. He's an egomaniac." He set his glass down again. "Considering how I feel about Rocco and his old man, it's pretty ironic that Rocco invited me to his wedding."

"Makes you wonder if he's got some ulterior motive," said Elmer.

"Wouldn't surprise me in the least."

"Either he doesn't know how you feel, or he doesn't have anyone else to turn to, or he's got something up his sleeve."

"All three," said Cosimo. "Typical narcissist. Nothing exists in this world except him. Nobody else matters. Impossible that anyone should not love him."

"Why'd you agree to come to this wedding of his?"

"I have my reasons." Cosimo turned his

glass around and around. "And you?"

"We belong to the same yacht club."

Cosimo looked up. "I wouldn't have guessed Rocco knew anything about boats."

"He doesn't." Elmer shrugged. "What he does know is that girls like guys with boats with big engines. It's not really a yacht club, but that's what he calls it. It's the municipal marina."

"Where's it located, in the city?"

"The 79th Street Marina."

"Had no idea there was a marina in the city."

"He has a boat and a slip there, and he spends weekends oiling his bare chest and telling any skirt who'll listen how great he is and how much money he has."

"So you're good friends, or what?"

"You can hardly call us friends," said Elmer. "I don't think he has a lot of what you might call friends." Elmer sipped some of his whiskey sour. "He texted me that he had to have someone sit on the groom's side of the church." Elmer laughed. "Gonna be pretty sparse on the groom's side, I'd say."

Cosimo nodded. "Why'd you agree to come? Doesn't sound as though you're any fonder of him than I am."

Elmer shrugged. "Trip to Martha's Vineyard seemed like a good idea. And like you say, I got my reasons."

"He offer to pay your expenses?" asked Cosimo.

"Rocco? Of course he offered to pay expenses. But after the wedding. You know his situation."

Cosimo lifted his martini glass in a kind of salute.

"Do you know anything about this bride of his?" asked Elmer. "He couldn't have known her long."

"He was engaged to another woman. Name's Bianca. They were planning to get married in September. Then this comes up."

"What about Bianca?"

"Good question."

"Why did he decide to marry this woman?" asked Elmer.

"All I know is Rocco calls her his rich bitch."

"Great way to start a marriage," said Elmer.

"Even greater way to get him out of the trouble he's in."

Charles came by. "Ready to order?"

"What do you recommend?" asked Cosimo.

"We have a couple of gourmet seafood dishes, but let me tell you, if you like meatloaf, the meatloaf here is something to write home about."

"Meatloaf it is," said Cosimo, sitting back. "I've had enough gourmet for a lifetime."

"Make it two," said Elmer.

"Just what the doctor ordered for a night like this," said Charles, and left.

While Cosimo and Elmer were ordering dinner, Bianca Diamond was pacing back and forth in the parking lot of the Edgartown Stop & Shop, raging into her cell phone.

The fog was not as thick in Edgartown as it was up-Island, but Bianca paid no attention to the weather. She had on a bright blue rain jacket with a hood she'd pulled over her hair. Moisture had caused her hair to curl in dark ringlets that nicely framed her face. At the moment, her dark eyes sparkled with fury and were magnified by tears welling up.

"Just wait until I get my hands on that two-timing, sleazy bastard." She flung her free hand into the air in a theatrical gesture.

Bianca was what Victoria Trumbull would call "pleasingly plump." She had a figure men turned to look at. A car horn honked politely and Bianca tossed a finger at the driver and kept pacing without looking up, the phone pasted to her ear. She stared down at the tarred surface of the lot. "What in hell does he think he's doing? We've been together a year, right? You know that. We planned to get married in September. That's only four months from now. The printer is printing up invitations as we speak. We went shopping, you and me, for the wedding gown, right?"

She kicked a stone out of her path with the toe of her boot. The stone moved a couple of inches, and she kicked it again. The car pulled around her, cutting unnecessarily close. She didn't notice.

She continued before the person she was talking to had time to answer. "Lucky I put it on layaway and didn't buy it. I'll lose the deposit, that scumbag. A year. We been together a whole goddamned year. Then this blond rich bitch comes into his life, and he ditches me without a word. Not a word!" She jabbed a finger at her chest, and the long, purple-painted fingernail ripped. "Oh, shit!" She bit off the torn end and spit it out on the pavement. "I came to this goddamned desolate place to keep my poor lonely sweetie company. Surprise him. 'Hardship assignment,' he tells me. Yeah. Sure." She took a breath. "I pick up the local paper and read he's getting married." She took another deep breath. "Married!

Like *this* week. This Saturday. Like three days from now."

She came to the end of the parking lot, turned, and started back, staring blindly at the wet pavement under her feet.

Another car horn honked. The driver shouted, "Hey, girl, watch where you're going!"

Bianca looked up and shouted back, "Fuck you!" Then, into the phone, "Not you." She pressed the phone even closer to her ear. "What am I supposed to do? I could kill him, I'm that pissed off." A slight pause. "Yeah, I could. That blond bitch too." She took another breath, and apparently the person she was talking to tried to say something soothing. "Believe me, I will!"

The tears flowed faster. Bianca's pretty face reddened. "Lucky? What do you mean by that? He's worth millions. His old man is a billionaire." Another pause. "Don't tell me money isn't everything. It is." Yet another pause. "You know me, Marybeth. Someone does me wrong, she and him better look out." She snapped her phone shut. She had reached her car, a blue Suzuki that matched her rain jacket. She yanked the door open, slid in, shoved the key into the ignition, backed out of her parking spot, and headed out with the screech of rubber on asphalt.

Her phone rang a chirpy melody. She ignored it and pressed her foot on the accelerator.

"You better believe me. I'm going to kill that bastard," Bianca muttered as she drove away from the Stop & Shop parking lot. She pounded her hands on the steering wheel. "And I'm killing that rich bitch too."

She turned right out of the lot without hearing the horn honk or the screech of brakes or the driver's shout. She followed the road that led along one of the Island's most peaceful settings, with Sengekontacket Pond on her left, Nantucket Sound on her right. Here, the fog was thicker. She never noticed the wild beach roses in bloom, patches of red, white, and pink, an artist's dream, with the colors bright against the fog. Nor was she aware of the fragrance of wild roses and honeysuckle that mixed with the smell of life returning to the warming ocean.

She drove on.

A gun? Knife? No. She shook her head. She didn't like guns. And knives were too messy. Too personal. She honked her horn at a Volvo ahead of her, whose driver had slowed, apparently to take in the fog-shrouded view of Nantucket Sound, blue-green against the gray. She jammed her foot on the accelerator and sped around the slower car.

An automobile accident? Here on this stupid place the top speed limit was forty-five, so no. Too iffy. *Poison?* Bianca chewed her lower lip. The logistics were too complex. *Hire someone to kill the both of them?* She slowed for a line of three cars that had come to a stop. She craned her head out the window to see what was holding up the line. A duck was waddling across the road, followed by a half dozen or more ducklings. She couldn't see around the cars in front of her to tell. She tapped her fingers on the steering wheel in exasperation.

"What a stupid patch of sand," she muttered. "Killer for hire."

She said the words out loud. "Not bad. Only how do you find a killer for hire here?" She tapped her fingers faster. "C'mon, people, move."

A gull swooped down low out of the mist and dropped something on the empty lane next to her with a splat, then dived down and swallowed it.

Where else in the world would two lanes of traffic stop because some duck chooses this minute to cross the road? She stopped tapping her fingers. *I wonder how much a killer would charge?* She thought for a moment.

83

Rocco's family would know that kind of thing. After all, his old man was always bragging about his "connections to The Family," and he didn't mean his wife and kids.

The ducks reached the Sengekontacket side of the road. There were about ten of them. She hadn't bothered to count them. The line of cars moved on. She followed.

If the family figures I want to kill one of them . . . No, that won't work.

She drove on past the Farm Neck Golf Course, where presidents have batted white balls into holes in the ground, past Harthaven and the small cove where a catboat lay at anchor.

Thinking, thinking.

Half the people in the family are killers. Maybe, if they're mad enough at someone it wouldn't matter if he's family. Unless . . . She had halfway convinced herself. *They're always squabbling, his family. Sometimes they seem to just like squabbling. Keeps them in practice. Who in his family hates Rocco?* She had almost reached the Steamship Authority dock and hadn't decided where she was going.

"Ahhhh!" She said aloud as she neglected the upheld hand of the ferry traffic controller and sped past him. *Angelo! That's who.*

84

His cousin Angelo. He hates Rocco. Really, really hates him. Don't know why, but it's a real hate. Wonder if he knows about Rocco's wedding? He'd never come here for that, of that I'm sure. But then family blood ties are pretty strong. They'd come to a family wedding even if they hate the groom. She passed the Flying Horses without noticing the white sign. *Maybe he'll show up just to kill Rocco. Just to show everyone he can. Yes! Now, how do I find Angelo?*

She started texting one after another of her contacts until she got her answer. "Angelo is on Martha's Vineyard for Rocco's wedding."

She thrust a triumphant fist in the air. "Yes! I knew it!"

She texted back, "Angelo hates Rocco."

"Go figure," came the answer.

"Where's he staying?"

"Dunno."

Bianca smiled. *I'll find him. This is a pretty small place. I'll find Angelo and he'll talk to me.* She slowed as she passed the Oak Bluffs Harbor and glanced at the boats tied up with sterns facing the road. A large old hotel loomed out of the fog on her left.

Creepy place, she thought. *Now, all I have to do is figure out where he's staying.*

Another half-dozen text messages and she

had an answer of sorts. She'd made the sharp left turn onto the road that went past the state police barracks and was facing the hospital.

"Angelo is at Victoria Trumbull's," said the message. "He sprained his ankle." Then a single word: "Maybe."

CHAPTER SIX

Lily brought the mattress down from the attic. Victoria heard it bump its way down, getting closer and closer to the library. She thought about the golden chain tree and the stairs and their ancient, flaking paint, and she hoped this was not the prelude to a semi-permanent stay.

She was not sure she could stomach hosting this couple, even for one night. But if they were destined to stay, she would make them comfortable. She got up from her seat in the cookroom, where she was working on a new poem, a sonnet that reflected her frustration at the audacity of some people.

The cookroom, now a pleasant room adjoining the kitchen, had been a shed that Victoria's grandfather had moved from the other side of the brook and attached to the main house as a summer kitchen. Victoria's carpenter friend, Dan Bradley, transformed her grandfather's rough shed into a pleasant breakfast room with windows to the south and west, a place where Victoria liked to write. Baskets and potted ivy now hung from the rough beams Dan had preserved. She still called it the cookroom, as her grandfather always had.

She retrieved lavender-scented sheets and pillowcases from the closet in the bathroom, and passed them to Lily.

"Thanks, Mrs. Trumbull." Lily sniffed the sheets. "Nice. Like, I hate to bother you, but do you know a place where we can get something to eat? I mean, if it's only a block or two away, I can pick up a pizza and we'll eat it in the library, where we won't bother you."

"I don't want food in the library." Victoria was determined to take a stand. "We have a problem with mice." She folded her arms across her chest and hoped Lily hadn't noticed McCavity, her mighty hunter cat. "The closest place is a half-mile from here, but it's closed now. You can hitchhike into Vineyard Haven. Several places have carry-out."

"Hitchhike?" Lily looked horrified. "You mean, now? It's going to be dark soon."

"It won't be dark for another couple of hours," said Victoria. "It's perfectly safe, as you know since you hitchhiked here. Eat your supper at the restaurant."

"It's kind of, like, foggy and rainy," said Lily. "And cold." She turned away with a look of pathos. "I guess we'll have to do without supper."

Victoria paused for the briefest of moments. She'd lost another round. "I can make an omelet."

Lily turned back, her face bright. "Would you, Mrs. Trumbull? How sweet of you. I'll tell Angelo. I know he's hungry."

Just as Victoria was adding grated cheese to the omelet, Penny returned from Edgartown, where she'd gone to do her shopping.

"It's just awful out there. My shoes are ruined." She kicked off her sandals, the ones with three-inch heels that made her taller than Victoria, then shed her raincoat and hung it on the coat rack in the entry.

"Oooh, Cousin Victoria, that looks and smells divine! I'm starving." She plopped down in a kitchen chair, dropped the bags and parcels she'd been carrying onto the floor, and slipped on the flats she'd left by the door. "Wait until you see what I bought."

"I thought you'd already spent all your money." Victoria was in a sour mood. She loathed shopping. Besides, she found it difficult to be civil to her young cousin, who seemed unaffected by the unsolved murder that loomed over them.

"I discovered a credit card I hadn't run up," Penny said with a note of triumph and a smile. She peered over at Victoria. "What are you cooking?"

"An omelet. I've made only enough for two." Victoria was reluctant to admit she had a fresh dozen eggs she'd picked up at Green's farm.

"Two?" asked Penny. "Has Dominic recovered?"

Victoria had momentarily forgotten Dominic. "We have two unexpected guests, cousins of Rocco's."

"Oh goody, who?" asked Penny, looking up from a plastic bag she was opening.

"Lily and Angelo."

"Lily? Who's Lily?" Penny stood suddenly, dropping a last package onto the floor. "Angelo? You don't mean Rocco's cousin Angelo?"

"Yes."

"Rocco hates him. What's he doing here? I never invited him. I don't want him in this house!" Penny stamped her foot with each sentence.

"He had an accident and hurt his ankle."

"Ankle, pankle," snorted Penny. "He's faking it."

There was the sound of retching and the clink of something hitting the china chamber pot in the downstairs room.

"Dominic," said Victoria. "I'd better check on him." She got up stiffly from her own chair.

"You've got to get rid of Angelo before Rocco shows up," said Penny, making fists of her hands and thrusting them down by her sides.

"I suppose he'll need something to eat when he returns," said Victoria. "I've got to check on Dominic."

"Cousin Victoria, you're not listening to me. You have to get rid of Angelo!" She stamped her foot again and hit one of the plastic bags with a crunch. "Oh, shit! Our two champagne glasses." She bent down, picked up the bag, and shook it. "Angelo will kill Rocco, Cousin Victoria. I'm serious. He will kill him! You need to get him out of your house."

"You're overreacting." Victoria had had enough. "A man is dead, in the mortuary, unidentified, and probably a relative invited to your wedding, and your fiancé's brother is ill."

Penny glanced out the window. "Somebody's coming, Cousin Vic."

Victoria looked too. "I have no idea who it is. Penny, please go out and ask the driver to park off to one side. Other people need to get by, and I have to check on Dominic."

Penny was back shortly, looking puzzled. The car, a white Malibu, had driven away.

"What's the trouble?" asked Victoria, who'd returned from the sickroom.

"I don't know what that was all about. Some blond woman wanted to know if we took in guests. I said no. Then she asked if a person named Angelo was staying here, and I told her no."

"But he is staying here," said Victoria, annoyed.

"Not for long, as far as I'm concerned," said Penny. "You've got to get him out of here before Rocco sees him."

Penny picked up the bag of crushed glass and deposited it in the trash. "I'm really freaked out about those champagne glasses. I went to a half-dozen stores before I found just what I wanted." She went to the refrigerator and opened it. "I haven't eaten all day. You must have something in here." She rummaged around and triumphantly produced the eggs Victoria had tucked behind the cheese box. "An entire dozen!" She handed the box to Victoria, who had turned the heat off under her omelet for two. "There's enough for all of us. Have you eaten yet, Cousin Vic?"

Bianca, in her blue Suzuki, googled Victoria Trumbull's address and punched it into her GPS. Because there are two Edgartown Roads on the Island, and because each has two names, depending on which end of the road one starts from, she got lost. After asking a woman who was walking a dog on a bike path for directions, she found her way to Victoria's sprawling, old, gray-shingled house. She waited for a white Malibu to pull out of the drive, then parked on the grass next to a VW convertible, its top held together with duct tape.

She was irritated about getting lost, angry about Rocco's impending wedding, determined to find a killer who would take care of both Rocco and his bride-to-be, and she was hungry. She hadn't eaten since breakfast, and her stomach growled.

Moisture dripped from the huge old tree she parked under. She zipped up her rain jacket and glanced in the rearview mirror, making a face at what she saw reflected there.

"Ick. Fatso." She stuck out her tongue, then set about making herself look presentable for Angelo. Lip gloss. Blusher, where it would slim those chubby cheeks. Eye liner. Eyes were her best asset, so she took special care with the artistry. She brushed her hair vigorously, then put brush and makeup back into her purse, and carefully pulled the hood over her hair.

Clearly, Angelo was faking that hurt ankle for some reason. One thing she knew for sure, Rocco had not invited this particular cousin to his wedding. So someone, she had convinced herself, had already hired Angelo to eliminate Rocco.

If she found out that someone else was paying for his services, that would make everything easier.

She smiled. She and Angelo really, really needed to talk.

Before she got out of the car, she studied this house of Mrs. Trumbull's. The main part was three stories high. Huge. It hadn't looked that large from the road. A second two-story section branched off of the main house, and a third one-story addition extended from that. And a long ell branched off of that. The ell had windows along its length. Skylights on the roof. That had to be a plant room or conservatory.

Victoria Trumbull must be rich to live in such a mansion.

Clearly Rocco was marrying into wealth. Damnation. He had enough money of his own. He didn't need to marry money. She, Bianca, needed Rocco's money a lot more than the rich bitch did. And now the rotten bastard was jilting her, Bianca. Killing was much too good for him. For both of them. A nasty, bloody killing. As long as she didn't have to get her hands dirty.

She checked herself once more in the mirror and, satisfied, got out of the car.

She crossed the drive to the side entrance of the house. Apparently no one on this crazy Island used front doors. She went up three stone steps into an entry lined with baskets, colored bottles, and geraniums. The door at the end was open, and Bianca could smell something fragrant in the kitchen. Her stomach growled. Her breakfast, an eon ago, had consisted of two cheese Danishes and three cups of coffee.

She knocked on the side of the open door. "Hello! Anybody home?"

An ancient women turned from the stove and glared at her.

"Are you Mrs. Trumbull?"

"I am," answered Victoria. "And who are you?"

"I'm a friend of Angelo's. He's Rocco's cousin."

"I know who Angelo is."

"Is he here?"

Victoria set down the spatula she'd been using to turn something in an omelet pan and shut off the heat off under the pan. She wiped her hands on a dish towel and faced Bianca. She waited.

Bianca was a bit disconcerted. "I, well, I heard he had an accident and hurt his ankle. And, well, I . . ." Her voice trailed off.

"I suppose you haven't had supper," said Victoria.

"Well," said Bianca, feeling an uncomfortable need for good manners. "No, ma'am. I haven't eaten since breakfast. What you're cooking smells great."

"Take your jacket off and hang it on the coat tree. I'm making a cheese omelet." Victoria broke another egg into a bowl, whipped it with a fork, poured it into the half-cooked omelet, and turned the heat back on under the pan. She flipped up an edge of the omelet to let the liquid egg run onto the hot pan. "You might just as well join us."

Bianca hung up her jacket as directed and patted her hair back into place. "Angelo?" she asked.

Victoria said, "Angelo is here with his cousin, Lily."

Bianca thought for a moment. *Lily?* What was she doing here? After what happened, Lily's father would never, ever have let her out of his sight.

Victoria tilted the pan and lifted another edge of the omelet, and the pan hissed. "Rocco's brother, Dominic, is here too, recovering from having drunk too much. He may join us if he feels up to it."

Dominic and Angelo? And Lily? In the same house? Bianca had no idea how Rocco's brother got along with Angelo. Angelo hated Rocco enough for an entire family. This was getting interesting.

"Are you going to eat with us, Mrs. Trumbull? That's five of us," said Bianca. "Are you okay with that?"

"We'll have six, unless someone else shows up," said Victoria. "The bride has returned from shopping."

"The bride?"

"Yes. Penny, the bride."

The bride I'm gonna kill, thought Bianca. "Will Rocco be here?" She wasn't sure things were shaping up in her favor.

"I doubt it. He's with the sheriff." Victoria turned the heat off under the omelet pan.

"The sheriff? What's he doing with the sheriff?" asked Bianca.

"He hopes Rocco can identify a body

97

found in my cellar this afternoon." Victoria moved the pan to one side. "Would you please set the table? Lily doesn't seem to want to leave her patient."

"A body, Mrs. Trumbull?" Bianca stood by the kitchen table, not able to move. Things were quite definitely all wrong.

"It's a long story, and I don't want to go into it right now. If you want to join us for supper, the utensils are in that drawer." Victoria pointed.

Bianca began to collect dishes and cutlery, moving slowly. "What happened to Angelo's ankle?"

"Apparently he twisted it getting out of a truck," said Victoria.

"He broke it?"

"I don't think so. Please hand me that platter." The platter was produced, and Victoria slid the omelet onto it. "In fact, I think he's making more of a fuss than his injury warrants."

"Oh," said Bianca feeling a rush of relief. "Can he walk okay?"

"With help of a branch from one of my trees."

As the last fork was set on the table, Penny breezed in. "Cousin Victoria . . . oh, I didn't realize you had company."

"This is" — Victoria paused — "I don't

believe I got your name."

"Bianca. A friend of the family. The groom's family." She smiled and held out her hand, all the while studying this rival, this blond bitch she was about to have killed.

"I don't believe Rocco mentioned you," said Penny, in turn studying this woman who looked too shapely and too nicely made up.

"He wouldn't." Bianca laughed her tinkly false laugh. "Mrs. Trumbull invited me to dinner, and I guess Angelo is invited too."

Penny flushed and turned to Victoria. "Cousin Victoria? I asked you to —"

Victoria interrupted. "Would you please ask Angelo and Lily to come into the cookroom. Supper is served."

There was no need to call.

"Hi, everyone! Oh, goody, something smells yummy!" Lily, followed by a limping Angelo, appeared at the kitchen door. "Can we help with any— ?" She broke off, apparently noticing Bianca for the first time. "Why are you here?"

"Lily, you can help serve." Victoria handed the platter to Penny. "Carry this to the table, if you will."

CHAPTER SEVEN

The white Malibu turned left out of Victoria Trumbull's drive and continued past the tiny police station and the Mill Pond, up a hill, and stopped in front of Alley's General Store.

Zoe Harrington, the blond driving the Malibu, locked the car and stepped up onto the porch. A woman sitting on a bench under a sign that read "Cans of Peas" nodded to her. She was wearing a gray sweatshirt with "Two Braves Hauling" printed on it. A stocky guy in a dingy red baseball hat was leaning against a post, chewing something, and a tall skinny guy in a worn plaid shirt was scratching his back against the doorframe.

"Howdy," said the skinny guy.

Zoe stopped, not accustomed to strangers greeting her, and not knowing what to say.

"Visiting the Island?" he asked.

"Sort of," she said. "I just flew in. Can I

100

get something to eat in there?" She nodded toward the interior of the store.

"Groceries," said the woman from the bench. "Like crackers and cheese and yogurt. That kind of stuff. But they close at seven." She looked at her watch. "That doesn't give you much time."

"Cans of peas," said the guy in the baseball hat.

"Ha-ha, Joe," said the woman on the bench. Then to Zoe, "The sign is an antique. They don't have cans of peas."

"If you want a sandwich or takeout, try 7A." The skinny guy jerked a thumb to a place she hadn't noticed behind the store's parking lot. "Pretty good food. Only I think they've already closed."

"Where'd you fly up from?" asked Joe. "New York?"

Zoe looked down at her high-heeled sandals as though they set her apart as a New Yorker. "Well, yes," she said. "How did you know?"

"People from New York lock their cars," said Joe.

"It's a rental car. Someone could steal it."

Joe guffawed. "Where's he gonna go if he does?"

"Come on, Joe," said the bench woman. To Zoe, "How long are you here for?"

"I thought just a couple of days, but I don't know. Maybe longer."

"This Island grows on you," said the skinny guy. "Like that mythical place you can't escape from."

The bench woman said, "Go on in and look around. It's worth a look even if you don't buy anything."

Zoe had a thought. "You don't happen to know a Mrs. Trumbull, do you?"

"Everyone on the Island knows her," said Joe. "She's related to most of us, and she is one tough old bird. What do you want to know about her?"

"Does she take in guests?"

"Sometimes," said the bench woman. "Not right now, because her cousin is getting married and the house is full of wedding people."

"You wouldn't happen to know if one of the guests is named Angelo, would you?"

The three looked at one another.

"Could be," said Joe. "The groom's name is Rocco, and we heard his brother, Dominic, just showed up. Someone named Angelo would seem to fit right in."

"You want to sit?" asked the bench woman.

She moved over and Zoe sat next to her.

"Is Rocco a friend of yours?" asked the

woman. "I'm Sarah, by the way."

"I'm Zoe. Rocco's a friend. Who's this cousin of Mrs. Trumbull's he's marrying? Kind of sudden, isn't it?"

"Penny something," said Joe. "Sudden. Yeah."

"Arbuthnot," said Sarah. "Penelope Arbuthnot."

"Close personal friend throws you for a loop, eh?" said Joe.

"No, no. Not like that," said Zoe.

"Stop it, will you, Joe," said Sarah.

"I'm trying to locate Angelo," said Zoe.

Sarah turned to her. "Who's Angelo?"

"Another friend," said Joe, smirking.

"*Stop* it, Joe," said Sarah. "You don't have to tell us, Zoe. What made you think Angelo was at Mrs. Trumbull's?"

"I know he's here on Martha's Vineyard, and someone told me they thought he was staying with Mrs. Trumbull. But when I went there, some woman with platinum blond hair said he wasn't."

"Long white hair. That would be cousin Penny, the bride," said Joe. "Don't believe anything she says."

"When's the wedding?" asked Zoe, who already knew when it was.

"It was supposed to be this Saturday, but

it looks like it might be postponed," said Sarah.

"Oh?" Zoe was surprised. "How come?"

"They found a body in Mrs. Trumbull's cellar," said Joe.

"Really? Who is it?"

"No one knows at this point," said the skinny guy, who hadn't identified himself. "Try Mrs. Trumbull's again and talk to her."

"Not that ditzy Penny," said Joe.

"Mrs. T might know of Angelo's whereabouts or could find someone who might." Sarah shifted slightly and crossed her legs.

"But a body in the cellar. What happened?"

"The electrician who was wiring stuff for the reception found him hanging from a beam," said Joe.

"So he was murdered?"

"Didn't hang himself," said Joe.

"And they don't know who he is," said Zoe. "How could it happen without Mrs. Trumbull knowing? I mean killing him in the cellar?"

"Maybe they killed him someplace else and carried him to the cellar," said Joe. "Who's Rocco to you?"

"None of your business, Joe," said Sarah.

"I've known Rocco since we were kids," said Zoe. "We were in grade school together." She got up from the bench. "He is — or was — engaged to someone, and they were planning to get married in September. I can't imagine him suddenly marrying someone else. Unless he's desperate for some reason. But somehow I'm not surprised that a body shows up on his doorstep."

"Mrs. Trumbull's cellar," said Joe.

"Whatever," said Zoe. "Well, thanks, people. Thanks a bunch."

"Don't lose the car keys," said Joe.

"Say hi to Mrs. Trumbull for us," said Sarah.

"I will. But I've got to get something to eat first."

"Lots of places open in Vineyard Haven," said Joe. "What d'ya say, Linc?"

"Try Oak Bluffs," said the skinny guy. "Linda Jean's is probably open. Good food and the price is right."

"Thanks again." Zoe got into her car and headed to Oak Bluffs.

"Cousin Victoria, the omelet is getting cold," Penny called out to her. "Everyone's sitting down. Is Dominic joining us?" A pause. "Cousin Victoria?"

"Sorry, Penny." Victoria had been pondering a decision she had to make. She agreed

105

with Penny that it would be well if Angelo and Rocco did not meet. She was trying to think of a diplomatic way to get Angelo and his cousin Lily to leave. The problem was that she had become intrigued by the two. Why were they here? And why was Lily putting on such a simpleton act? And Angelo was clearly faking the hurt ankle. She would like to solve that mystery before she sent them away. She had another thought. *Might they be linked to the body in the cellar?* She couldn't imagine how, but she would leave the question open.

"Yes, Penny, I'm coming," she said. "I don't think we need worry about Dominic wanting food for a while."

Angelo was already seated at Victoria's usual place at the head of the table, and Lily was to his right, fussing with her magenta hair. Bianca was on his other side, and Penny sat as far from the charming Bianca as she could get. Victoria took the only available seat, with Bianca on her right and Penny on her left.

This didn't seem to be the proper time for Victoria to evict Angelo and Lily. But she would have to get them out of the house before Rocco returned from the funeral home.

Lily broke the awkward silence. "This is

so nice of you, Mrs. Trumbull. Taking us in and, like, feeding us too." She stopped fussing with her hair and looked up at Victoria. "You have a nice house. I saw a harpoon in the front hall."

"It was my grandfather's," said Victoria, surprised that Lily had noticed the weapon that hung above her great-grandparents' portraits.

"In 200 BC the Greeks hunted swordfish with harpoons," said Lily. "They had detachable heads."

Victoria looked at Lily with astonishment. "How interesting."

"Eskimos used harpoons before the nineteenth century," continued Lily. "And in addition —"

Angelo interrupted. "I will pour the wine," he said, uncorking one of the bottles of Concha y Toro red that Victoria had been saving for a special occasion. This was not it. "Pass your glass, please, Mrs. Trumbull. You are first."

Victoria reluctantly handed over the wine glass that had been set at her place. How strange, she thought, that Lily, who seemed so simple, knew so much about harpoons. Far more than she did.

"Penny, the bride, next," said Angelo, holding up the bottle.

Once the wine had been poured and the omelet divided, the conversation was the getting-to-know-you sort, with awkward overtones.

Lily sat quietly.

Angelo turned to Bianca. "You are familiar to me. Have I seen you at some Bufano family gathering?"

"Maybe." Bianca picked up her wine glass and took a sip.

Penny said, "Are you another cousin of Rocco's?"

Bianca smiled and set her glass down. "Close personal friend."

"Oh," said Penny.

Victoria was silent.

Bianca smiled again and turned to Penny. "How did you and Rocco meet? Not too long ago, was it?"

"It was a while ago," said Penny. "We met in Boston at the Parker House about three months ago."

"That's so romantic," said Lily.

"At the bar?" said Bianca.

"He was at the bar," said Penny. "I was there with friends, and he came over to our table and introduced himself to me."

"I suppose he told you about his wealthy family?" asked Bianca.

"Not at first. We talked about the usual

things — you know, jobs, where we lived. I talked about my family and Martha's Vineyard, and, well, one thing led to another."

At the sound of breaking crockery coming from the downstairs bedroom, conversation stopped.

Victoria stood. "Dominic must have fallen out of bed. I'd better check on him."

"I'll go with you," said Penny.

After Victoria and Penny left, the remaining three were quiet for a brief time.

Bianca leaned toward Angelo, who was to her right. "I didn't think I'd find you here, Angelo. I've been looking for you."

"Accidents happen," said Lily brightly, not giving Angelo a chance to respond.

"Sure," said Bianca. "Like I accidentally ended up here too."

"What do you want?" said Angelo, dropping his Italian accent.

"I want to talk to you when that cutesy blond" — she nodded in the direction Victoria and Penny had taken — "is somewhere else."

"Angelo can't walk," said Lily.

"Yeah, I believe that too," said Bianca. "Where can we talk? Does the groom, whose name we won't mention, know you're here?"

"Mrs. Trumbull said he's at the funeral parlor with the police," said Lily.

"Oh, for God's sake, shut up and let Angelo talk for himself," said Bianca. "Those two are coming back any second."

"Where are you staying?" asked Angelo.

"Oak Bluffs. We could meet in that park near the ferry dock and talk," said Bianca. "How come you're here?"

"On business," said Angelo.

"How long are you staying?"

"Until I finish my business," said Angelo with a smile.

"Can we meet tomorrow morning?"

"Hey, I'm coming too," said Lily.

"You can feed the pigeons while we talk," said Bianca.

"They're not pigeons, they're seagulls," said Lily.

In the Shirt Factory's penthouse, Giovanni Bufano's call had gone through to Leonardo Caruso. Giovanni was Rocco's father. Leonardo was Lily's father. They were third cousins.

"This is Dottore Caruso."

"Giovanni, here, Leonardo." Giovanni lifted his feet off the ottoman and sat up straight.

"Ah."

"You know why I'm calling, of course," said Giovanni.

"Perhaps you will remind me. I wish to record this."

"I'd prefer this to remain unspecific, if you don't mind, Leonardo. You understand, I'm sure."

"It doesn't hurt to have a record of one's conversations," said Leonardo. "That way, there can be no misunderstanding. Go ahead. You can speak in generalities."

"We're family, Leonardo."

"Of course. And we are about to talk about your son Rocco and my daughter, Lily."

"I have disowned him. He is no longer my son."

"Yes, yes, I know."

Silence.

"Are you still there, Leonardo?"

"I'm thinking. I'm thinking." A pause. "I have a concern about my daughter at the moment. But I won't trouble you with it."

"Do you wish to unburden yourself, Leonardo?"

"Not now. What I want now is to know why you called."

"As I have already told you, I have disowned Rocco. Rocco is no longer my son. As far as I am concerned, my son is dead."

"He's not dead yet." Leonardo barked out a short, humorless laugh.

"It was almost two years before I learned what he had done. Immediately after I learned . . ." Giovanni stopped.

"He may be dead as far as you are concerned, Giovanni, that may be so. But I? I am suffering at this moment because of Lily and something related to that incident two years ago. I fear greatly what is coming. But go on."

"I heard that a body was found on Martha's Vineyard," said Giovanni. "That the body was found hanging in the cellar of the bride's family home." His mantel clock made a whirring sound.

"What do I hear?" asked Leonardo.

"My clock is about to tell me the time."

Two bronze figures, each about six inches tall, one on either side of the clock, turned to face one another. They raised their arms in unison and struck a gong. One, two, . . . seven times. The figures then lowered their arms and turned again to face out into the room.

"A clock," said Leonardo. "A clock one can hear from the other side of the city." He laughed. "Where does one find such a clock?"

It was a rhetorical question and Giovanni

didn't answer.

"To answer what you did not ask, my helper's first attempt went awry," said Leonardo. He paused and they were both silent again for several moments. "Who winds such a clock?"

"I wind it," said Giovanni. "Every Sunday morning. Can you give me any specifics?"

"Most unfortunate," said Leonardo, not answering the question. "I want to assure you, as I have before, that I have nothing against you personally, you understand? This is not to become a family feud."

"And as I told you, I have only one son now," said Giovanni. "Dominic is my only son. And Caesar. I accept him as my son. I have no other. You and your daughter are my family."

"Caesar is your stepson, no?"

"Yes."

"I know about the accident. And he has a brother?"

"A brother, Cosimo."

"You and Cosimo are not simpatico?"

"He was a difficult boy. Enough of my stepsons. What happened to Lily can never be forgotten. Or forgiven. I would give you everything I own, even my cherished clock, if I could turn back the time."

"Here today, tomorrow in the grave. *Oggi*

in figura," said Leonardo, "*domani in sepol-tura.* Right, my good cousin?"

"I assure you that I wash my hands of the whole affair," said Giovanni. "You recorded this?"

"Need you ask?" replied Leonardo.

CHAPTER EIGHT

Victoria, with Penny right behind her, reached the bedside of Dominic and found him sprawled out on the floor beside the broken chamber pot. He was lying on his side, his legs bent, his right arm under him, his left flung out to the side.

Penny knelt down beside him and looked up at Victoria. "He's unconscious, Cousin Vic. Should I call 911?"

"Yes. Of course," said Victoria. "Then call Rocco and let him know his brother had a bad fall and we've called for the ambulance."

Victoria and Penny stayed with Dominic. The three remaining diners, Angelo, Lily, and Bianca, were still at the table in the cookroom when the ambulance arrived.

"Should we help?" asked Lily. "I mean, he might be hurt bad."

"We'll stay out of the way," said Angelo.

"They don't need us."

"You can clear the table, Lily," said Bianca, stacking the dirty dishes off to one side. "Then how about you disappear for a while. I need to talk to Angelo."

Lily, sulking, carried the plates into the kitchen.

Angelo leaned back in his chair. "I'm trying to think how come I know you. At some Bufano get-together, right?"

"Right," said Bianca.

Angelo set his elbows on the chair arms, steepled his fingers under his chin, and thought. "Got it," he said after a bit. "You and Rocco the Rat."

"Rat," said Bianca. "Don't insult rats."

"You were engaged or pinned or something cute like that."

"Cute," said Bianca. "The wedding invitations are being printed right now."

"I see," said Angelo. "So, knowing my reputation for solving problems, you looked me up when you learned this rich woman from Martha's Vineyard is about to marry your sweetie."

"He wasn't my sweetie. He was my fiancé. We were getting married in September. Four months from now. And he does this to me?" said Bianca, her voice rising. "To me! I come here to this Island thinking we're about to have a nice get-together, me and Rocco, who was here on a hardship assignment, so he said. So I look in the paper — in the local newspaper, mind you — and read that he's getting married in three days. But not to me. Never had the decency to let me know."

Angelo nodded. "Consider yourself fortunate. Do you have plans of some kind?"

Bianca changed the subject, sort of. "What are you doing here?"

Angelo laughed.

"What's he done to you?"

"Please. I won't get into that."

They were interrupted at this point by an EMT checking the kitchen door. "Too tight a turn for the stretcher," he said to someone out of sight. "Take him out through the front door. I'll move the ambulance around to the front."

Angelo got up. "Everything okay?"

"He'll live," said the EMT. He went out into the entry, and in a moment they heard the ambulance start up.

Rocco, still in the police car that Smalley had parked behind the Dairy Queen, his burger still untouched, opened the door and swiveled his legs out. He was taking a deep breath when his phone sounded the Darth

117

Vader theme. He was about to let it go to voicemail when he heard Sergeant Smalley on *his* phone, telling someone that he was bringing in a person of interest.

Rocco glanced over his shoulder. *Person of interest? A suspect? You talking about me?* His phone continued to sound, and Rocco checked to see who was calling. *Penny. Hell. What timing.* He jabbed the talk button. "What's up, Penny? Make it quick."

"Dominic is in an ambulance on his way to the hospital."

Rocco held the phone closer to his ear. "Drying him out?"

"No, no," said Penny. "He fell out of bed. He doesn't look good."

"Shit!" said Rocco. "I don't need this. What kind of shape is he in?"

"I don't know, darling. The ambulance just left."

"Damn," said Rocco. Then he had a thought. Dominic may have saved his neck. "We'll have to cancel the wedding."

"But Rocco. The caterers. Our guests. I —"

"Penny, my dear, we must cancel the wedding. Therefore, no reception, do you understand? No wedding. No reception."

Rocco pulled his legs in and sat up straight, keeping the phone close to his ear.

"Dominic comes first," he said with a touch of self-righteousness. "He's my brother, after all." That said with a hint of pathos.

"Yes, of course," said Penny. "But we don't need to cancel our —"

Rocco disconnected without answering.

Smalley finished his own call and set his phone on the dashboard. "So," he said, "now what's your problem?"

Rocco slammed the door shut. "I need to get to the hospital. Right away. My brother had a bad fall."

"Sorry," said Smalley, starting the engine. "I'm taking you to the jail."

"Jail?" repeated Rocco. "You can't do that."

"You think not?" Smalley smiled. "Fasten your seat belt." He released the emergency brake

"What are you talking about?"

"You are going to tell me about that man lying on that table in the funeral home." He headed out of the Dairy Queen parking place. "That man you don't know, who looks like you, who was tailing you, you say, and who, you also say, someone killed to give you a message." Smalley glanced at him. "Your brother can wait." He turned right onto Main Street. "You going to eat your hamburger?"

"He might die," said Rocco.

"If he dies, there's not much you can do about it," said Smalley. "If he's in intensive care, you won't be welcome. Anything else, you got nothing to worry about."

"Where are we going?"

"To the jail."

"Shit, man!" said Rocco.

"You got one bright spot in your day," said Smalley. "Pretty slick the way you squirmed out of your wedding with Penny the Pauper."

Penny, still in the downstairs bedroom with Victoria, punched the off button on her phone with her shell-pink fingernail. The EMTs had come and gone, and Victoria was picking up fragments of the broken chamber pot. "He can't do this to me, Cousin Vic."

Victoria looked up.

"He's canceling the wedding."

"Oh?" said Victoria.

"He doesn't care about me at all. Not one little bit."

"It's fortunate you found out now instead of after you were married." Victoria stood up straight with the broken pieces in her hand. "I may be able to repair this with Gorilla Glue."

Penny burst into tears. "You don't care

either. I spent every cent I had on this wedding." She hiccupped. "A real Vineyard wedding. Picture perfect. Tents, raw bar, DJ, caterers. Then that awful man let himself get killed, and now Dominic falls out of bed, drunk." Penny's sobs intensified. "He's ruined everything. I hope they keep him in jail and he dies."

"You can probably get most of your deposit back." Victoria handed her a used paper towel from her own pocket. Penny wiped her nose with it and offered it back to Victoria.

"Keep it," said Victoria.

Angelo sat again after the EMT left, and Bianca picked up where they'd left off. "I guess you won't go into mourning if something happens to Rocco?"

"It would be only decent to mourn," said Angelo with a smile. "He is, after all, my cousin."

Lily returned from watching the departing ambulance. "They're taking Dominic to the hospital. I think he just needs to be, like, dried out. You two done talking?"

Bianca glanced at Angelo. "What's with Lily?"

"Lily is my cousin," said Angelo.

"I know *that* much," said Bianca.

Lily faced Bianca. "You're rude," she said.

At which point, Victoria returned, with Penny following, blotting her eyes.

Victoria looked at Angelo, who was leaning back in his chair. "That chair is fragile. Don't lean back like that."

He set the chair legs down, looking sheepish.

"Are we interrupting something?" she asked.

Bianca said, "No. We were just talking. Is Dominic going to be okay?" She indicated the damp paper towel Penny still held. "I didn't know you two were close."

Penny turned away. "I'm going upstairs to lie down, Cousin Vic."

"I'm leaving too," said Bianca. She tore a sheet of paper from the note pad on the telephone table, wrote a number on it, and handed it to Angelo. "I'll see you tomorrow. Call me," she said, and left through the kitchen door, the door that Dominic's stretcher hadn't been able to get through.

After Bianca left, Victoria sat in the seat Bianca had occupied during supper. Angelo was still seated at the head of the table in Victoria's usual place, and Lily was sitting next to him, her chair pulled up close to his, running her fingers through her spiky hair. Victoria wasn't quite sure how to begin. Fortunately, Angelo spoke first.

"I am so sorry you had to contend with this awkward situation," he said, the Italian accent in full bloom again. "You are a person to turn to when one is in need."

Victoria felt a pang of sympathy for the two. Angelo and the naïve-acting Lily. Was Lily really as naïve as she seemed? Angelo clearly did not have an injured ankle. Why the pretense? It was a mystery to her, and in a way, she wanted to solve it. But Penny was right, if Rocco and Angelo did not get along. She cleared her throat, sat up straight, and put both hands on the table.

Lily looked from her to Angelo and back. She offered Victoria a faint smile. "Thank you, Mrs. Trumbull, for supper and for everything you've done for us . . ." Her voice trailed off.

Angelo said, "Mrs. Trumbull, you have been most gracious."

"I'm afraid I have to ask you both to leave." Now she'd said it, Victoria felt her confidence return. "I don't like sending you off like this, but . . ." Victoria paused.

"I understand," said Angelo. "My meeting Rocco here is inadvisable."

"Why is there such animosity between you?"

"Mrs. Trumbull, it is a long, sad story, and I can't go into it now."

"I have a great many questions, but I suppose they will have to wait. I think it would be wise for you to leave before Rocco returns."

"Now?" asked Lily. "You mean, right now?"

"Yes."

"But . . ." said Lily, looking again from Angelo back to Victoria.

"Please take the mattress back upstairs where it belongs, Lily."

"But, Angelo . . . ?" said Lily, looking at him with a helpless shrug.

"If you'll hand me the telephone," said Victoria, reaching for it, "I'll call the ambulance, and they can take Angelo to the hospital where *he* belongs."

"That won't be necessary, Mrs. Trumbull," said Angelo. "We have imposed upon you." He got up stiffly from his seat and stood.

"I'm sure he just needs to, like, rest a day or two," said Lily.

"Hand me the phone," said Victoria.

"All right. If that's the way you're going to be," Lily pouted. "We'll leave. But we have no place to go."

Angelo turned to her. "We will be fine,

Lily. You may take the mattress back upstairs.

Lily left and Angelo followed.

It didn't take them long to get ready. Victoria was wiping the kitchen counters when they came to say goodbye. Lily had packed up her and Angelo's few belongings, and she was carrying her backpack. "I took the mattress back upstairs, Mrs. Trumbull. We're leaving."

"Thank you," said Victoria.

Angelo, a hand on Lily's shoulder, said, "I imposed upon you, Mrs. Trumbull. We did, that is. Our plans for the next few days are uncertain." He bowed slightly.

"Let me have a phone number where I can reach you if I need to," said Victoria.

Angelo turned to Lily. "Give Mrs. Trumbull your cell number, please."

Lily scribbled a number on the message pad.

They gathered up their possessions and paused at the door.

"*Grazie,* Mrs. Trumbull. We hope we have left no ill feelings."

"Good luck." Victoria didn't want to ask where they planned to stay, afraid they might tell her they were sleeping in the park. She felt as though she might have doomed them to a wet and chilly night of sheltering under bushes. But she felt she had to ask. "Where will you go?"

"To Edgartown. There are a number of places we can stay. Thank you for asking."

Victoria watched them leave. Angelo limped down the drive with Lily by his side, and the fog closed them off from her sight.

CHAPTER NINE

Lily and Angelo stopped at the end of Victoria's drive. "Will we stay at the Youth Hostel?" asked Lily. "That might be fun."

"No, we don't need to stay there." Angelo was no longer limping now they were out of sight of Victoria's house, and he had dropped his Italian accent. A car passed. Tendrils of fog swirled after it.

"Angelo, why were we, like, trying to stay with Mrs. Trumbull?" Lily set her backpack down. "That was dumb. She didn't want us there."

"I had my reasons," said Angelo.

"I don't know why, though." A car drove by, heading up Island, tires swishing on the wet road. "Where will we stay?"

"I have a nice place in mind," said Angelo. "Don't worry."

Victoria watched from the entry until Lily and Angelo were out of sight, then waited until she heard a vehicle on the Edgartown Road slow down and stop. She hoped it had stopped to pick them up. She had mixed feelings about their departure. Why had they come here? And how did they figure in Penny's wedding? Did their appearance have any connection to the body in the cellar?

In a way, it was a relief to have them out of the house. It was also a relief to have the wedding canceled. Penny would recover, she was sure. She did feel a pang of guilt about Angelo and Lily. She hoped they could find a place to stay. Someone had picked them up, she was sure, almost right away, and if it was a local driver, he or she would make sure they were all right.

The fog had turned into a gentle rain, perfect for the garden, and perfect for a quiet evening. She went into the parlor and set about laying the fire.

Lily and Angelo hadn't had to wait long before a pickup approached heading toward Edgartown.

Angelo stuck out his thumb and the pickup slowed and stopped. The driver, a thin, sandy-haired guy wearing a plaid shirt, lowered the passenger window and leaned over. "Heading to Edgartown?"

"Yes, sir," said Angelo. "You have room for both of us?"

"Kind of cramped, but it's only eight miles." He nodded at the back of the truck. "Put your backpacks there then hop in."

Angelo followed Lily into the truck, and they set off.

"You visiting the Island?" asked the driver.

"Yes, sir," said Angelo, hoping the driver wouldn't expect conversation for the entire eight miles.

"Friends of Mrs. Trumbull's?"

"Sort of," said Lily. "We're here for a wedding, but it's been canceled."

"Finding a dead body in Mrs. Trumbull's cellar sure puts a damper on things," said the driver.

"News gets around fast on this island," said Angelo.

"Sure does," said the driver. "Better than any of your e-stuff. By the way, my name's Linc."

"He's Angelo. I'm Lily."

"Friends of the groom, I guess."

Lily nodded at Angelo. "He's —"

Angelo interrupted. "Is that building on the left the Youth Hostel?"

"Sure is." said Linc. "One of the first Youth Hostels in the US of A, only they don't call it 'Youth' anymore."

A few minutes later they were well past the hostel. Lily started to say something.

Before she could, Angelo said, "I suppose you have to bike or hike to stay there at the hostel?"

"Not anymore. They even have parking for cars."

"Dorm rooms with bunk beds?" asked Angelo.

"You got it. Four bunks to a room."

"Eight snorers," said Angelo.

Linc laughed. "They got other rooms too."

They were quiet for a couple of miles. Then Linc asked, "Where are you staying?"

Before Lily could answer, Angelo said, "Edgartown. This area on the left" — he indicated the dense scrub oak woods they were passing — "I expected the Island to be more built up."

"You're looking at the State Forest. Five thousand acres of protected land. Takes up the whole center of the Island. Our single-source aquifer. No building allowed."

"Wow," said Lily, temporarily deflected from explaining all about Angelo's relationship to the erstwhile groom and their reason for being here.

"Started out as a sanctuary for the heath hen," said Linc.

"What's a heath hen?" asked Lily.

130

"Like a prairie chicken," said Linc. "Last one died off in the early 1930s. Right here on the Vineyard."

"Well, we're here because —" Lily began.

"And I bet this is the airport," Angelo interrupted. They had come to a cleared area set off from the road by a chain link fence.

"Yup," said Linc. "The County of Dukes County Airport." He laughed. "That's where we live. In the County of Dukes County."

"Pretty good-sized airport," said Angelo.

"It was the Navy's during World War Two," said Linc. "Cut out part of the State Forest for it."

They passed the airport and the State Forest and were silent for another few miles.

Lily, clearly uncomfortable with the silence, said, "You know, Mr. Linc, we were going to —"

Angelo interrupted, "Does Air Force One land at the airport?"

"Marine One does," said Linc. "Helicopter. Air Force One landed on the Cape, and they brought the prez here by 'copter. We get a lot of celebs here in the summer besides presidents and movie stars."

They were quiet for another few miles. Then Linc said, "You folks planning on sticking around for a while?"

Lily shifted in her section of the seat.

"Probably not," Angelo said. "Beautiful place, but we've got to get on home."

"Actually," said Lily, "what we really plan to do is —"

"Say, that's interesting," said Angelo, twisting in his half of the seat. "That's a pretty big windmill."

"Morning Glory Farm," said Linc. "We're on the outskirts of Edgartown. Where do you want to be dropped off?"

"The road ends pretty soon, doesn't it?"

"Makes a T at Main Street," said Linc. "Near Cannonball Park."

"Cannonballs?" said Lily.

"Drop us off there. That's fine. Give us a chance to do some sightseeing and window shopping."

"You can also see the County of Dukes County Jail," said Linc with a laugh. "Looks like an old captain's house, but if you give it a closer look, it's got bars. Some call it the Graybar Inn." He laughed again. "Well, here we are. I'll drop you off before I turn onto Main Street. That's the jail." He pointed. "Have a good evening."

He pulled over to the side and Angelo and Lily slid off the seat.

"Thanks, Linc. Appreciate it," said Angelo,

giving a wave as he slammed the door shut.

They retrieved their backpacks, damp from the misty rain, from the back of the truck, and it took off. Before the pickup was out of sight, Angelo turned to Lily. "Lily, please, I want you to keep quiet."

"I didn't say anything," said Lily. They were standing next to the stop sign on the corner of the Edgartown Road, which, now that they were in Edgartown, was called the West Tisbury Road. Several cars passed them, stopped, and turned onto Main Street. "He asked perfectly nice questions and I was, like, just trying to answer, and you kept interrupting me."

"I interrupted you because you were going to tell that guy our life histories, and he'd broadcast it all over this Island."

"I wasn't going to tell him our life histories, Angelo."

Two bicyclists coming up on their left stopped, a man and a woman. Both wore yellow slickers. The man asked, "Can you tell us the way to the Chappy Ferry?"

"Sorry, sir," said Angelo. "We're just visiting the Island."

The man, both feet on the ground, legs straddling the bike, pulled a map out of his pocket, opened it, and conferred with the woman biker before turning back to Angelo.

"We're not even sure where we are now."

"Perhaps I can help you there," said Angelo, stepping off the curb to check the map. He examined it briefly. "Here you are. Looks like the Chappy Ferry route is here." He traced the way. "Turn right here, and then left shortly after. Probably marked."

"Thanks so much," said the man, folding up the map and putting it back in his pocket. "Left, then left again. Thanks."

"No," said Angelo. "First right, then left."

"Yes, thank you," said the woman. "You Islanders are so helpful." They took off.

"Not," said Lily to their retreating backs. She turned on Angelo. "You do all the talking and won't let me talk. You're mean, Angelo."

Angelo took a deep breath and held it.

"Are you going to tell me where we're going to spend the night?" asked Lily. "I wanted to stay at the hostel. Will we sleep under a bridge somewhere? I wouldn't mind."

Angelo shrugged his backpack over his shoulder, crossed Main Street, and turned right. He strode past the big white Whaling Church and the brick courthouse.

Lily had trouble keeping up with him. "Wait for me, Angelo! Please slow down. I can't walk that fast."

"I'm sorry," said Angelo. "I keep forgetting I have longer legs than you do." They passed shops. They passed cars inching along congested Main Street. They passed a gray-haired man in barn-red slacks and a yellow foul weather jacket.

"Good afternoon," said the man. "Good day for a walk."

"Good day for ducks," said Angelo.

He turned left onto North Water Street, and Lily followed, no longer trying to keep up with his strides, which had increased in length again. He was far ahead when he turned, saw her, and waited for her to catch up.

"Sorry," he said again.

On their left were large white houses. All of them faced the harbor at an angle to the road.

Lily stopped and leaned against a white fence, breathing hard. Angelo too stopped.

The misty air carried the scent of lilacs and the salt sea beyond. A passing white-haired man nodded to them.

Lily smiled. "Nice day," she said to him.

After a brief rest they moved on. The houses on their left had small, tidy front yards bounded by white fences laden with budding roses.

At last they stopped in front of a large

gray-shingled hotel. Angelo checked his phone while Lily stared up at the place. It was huge. It was several stories tall and, if it had been in the city, would have covered a large part of a city block. The trim was freshly painted. The multiple windows shone. A flight of steps led up to a wide porch with a dozen rocking chairs. The path leading up to the steps was lined with newly planted blue, red, and yellow flowers.

"We're staying here," said Angelo.

"Here?" asked Lily. "Where are we?"

"The Turkey Cove Inn."

"Why did we want to stay with Mrs. Trumbull if we could've stayed here?"

"I had my reasons, Lily." Angelo went up the steps, and Lily followed. They crossed the wide porch and he opened the door for her. They entered a spacious lobby. The voices of the dozen or so people scattered around were muted, absorbed by thick carpets, heavy draperies, and soft cushions on sofas and chairs. A broad stairway faced them. To their right, windows separated the lobby from a restaurant, its empty tables set with dazzling white linen. To their left, a log fire blazed in an enormous fireplace.

Angelo led them to the registration desk, set discretely at the back of the lobby. "A reservation for Angelo Ferrari, please."

"Certainly, sir." The desk clerk turned to his computer.

"But you are —" Lily began. "Ouch, Angelo!"

He had stepped on her foot.

"Your room is on the second floor, sir. Front of the hotel with a view over the harbor." He gave Angelo two key cards. "Would you like assistance with your things?"

"Thank you, but we can find our way," said Angelo. "Come, darling." He took her arm firmly in his large hand.

Angelo hustled her away from the desk. He bent down to her. "Please, Lily, don't say anything. And smile, okay?" He squeezed her arm. They were nearing a group of four solemn guests, a woman in a gray suit and three men, all in dark suits and ties.

"Afternoon," one of the men said. "Great place for the memorial service, this."

"Yes, it is," said Angelo, slowing his pace slightly.

"Where are you from?" asked a second man, older than the first.

Lily began, "We're from New —"

"Chicago," Angelo interrupted.

"You here for the memorial service?" asked the first man.

Angelo smiled. An engaging smile. "We're on our honeymoon."

"Congratulations," said the older man. He held up his hand, palm outward. "God bless you."

"Thank you," said Angelo.

Lily said nothing until they were out of earshot, climbing the broad stairs to the second floor. Then, "Why did you tell him that, Angelo?" They were halfway up the stairs. "We're not from Chicago; we're, like, from New York." She stopped climbing. "And we're not on our honeymoon. I don't want to be married."

Angelo said nothing in response.

They reached the top of the stairs and Angelo turned toward the front of the hotel. They came to the end of the hall. Angelo checked the number on the door, inserted a key card in the slot, and a green light went on.

"How come you gave your name as Ferrari?" asked Lily. She pushed her glasses back into place. "Your name is Federico."

"Trust me, Lily." He turned. "I know it's hard for you, but please, you must keep quiet."

He pushed the door open, and they walked into a large room with a king-size bed and a view overlooking the harbor.

Lily dropped her backpack on the floor and looked around. "Where are you going to sleep, Angelo?" she asked.

CHAPTER TEN

Victoria looked forward to a bit of peace and quiet after such a day. She would light the fire she'd laid earlier.

She felt bad about evicting Angelo and Lily. There was something about them she didn't understand. If it hadn't been for Penny's adamant refusal to have them stay, she might have let them remain a day or so longer while she figured out who they were.

She needed to get her mind off everything that had happened today. Was it still the same day that Penny so happily supervised her planned reception — the tents, the caterers, the DJs, the raw bar, shopping, all the wedding details? The body in the cellar. Dominic drunk in Penny's car, Dominic taken to the hospital. Rocco at the mortuary. The wedding canceled.

What had happened at the funeral home to make Rocco change his mind so suddenly about the wedding?

Victoria's mind was a muddle. The solution was poetry. She would escape into her poetry. She needed to get her mind off the murder of the man in her cellar and the violence and misfortune that was accompanying her cousin Penny's hopes for a suitable marriage.

For the past week or so, she hadn't been able to think about writing. Now she realized it was necessary for her peace of mind.

She had always loved formal poetry, the constraints that a sonnet or a sestina put on the poet, the requirement to distill vast and cosmic thoughts into only a few words, and those few words in a prescribed form.

She settled herself into her mouse-colored wing chair and set to work. She heard Penny come downstairs and go into the kitchen. To finish the last of the kitchen chores, she supposed.

Victoria was organizing her thoughts when Penny came into the parlor with a glass of red wine she'd poured for herself.

"Would you like a glass of wine, Cousin Vic?"

"No, thank you. I'm all set."

Penny was about to sit, when she glanced out the window.

"That woman in the white Chevy is back

again, Cousin Vic. The one looking for Angelo."

"I'd better speak to her this time." Victoria eased herself out of her comfortable chair and went to the kitchen door. The woman parked where Bianca had parked, slid out of her seat, and closed the car door. She put the car keys in her pocketbook without locking the car.

She had strawberry blond hair and was about the same age as Penny and the others who'd gathered around the cookroom table. Victoria went to the outer door, stood at the top of the stone steps, and watched the woman approach.

"Mrs. Trumbull?" A soft voice salted with a New York accent.

"Yes."

The woman paused at the foot of the steps. "My name is Zoe Harrington. I stopped by here before supper, looking for my friend Angelo." She rested her hand on the railing and looked up at Victoria. "I thought he might be staying here, but some woman with platinum hair said he wasn't."

Victoria waited, saying nothing, curious to hear what would come next.

"After I left here, I went to the general store to get something to eat, but they were about to close."

"They close at seven," said Victoria.

Zoe nodded. "I got to talking to some people sitting on the porch, and told them I was looking for my friend Angelo. They said you might know where I could find Angelo because you know everything." She smiled, and Victoria warmed to her. "It's quite important that I find him. They suggested I come back here again and talk to you rather than to that other woman."

"You'd better come in out of the rain," said Victoria. "Did you get something to eat?"

Zoe climbed the steps and followed Victoria through the entry and into the kitchen. "Yes, thank you. I went to Oak Bluffs and had a marvelous home-cooked dinner at Linda Jean's."

Victoria decided to override Penny's objection to this woman. "Would you like to come into the parlor?"

"Yes, thank you." Victoria led her into the parlor, where Penny was perched on the uncomfortable horsehair sofa.

"This is Zoe Harrington, Penny. She's trying to locate Angelo," said Victoria, introducing the two.

Penny stood. "When you came by earlier, I told you Angelo wasn't here," said Penny. "He was here, but he left. My fiancé and he

143

can't stand each other, and I wanted to get him out of the house before they met up."

"I know both Angelo and your fiancé," Zoe said. "I understand the situation fully. Angelo and I are quite close."

"Please have a seat," Victoria said. "Penny was going to get me some wine, and I said no. But I've changed my mind. Perhaps you'd like a glass?"

"Thank you, I'd like that." She sat on the big chair Victoria called the throne. "It's a pleasure to meet you, Mrs. Trumbull. My company publishes books of poetry, so I'm well acquainted with your wonderful work."

Victoria nodded her thanks.

Zoe turned to Penny. "You're quite right about keeping Angelo and Rocco apart. Those two should live on separate planets. When did Angelo leave?"

"About an hour and a half ago," said Victoria.

"Do you know where he went?"

"I'm afraid not," said Victoria.

"I've got to find him."

"Is there an emergency of some kind?" asked Victoria.

"Sort of," said Zoe. "I have to talk to him before the wedding." She glanced at Penny. "I gather you're the bride?"

Penny said nothing.

144

"Do you know where Angelo went?" asked Zoe.

"They were heading toward Edgartown," said Victoria. "That doesn't narrow the search a great deal, but I'm afraid that's all I have. What's the problem?"

"Angelo's cousin is missing, and her father is terribly upset."

"I'm not sure I understand. What relationship does Angelo have with his cousin?" Victoria had a feeling she knew what was coming next.

"He's one of the very few people the girl trusts. She may have told him where she was going."

"How old is the girl?" asked Victoria.

"She's in her twenties, but she's autistic, what one calls developmentally disabled. She's like a ten-year-old, with all the enthusiasms and lack of understanding of a ten-year-old." Zoe clasped and unclasped her hands. "She lives with her father, who's quite wealthy, and he keeps her under close supervision. Somehow, she avoided his watchful eyes and ran away."

"And you think Angelo might know where she is?" Victoria was sure, now, that she knew who this cousin was.

"Angelo's close to her. He and her father are the only men she's able to be around.

She had a traumatic experience a couple of years ago, and she's terrified of men."

"Does she have magenta hair and glasses with black frames?"

"Yes," said Zoe. "That's Lily. Lily Caruso." Zoe half-rose from the throne. "You've seen her. She was here with Angelo? I've got to find them. I've got to find Angelo."

"They came by, hoping to stay here. Angelo was pretending to have a sprained ankle. They didn't seem to have any money. I'm afraid I did a very wrong thing by sending them away."

"No, no, don't worry about money. Money isn't a problem for them," said Zoe. "They have plenty. That's one thing I'm very sure of. They can afford the best hotel."

"Why were they here, then, pretending to have nothing?"

"I can't imagine why," said Zoe. "Angelo may have been trying to get information he could get in no other way. That would be like him."

"Why are you concerned about reaching her before the wedding?" asked Penny.

"This is a confidence I'd rather not tell anyone, but in this case . . ." Zoe looked down at her hands.

"Don't feel you need to reveal a confidence to us," said Victoria.

Zoe looked up. "I think in this case it's important for you to understand what's going on. Lily has every intention of killing Rocco."

"A ten-year-old in a woman's body. That's scary," said Penny.

"Yes, it is. Especially since money is of no concern," said Zoe.

"How does a mentally challenged person plan to go about killing anyone?" asked Victoria.

"She's what used to be called an idiot savant," said Zoe. "It's now called savant syndrome, or autistic savant. She's only about ten years old emotionally and mentally, but she has an amazing, prodigious knowledge of one narrow field. She knows more about that specific field than all of us put together, and that field happens to be murder. She knows more than most criminologists about murder weapons."

"Does her knowledge of weapons extend to her knowing how to use them?" asked Victoria, remembering Lily's interest in the antique harpoon.

"I don't want to find out." Zoe stood. "As long as Angelo is with her, she'll be all right. Knowing Angelo, he'll head for a good hotel — I'm sure of that. The best."

"That would be the Turkey Cove Inn,"

said Victoria.

Zoe brightened. "That's where I'm staying. They had a last-minute cancellation. If Angelo has registered there, I'm sure I'll run into them. But if not, if he does call you, please tell him to get in touch with me. His phone is turned off."

"Leave me a number where we can reach you," said Victoria.

"I'll write down my cell number." Zoe dug in her shoulder bag, extracted a business card, wrote down her phone number, and gave the card to Victoria. "Angelo needs to know I'm here on the Island. It's critical that I get in touch with him about Lily."

Sergeant Smalley drove Rocco from the Dairy Queen to the county jail, where he and Rocco sat facing Sheriff Grimsey Norton across his desk. The cramped office felt as though it had been shrink-wrapped around Sheriff Norton, who was well over six feet tall and built like a linebacker.

"Thanks for coming in after hours," said Smalley.

"No problem," said the sheriff. "After hours is what I do best."

"I want my lawyer." Rocco shifted uneasily in the hard wooden chair. "Why am I here?"

"We're not holding you, Mr. Bufano," said the sheriff, leaning back in his swivel chair. "My understanding is that you are in imminent and likely mortal danger, and from someone unknown. Am I right?"

"I want my lawyer," Rocco repeated.

"There's no need for a lawyer," said Smalley. "We want the identity of the victim who's laid out in the funeral home."

"I tell you, I don't know who he is," said Rocco, avoiding the sheriff's gaze. "I told Sergeant Smalley that I don't know him." He thumped his fists on his knees. "I don't have any idea who he is!"

"Tell us what you can about him then," said Smalley. "You told us he resembled you. He's too far gone for us to recognize the resemblance."

Rocco lowered his head. Rocco was a tall slender young man. Compared to his buddies, he seemed large and invincible. But here, compared to the sheriff and the sergeant, who was almost as big as the sheriff, he seemed slight.

"Someone killed him thinking he was you," said Smalley. "Or they killed him to give you a message. Why?"

Rocco didn't answer. "Why did you bring me here?"

"For your protection," said the sheriff,

swiveling his chair as far as it would go given the narrow quarters. The springs squealed. "We need answers from you, Mr. Bufano. You may not know the victim's name, but you know something about him."

"Why were you being tailed?" asked the sheriff.

"I don't know," said Rocco, looking away.

"Yes, you do know," said Smalley.

Rocco said nothing. He looked down at his hands, now folded in his lap.

The sheriff got to his feet. "We can hold you for twenty-four hours without charging you. I can make application to hold you for up to ninety-six hours. This is a murder investigation, you know." He leaned his knuckles on the desk and loomed over Rocco. His body seemed to fill the small room. "Ninety-six hours is four days." He paused, still leaning on the desk. "Do you know what four days in a jail cell is like? Well, Mr. Bufano?"

Sergeant Smalley stood too. "Take him to his cell, Sheriff."

"I want my lawyer!"

"We want answers," said the sheriff. "You're welcome to your lawyer. We'll hold you until he or she gets here."

Rocco sighed. "What questions?"

Both Smalley and the sheriff sat again.

Smalley said, "You told me the victim looked like you and that he'd been tailing you, apparently not trying to conceal himself. You must have some idea why."

"I owe somebody money."

"How much, Mr. Bufano, if I may ask," said the sheriff.

Rocco continued to look down. "Less than a hundred grand."

"Eighty thousand? Ninety thousand?" The sheriff picked up a pencil and tapped it on his desktop.

"Something like that."

"You mean that's all it took for you to decide to get married?" asked Smalley.

Rocco glanced up. "I thought she was rich."

"You come cheap," muttered Smalley, looking away.

The sheriff continued to tap his pencil, then wrote something on his desk pad. "Eighty thousand. Ninety thousand. I'm surprised they planned to kill you for a debt as small as that, Mr. Bufano."

"Think, Rocco," said Smalley. "Possibly you borrowed a bit more than that? Gambling debts mount up, you know. Or something else? Perhaps you offended the wrong person."

"They intended to kill me. When they hit

the wrong person, they decided to let it be a warning. They're going to kill me."

"Sounds that way," said Smalley. "Like it or not, you have to consider we're on your side. Unless, of course, you killed him."

"I didn't kill him! I would never have killed him."

"Then you did know him," said the sheriff.

"No, no. I didn't mean that," said Rocco.

"Then somebody's out to get you, Mr. Bufano," said the sheriff. "Am I right?"

"Oh, God!" said Rocco, burying his face in his hands.

"Marrying well, Mr. Bufano, would solve your problem, I gather,"

Rocco said nothing, his face still hidden in his hands.

"You have to think you're a lucky bastard," said Smalley. "You slipped out of marriage to a pauper, and the killer killed someone other than you."

The phone rang across the hall. A voice answered it.

Smalley was the first to speak after a long few minutes. "Looks to me as though you've got two problems, not one."

Rocco looked up at him.

"Person or persons number one hired someone to follow you, twitch your nerves. I can't see person number one doing that to get his hundred grand back. Wouldn't get his money back if he kills you."

Someone knocked and opened the door. A pale young man stuck his head in. "Court is sending a prisoner over. Want me to handle it?"

"Yes," said the sheriff. "Thanks."

The door shut.

Smalley continued. "Person number two has a serious issue with you and wants you dead. Thought your stalker was you. Reason for wanting you dead is unknown to us, but perhaps you have a clue?"

The sheriff put down his pencil and folded his hands on his desk pad. "I understand your father is Bufano of Bufano Industries. Way up there. Billions. Not mere millions. Right? That your old man?"

Rocco refused to look up. His head dropped lower.

"If you were my kid and I was the senior Mr. Bufano — is he Rocco, also?"

"No," said Rocco. "Giovanni."

"Now if I were Papa Giovanni, I'd take care of the person or persons who are hassling my little boy, right?"

Rocco didn't move.

"Your father is pretty well known as ruthless," said the sheriff. "Want to tell us something about your relationship with him?"

Rocco continued to look down at his hands. "He disowned me."

The sheriff said in a soft voice, "I can't believe that your old man would put a contract out on you, but something tells me he's not discouraging whoever has that contract." The sheriff's voice got louder. "What's your old man's role in this?"

Rocco shrugged.

The sheriff sat back and the chair squealed. "Gotta put some WD-40 on that one of these days."

CHAPTER ELEVEN

After Zoe left, Penny went upstairs and Victoria went back to her planned poem, relaxed in the welcome peace and quiet, with the humming of burning logs.

She went into the kitchen to make herself a cup of tea and was ready to start work on her poem, when someone knocked on the side of the open kitchen door.

"Come in," said Victoria, not pleased with the interruption.

It was Mark Johnson. He was wearing a baseball cap with the local fish market's logo, "The Net Result," embroidered on it.

"Good evening, Mrs. Trumbull. Sorry to bother you. I'm the electrician."

"Yes, of course. I know who you are," said Victoria. "This is not your first visit today."

"Sorry about that," he said.

"Have you been able to retrieve your tools from the cellar?"

"That's why I'm here. Just wanted to let

you know, I'll be working in your cellar tonight. The cops told me I can get at my gear now and finish the wiring job for Penny's wedding." He turned, about to leave.

"Wait!" said Victoria. "There's a problem."

Mark turned. "The bride? How's she doing? Some shock for her, dead body and all. And that drunk falling out of her car."

"Penny's fine. At least as far as dead bodies and drunks are concerned. But the wedding has been canceled."

"Is that right!" He seemed pleased. "I'll take my stuff away, then. I don't blame her for canceling."

"She didn't cancel the wedding," said Victoria. "The groom did."

"Wow." Mark leaned against the doorframe. "She invested some big bucks in the reception. I have to send her a bill, I'm afraid."

"Better for her to find out about him before the wedding," said Victoria.

"Why'd he cancel?"

"It's not entirely clear to me."

Mark laughed. "The bride . . . guess she's not a bride now. Has Penny recovered from that drunk falling out of her car?"

"The groom's brother," said Victoria.

"How'd he get in her car, anyway?"

"Apparently he had a few too many drinks with people he met on the ferry, and they delivered him here. He'd mentioned my name, and, well . . ."

Mark laughed. "Everyone on the Island knows you, right?"

Victoria smiled and continued. "He fell again this evening, this time out of bed, and he was taken to the hospital.

"Hurt bad?"

"I doubt it," said Victoria. "I believe he's still suffering from his excesses. I'm sure he'll recover."

Light footsteps sounded on the front hall stairway and Penny appeared, face washed and looking more like her usual self.

"Cousin Vic, have you seen — Oh, sorry!"

Mark pushed his baseball hat toward the back of his head. "Nothing like a bit of excitement around this place. I'll try to get out of your hair before something else happens."

"Didn't mean to interrupt," said Penny. "I just didn't notice you, is all."

"Figures," said Mark.

"I never thanked you for hauling that pig out of my car. So thank you."

"Any time," said Mark. "I hear he's at the hospital."

"They're drying him out," said Penny. "I

suppose Cousin Victoria told you I won't need the electric hookups after all?" She tossed her long hair over her shoulder. "I guess I owe you some money."

"I'll send you a bill. But I won't charge you full price."

"At least that's something." She smiled. "Thank you."

The phone rang and Victoria went to the cookroom to answer. "Rocco? Where are you?"

"That asshole," said Penny, frowning.

"The groom," said Mark, grinning.

"What are you doing in jail?" exclaimed Victoria.

"Ha," said Penny, crossing her arms and tapping her foot on the floor.

Mark straightened his hat. "I gotta get my equipment out of the cellar. Four other weddings to wire."

Penny glanced at his left hand. "You're not married, are you?"

He grinned again. "No ma'am."

"Don't," said Penny.

Victoria came back into the kitchen.

"What's he done now, Cousin Vic?"

"I'm not sure," said Victoria. "He recognized the body. He claimed it was a man who'd been stalking him."

Mark was still standing by the door.

"We're referring to the body in the cellar?"

Victoria nodded.

"You believe him about this guy stalking him?"

"I don't know what to believe," said Victoria.

"Bet you five bucks he knows the vic and can't admit it for who knows what reason."

Victoria glanced at him. "I don't care to bet against you."

Penny plopped onto a chair. "Do they think Rocco killed him?"

"I don't know what the police think," Victoria said. "But they need answers from Rocco, and he's reluctant to give answers. He's being held until he changes his mind."

"Can they do that, Cousin Vic?"

"Sure they can," said Mark.

Zoe Harrington drove slowly out of Victoria's drive, pondering her next move. She must call Leonardo Caruso, Lily's father, before she did anything else.

She pulled over and parked in a wide space in front of a small firehouse on her left. She punched in Leonardo Caruso's number.

"Dottore Caruso speaking."

"This is Zoe Harrington, Dottore, calling from Martha's Vineyard."

"Have you located him, my dear Zoe?"

"I think so. At least I'm getting close. Lily is here with Angelo."

There was a moment's pause. "You've found her. Is she safe?"

A string of bicyclists zipped past, heading toward Edgartown, headlights bright, red taillights flashing. Where could they be going at this time of night? Their helmets and goggles, spandex, the whirr of their well-oiled gears — all made them look and sound like a swarm of bugs, and Zoe had the feeling that she had narrowly missed being eaten by these strange insects.

"Are you there still, Zoe? My daughter . . . ?"

"Lily and Angelo were at the home of Victoria Trumbull, the poet. Her cousin Penny is the woman who was to marry Rocco."

"You say, 'was.' "

"Rocco canceled the wedding."

"May I ask why?"

"It's complicated," said Zoe. "They found a corpse hanging in the cellar. That may have had something to do with the cancellation."

Leonardo was silent for a moment. "Has the body been identified?"

"No one seems to know who it is."

"Ah," said Leonardo.

160

Zoe continued. "But I think the real reason that Rocco backed out of the wedding is that he discovered the bride was not as wealthy as he'd been led to believe. In fact, she's penniless."

"Interesting," said Leonardo. "Getting back to Lily. You said she was at the house of Victoria Trumbull. Where is she now?"

"I'm not sure," said Zoe.

"You must find her," said her father. "She has every intention and every means of killing Rocco. If she does kill him, she doesn't have the ability or wits to avoid capture. In fact, she will brag about it to the police, and they will have her tried and she'll be locked up. I cannot allow that to happen."

"I'm heading now to Edgartown. They may be staying in the hotel where I've booked a room."

"Please, I will cover everything — all your expenses. Don't worry. You must find Lily. She must be prevented from getting anywhere near Rocco. Convince her that others will take care of him."

"Yes, Dottore, I understand," said Zoe.

She waited for another bicyclist to pass before pulling back onto the road and continuing on her way to Edgartown.

She thought about Lily. Childlike. A ten-year-old mind with an expert's knowledge.

A woman, with a woman's body and a woman's desires. But a child who hadn't a clue about dealing with those desires. A child-woman who could so easily be crushed by Rocco, a man who cared not a whit about her, but only about satisfying his own hungers.

Edgartown was almost a half-hour away, time for her to think about the vast difference between the two cousins, Angelo and Rocco. Both were bright, but Angelo was brilliant. He spoke four languages that she knew of: Italian, English, French, German. Probably others as well. He'd gone to Dartmouth. Had an MBA from Harvard. He talked like a college professor, when he wanted to. When he was with her, Angelo was gentle, sweet, and kind. Definitely warm-blooded. He'd never once raised his voice to her, although she had given him cause enough times. She loved him more than she wanted to admit.

Yet she didn't really know what made him tick. He held back something big and frightening, and she found that extremely erotic. Hints of his hidden self showed up unexpectedly. His eyes, warm and loving, could suddenly ice over at the mention of Rocco, for instance. Never at something she said or did — never. But at the mention of

162

his cousin Rocco, he became something else. She had known Angelo since they were in high school together, and had long assumed that Angelo had another self. She had seen that other self throughout the years. He would disappear without notice, and when he reappeared, his explanation was always, "I was on a job." There had been a couple of times when Angelo's disappearance coincided with a newspaper item about a missing person. She had convinced herself, long ago, that his alter ego was a hired killer. A cold-blooded killer.

She'd often wondered why he hated Rocco so much. She suspected she knew. Lily was involved, but she was not sure how. When she and Angelo were last together, he'd told her he was going to Rocco's wedding, that he had a job to do and perhaps they could meet up when he finished the job.

So when Dottore Caruso asked her to go to Martha's Vineyard to find Angelo, to find out if he knew where Lily was, this was her opportunity to find Angelo and surprise him. She didn't expect a murder, a canceled wedding, and Lily on the loose.

She slapped her hands on the steering wheel. An approaching pickup swerved out of her way.

Calm down, she told herself.

And then she thought, *Angelo is here to kill Rocco.* He would know how to do it. If he gets there first, Lily will be in the clear. But why was Lily with him? Angelo knew how Lily's father protected her. Did he intentionally bring her here despite her father's concern?

And then she thought, *But would he kill his own cousin?*

And then she thought, *Yes, he would.* If it was a matter of principle, he would kill. If the fee was generous enough, he would kill.

It was close to nine o'clock. She passed the airport, its runway lights bright after the acres of drab oak trees her headlights had picked out in the State Forest. She'd been on Martha's Vineyard only once, several years ago. When she recalled from that visit that wonderful old hotel in Edgartown called Turkey Cove Inn, she called and was fortunate to get a reservation. She looked forward to staying there. She'd find Angelo and Lily, quite possibly at the hotel, and she and Angelo would work together. She and he would be a shield for Lily.

Lily's presence gnawed at her, though. What was it like to have a mind like hers, capable of soaking up an arcane field of knowledge that most PhDs took years to acquire. Yet to be unable to function like a

grownup in most ways. Someday research-
ers would find the key to unlock the promise
held in brains like Lily's.

The Edgartown Road ended. Directly
ahead of her was the jail, a structure built in
the 1800s that looked like the other captains' houses that lined the street. She didn't
know it, but Rocco was at that very moment in the sheriff's office, talking to the
sheriff and the state police sergeant.

She turned onto Main Street and passed
the county courthouse and the magnificent
old white Whaling Church. Main Street
ended and she turned left onto North Water
Street, where large old captains' houses
lined up en échelon facing the harbor.

By the time she parked in front of the
grand hotel and walked up the broad front
steps, onto the porch, and into the comfortable, elegant lobby where a concierge
greeted her warmly, she was feeling better.

"You must have a guardian angel, madam.
You got your reservation only minutes after
someone canceled. We are fully booked —
unusual this early in the season."

Zoe nodded and went to the registration
desk, where she filled out the form and the
desk clerk accepted her credit card.

"Would you like to be shown to your
room, ma'am?"

"Thank you, that won't be necessary," said Zoe. The world looked brighter.

CHAPTER TWELVE

Victoria returned to the fireside, but Mark, the electrician, hung around. He was seated on the captain's chair by the door, still wearing the ragged jeans shorts and boots he'd worn earlier that day when he'd discovered the body.

"Can I offer you a hot chocolate?" asked Penny. She stood by the door that led out to the kitchen garden. "Cousin Vic hauls out hot chocolate when she thinks someone's stressed out."

"Stressed out is right." Mark pushed his hat to the back of his head. "Four weddings coming up. Four brides and four mothers of the brides."

Penny reached into the cupboard above the dishwasher, where Victoria kept the mugs, and selected three of them.

"If you're so stressed out, why are you hanging around here?" Penny flipped a strand of her platinum hair over her back.

"Shouldn't you get to work? And further-more, Cousin Vic thinks it's disrespectful for a guy to wear his hat in the house."

"Sorry." Mark tugged his hat off and perched it on his knee. "I've got to get my stuff out of the cellar. And I don't much feel like going back down there by myself right now."

Penny opened packets of chocolate mix and poured them into the mugs. "Why don't you get a helper?"

"This late? I called everyone I knew, guys I usually call on, and they're all busy."

At this point, Victoria came back to the kitchen. "I think I heard the words *hot chocolate.*"

"You did," said Penny, "and I've got a cup ready for you."

"I also heard you say, Mark, that you're looking for a helper. Why don't you ask Penny to help you?"

"Moi?!" Penny placed a hand on her chest.

"Her?" said Mark at the same time, look-ing incredulous. "No way."

The kettle began to whistle, and Penny turned off the burner.

"I don't know why not," Victoria said. "Since her plans have changed, I'm sure she's available. Do you pay your helper?"

"Not even minimum wage."

168

"I don't know anything about electricity," said Penny. "I don't want to know anything about electricity." She poured hot water into the mugs and handed them out.

"What needs to be done?" asked Victoria.

"Answer my phone. Untangle wires and put them in order. Hand me tools. Deal with four brides and their mothers. That kind of stuff." He looked down into his hot chocolate and lifted it to his mouth. "Gofer work. I don't need someone with brains."

"Thanks a lot," said Penny. "Just the job I'm looking for. I'm going back upstairs." She started to leave.

"How soon do you need Penny to start work?" asked Victoria.

"Hey!" said Penny, turning around.

"Now," said Mark. "I need someone now."

Penny studied him for a moment, from his ruffled hair and beard, past his ragged shorts, down his muscular legs, to his worn boots.

She sighed. "Can I at least change into something else?" She indicated her own shorts and bare feet.

Mark smiled.

"O-kay," she said, and left the kitchen, her hot chocolate untouched.

"Thanks, Mrs. Trumbull," said Mark. "I do pay, but not much."

"She can use the money," said Victoria.

"I know," said Mark with a broad smile. "I heard all about it."

After checking in at the Turkey Cove Inn, Zoe went up to her room and tidied up. Then she walked down the stairs to the hotel's pub and sat where she could look out at the view of the harbor now that the fog had cleared: a lighthouse, and boats coming in for the night, green running lights to starboard making a pleasant moving pattern. She could see the small ferry that shuttled back and forth across the narrow mouth of the harbor between Edgartown and Chappaquiddick. She watched as the line of cars waiting to board the ferry inched forward, three cars at a time. The cars were loaded with great efficiency onto the ferry, which took off for the two-minute run across the harbor. It was a peaceful scene, just what she needed.

Today had been a killer. Talking to Dottore Leonardo Caruso, who was clearly more than upset about his daughter's disappearance, trying to calm him down. Arranging for Bev, her personal assistant, to cancel her appointments. And giving instructions for those she couldn't cancel, arranging for a flight to the Vineyard, renting a car. Then, upon her arrival, learning about the murder at the bride's place. The wedding cancellation. The disappointment of learning that Angelo and Lily had been at Victoria Trumbull's and she had narrowly missed them.

The bright spot was meeting the renowned poet, Victoria Trumbull. She hoped she could find time later to sit down with Mrs. Trumbull. She sat back and looked out at the view. What next? To find Angelo and Lily. But first, a drink.

"Would you care to see a menu?"

She looked up, taken away from her thoughts. The server, a young woman with long blond hair tied back in a ponytail, held up a large menu. Her nametag read "Amanda."

"Yes. Thank you, Amanda." Zoe took it.

"Would you care for something to drink, first?"

"Definitely."

Amanda smiled. "That kind of day, was it?"

Zoe nodded. "More than that kind of day. A double scotch on the rocks, please."

"Got it. Would you like to order something to eat, or would you like to wait a bit?"

"I've had dinner already, thank you, but I might order something light a bit later."

Amanda left and Zoe went back to watching the harbor settle for the evening. After such a jarring day, she'd been wise to come to this grand old hotel. She'd sip her scotch slowly. Maybe sit in the lounge and wait in hopes that Angelo would appear. She didn't need to go anywhere. Bed would feel good.

"Mind if I join you?"

She was jolted out of her reverie by a deep voice. She looked up. Dark hair, dark eyes, a thin scar. A familiar face. Menacing. Not someone she wanted to see. Especially not now.

"Cosimo. What are you doing here?"

"I came here for Rocco's wedding, of course." He pulled out the chair next to her and sat. "My dear stepbrother invited me. I wouldn't think of missing it." He laughed. "I might ask you the same question. What are you doing here? Keeping track of Angelo?"

Zoe felt her face flush.

"Guess that's yes," he said and smiled.

"Are you staying here? Zoe asked.

"Certainly not. Couldn't afford it."

Amanda returned with Zoe's drink and set it on the table. "And you, sir? May I get you something to drink?"

"Vodka martini with two olives."

"Would you like to change your mind about ordering, ma'am?"

Zoe shook her head. "Not yet, thank you."

Amanda left.

"So why are you here at the hotel if you're not staying here?" asked Zoe.

"That's my business." Cosimo leaned forward. "I saw that Angelo's here with Lily."

"Here at the hotel?"

"Yes."

Zoe turned her glass around and around. "I thought they might be here."

He smiled. "Rocco certainly wouldn't invite Angelo to his wedding."

Zoe said nothing.

He sat back again. "You heard they found a body where the reception was supposed to be, didn't you?"

"Yes. I heard." Zoe continued to turn the glass around.

"They haven't identified the victim yet," he said, "but according to Rocco, who called me, it was a guy who'd been stalking him. Apparently looked a lot like Rocco, so the police think it could be a case of mistaken identity."

"Cosimo," she said, "I don't know why you're telling me all this."

"I'm telling you because you've arrived in the midst of a nasty situation you didn't anticipate." He leaned forward. "I think it's

173

obvious that someone else is about to get hurt."

"What are you saying?" She stopped turning the glass.

"I'm saying you probably don't want to be around here when it happens."

"You followed me here to tell me that?"

He sat back again. "I didn't follow you. I saw you come in. I'm not staying at the inn. I'm here for quite another reason."

"Oh?"

He smiled. "I was led to believe Rocco had booked a room here, but apparently he canceled. My best guess is he's now hiding out somewhere."

Amanda returned with his martini. "Would you like to run a tab?"

"Put both on my bill," said Cosimo.

"Yes, sir." She jotted something on her note pad. "Everything okay for now?"

"It's fine, thank you," he said, waving her off.

"Well thanks for warning me," Zoe said after the server left. "And thanks for the drink. Now, how about you taking your martini to the bar and leaving me alone."

Cosimo grinned. He stood, picked up his glass, and reseated himself at the bar.

At the jail, the sheriff was considering Rocco's comment. "Disowned you, eh? Sounds as though your old man hates you, huh?"

Rocco nodded.

Sergeant John Smalley, sitting in the chair next to Rocco, leaned back and put his hands in his pockets.

"You think your old man would put out a contract on you?" asked the sheriff.

"He's too cheap."

"But he wouldn't discourage someone else?"

"Look, I don't feel so hot," said Rocco, leaning forward in the chair on the other side of the sheriff's desk.

"Can't say as I blame you." The sheriff leaned back in his own chair, and the springs squealed again. "Let's go over your situation. You owe someone one hell of a lot of money. Enough so you're willing to marry a gorilla if she had money. Right?"

Rocco looked down at his lap.

Sergeant Smalley took out his nail clippers and began working on his nails.

The sheriff said, "Someone put a tail on you, but the tail was so obvious, they were just telling you they were watching you, right?"

"I guess," said Rocco.

"Doesn't sound as though that's where the problem is. Whoever put a tail on you is

175

just threatening you." He stood up and leaned his fists on the desk, looming over Rocco. "So the tail's not out to kill you. Someone else is, sonny. Who?" he demanded.

Rocco looked over at Smalley's manicure in progress. "I don't know."

"I think you do." The sheriff sat again. "You're dead meat, you know. Unless you can tell us who wants you dead. Sounds like your old man won't intervene, am I right? You understand what 'dead' is?"

Rocco continued to look away.

"This is a murder investigation," said the sheriff. "We can hold you for up to four days, since you're a person of interest. We can also hold you in protective custody. Your would-be killer can't get at you here." He waited for Rocco to respond, and when he didn't, the sheriff said, "Or we can let you go. Your choice."

Rocco got shakily to his feet. "I want outta here."

The sheriff sighed and turned to Smalley. "John?" he said.

Smalley put his nail clippers back in his pocket and smiled. "He'll be dead in three days. Wanna bet?"

"No bet," said the sheriff.

"Cut out the comedy, will you?" Rocco

looked from one to the other. "I'm not getting stuck in some rotting jail cell. I'll take my chances."

"Looks like your old man is about to get his wish," said the sheriff.

Sergeant Smalley stood and hitched up his trousers.

Rocco looked from one to the other and eased himself out of his chair. "I'm free to go?"

"If you can call it that," said the sheriff. "Change your mind, that French chef is still serving time here."

"Want a ride someplace?" asked Smalley.

"No thanks."

"Your car's at Mrs. Trumbull's, right?"

"Look, I don't need a ride. I don't want a ride. I can find my way back to Mrs. Trumbull's without your help."

Rocco left the cramped sheriff's office, slamming the door behind him. The front door opened and shut again.

"Someone tailing him, John?" asked the sheriff.

"Guess I'm it," said Smalley. "He'll hitch a ride to Mrs. Trumbull's, and I can follow him from there."

CHAPTER THIRTEEN

Amanda, the server in the pub at the Turkey Cove Inn, returned to Zoe. "Are you okay, ma'am? That guy" — she nodded over at Cosimo, who had seated himself at the bar — "that guy bothering you?"

"Not really," said Zoe. "An old friend. I'm just tired." She stood. "Would you please put my drinks on my room bill."

"Your friend has already taken care of that."

Zoe dropped a twenty on the table and left the pub. Damned if she would accept a drink from him. Let Amanda have it as a tip. She'd understand. She had turned into the hallway that led to the lobby when she heard a familiar voice on the other side of the stairway. She knew his voice well enough.

". . . on our honeymoon," she heard him say, and she heard a guest congratulate him, and then heard him say, "Thank you."

She waited until she was sure he'd gone up the stairs out of sight, and then went to the reservation desk.

"My friend Angelo Federico is staying here. Can you tell me which room he has?"

The reservation clerk checked his computer. "We have no Angelo Federico, but we do have an Angelo Ferrari." He looked up at Zoe.

"I misspoke. That's what I meant — sorry," said Zoe, giving him her best innocent smile.

"Certainly, madam." He smiled back. "No problem. We're really not supposed to give out room numbers."

"His phone number then, please. We're family. A wedding."

"Certainly, ma'am." He wrote the number on a card.

She looked up with a smile. "Thank you."

The phone number he'd given her was, instead, a room number, and he smiled when he gave it to her. Zoe turned away from the desk.

She trusted Angelo. She and Angelo had known each other a long time, and she trusted him. Why had he told that man in the lobby that he and Lily were on their honeymoon? That seemed like an unnecessary thing to say to a stranger. It was beyond impossible that Angelo had married Lily. If he and she were here together, it had to be because he was here to keep her out of trouble. Had he anticipated Dottore Caruso's concern?

Then an uneasy thought snuck in. They were cousins, true, but distant enough. Third or fourth cousins. Was it just barely possible that Angelo had married her? If so, Angelo was marrying into big money. Leonardo Caruso, Lily's father, was a multibillionaire, and Lily was his only child. Too, Lily's marriage to Angelo would please Leonardo, who clearly trusted Angelo. His daughter would have a caretaker; Leonardo's fortune would be safe; and perhaps, by some miracle, there would be grandchildren.

Angelo had no way of knowing she was here on Martha's Vineyard. Her drink, instead of calming her, roiled in her stomach. She would have to find the truth, and the only way to do that was to confront Angelo.

She turned away from the reception desk and almost bumped into a heavyset man in a dark suit and somber tie. "So sorry!" said Zoe.

"My fault. I wasn't paying attention," said the man. "Are you here for the memorial service?"

"No," said Zoe, thinking of Angelo on his honeymoon. "Not this one."

"Oh," said the man. "I'm so sorry. My condolences. I didn't realize there was another . . ."

But Zoe was on her way up the broad stairway to the second floor. She reached the top and turned to the right, where Angelo's room was located. She hustled to the door and knocked.

Angelo's voice responded. "We're all set, thank you."

Zoe pounded again. "Open up, Angelo."

The door opened. "Zoe!" Angelo's look of astonishment faded quickly. "Zoe! What are you doing here? Come in."

"I've been trying to track you down, Angelo."

"And you've found me." He ushered her in and closed the door. "You know Lily, of course."

"Hello, Lily." Zoe looked around the room, at the king size bed, the windows that overlooked the dark harbor, two armchairs pulled up next to a small table, a china-based lamp casting a soft glow over the polished wood.

Lily, looking uncertain, was standing next

to a backpack dropped on the floor. "Hello, Zoe."

"I thought you were staying at Mrs. Trumbull's place, but when I got there, you'd left. Hitchhiked to Edgartown. Why were you at Mrs. Trumbull's? And why were you hitchhiking?"

"As far as hitching a ride is concerned, I couldn't get a car reservation on the ferry. Hitching is easier than finding a cab on this Island," Angelo said. "And why was I — we, that is — at Mrs. Trumbull's? I figured the only way to check out the wedding plans was to stay at her place. I'd made a reservation here at the inn as soon as I learned Rocco was getting married. It's where he's registered."

"Rocco's not staying here, you know."

"He made a reservation a couple of weeks ago," said Angelo.

"He checked out when he found the bride is broke. I was fortunate enough to book his room."

Lily picked up her backpack from the floor, opened it, and started pawing through the front section.

"Where's he staying now?" asked Angelo.

"Good question," said Zoe. "Do I understand you're on your honeymoon?"

Lily said, "That man in the lobby . . ."

She looked at Angelo and didn't get any further.

"Please, have a seat, Zoe," said Angelo. "Then tell me, what are you doing here?"

"First, I'd like to know if I should be congratulating you two. I heard you said to someone in the lobby that you're on your honeymoon," said Zoe. "And I believe you've registered under the name Ferrari?" Zoe went over to the two chairs and sat down. "What is going on, Angelo? As you can imagine, all sorts of questions are running through my mind."

Lily said, "Angelo just said that out of the blue about the honeymoon. He didn't mean it."

"Lily, please," said Angelo. He turned back to Zoe. "Before I say anything, what brought you here? Did Leonardo send you?"

"Before I answer that," said Zoe, "are you and Lily married? If you are, I'll leave immediately. I'll let her father know, and then I'll return to the city. If you're not, I deserve some explanation of the subterfuge and the room with the king-size bed."

"We're playing a game of tennis, aren't we," said Angelo. "All right. It's my move. Lily and I did not marry. This is Lily's room. My room is next door." He smiled. "Your turn. Did Leonardo send you?"

"Yes," said Zoe.

"Why?" asked Angelo.

"Lily was missing and her father is desperate."

"I wasn't missing," said Lily.

"It's okay, Lily," said Angelo.

"Her father suspected I might find you here on the Vineyard because of Rocco and the wedding. He hoped you might know where his daughter was."

"We need to talk," said Angelo. He turned to Lily. "Are you hungry?"

"Starved," said Lily. "All we had to eat today was that omelet at Mrs. Trumbull's, and that was, like, hours ago."

"I'll order something from room service for you. Whatever you like, okay? Zoe and I are going downstairs."

"I want to come too."

"You can order whatever you want. We'll be back before you finish." He handed her the room service menu and she pored over it, writing out a list.

Angelo checked the list. "Are you sure you want steak tartare?"

"I like steak. That's what I want."

"Steak tartare is raw meat mixed with raw egg."

"Yuck." She crossed it out.

"How about filet mignon. I bet you'd like

184

that better." Angelo called in the order — cheeseburger, chili dog, filet mignon well done, chocolate ice cream, chocolate cake, banana cream pie.

"Someone will knock on the door and tell you it's room service," said Angelo. "You can let him in, but don't open up for anyone else, okay? We won't be late. You can unpack your things, if you want."

"Will we stay here long?"

"A couple of days, probably," said Angelo.

"This is a nice place." Lily picked up the backpack, walked over to the far corner of the huge bed, and settled down on it.

Angelo escorted Zoe out the door, and they started down the stairs. "How about the pub?"

"Fine," said Zoe. "I was there earlier this evening. Cosimo showed up and bought me a drink."

"What was he doing here?"

"He was evasive," said Zoe.

They walked past the restaurant, busy this time of evening. Voices of diners blurred into a pleasing background hum, accompanied by the clink of utensils against china, glasses touching other glasses. An occasional burst of laughter.

"Is Cosimo staying here? I didn't think he had that kind of money," said Angelo.

"He said he's staying in Oak Bluffs."

They walked past the restaurant, down a long hall hung with sepia and black-and-white photographs of the hotel in the late 1800s.

"Doesn't it occur to Rocco that maybe Cosimo despises him? That a lot of people dislike him?" Zoe said.

"In Rocco's world, he's convinced everyone loves him. Whatever nasty thing he does to them doesn't register in his world."

They turned in at the pub and selected a table near the wide windows that looked out on the harbor, now dark and speckled with light from boats, some moving and some at anchor.

"Your problem with Rocco is Lily, isn't it?"

Angelo nodded.

"You hate him for what he did to her, don't you."

"Yes. He was thoughtless, selfish, and cruel. He took advantage of a ten-year-old girl child. He claims she was a willing adult."

"You know why her father, Leonardo, wanted to find Lily?" asked Zoe. "I feel as though I'm being disrespectful calling him by his first name. I always call him Dottore Caruso."

"He deserves the respect. I know why he's

worried," said Angelo. "Lily, let loose from his supervision, will kill Rocco. She's planned it out. She's told me every detail. However, she could never get away with it. Her mind is not sophisticated enough. She would be caught, and she would brag to the police about how she'd done it. She'd be tried and possibly be incarcerated. Because she's really twenty-two, not ten, and she is not that seriously retarded. Her father, Dottore Leonardo, will never let that happen. The trial alone would devastate her. And him too."

Amanda, the same server who'd waited on Zoe earlier, came to their table. "Good evening, ma'am, sir. What can I get you?"

"Just coffee for me, thank you, Amanda," said Zoe.

"You have Sam Adams on draft?" asked Angelo.

"We do." She made a note of their orders. "Will that be all?"

"Yes, thank you."

Amanda left.

"You'd kill Rocco yourself to prevent Lily from doing it, wouldn't you," said Zoe.

"I would. The authorities would never catch me."

They were quiet, both watching the lights on the harbor.

Zoe broke the silence. "You know, Angelo, I wouldn't have been too surprised to learn you'd married Lily. You'd not only be her protector, you'd be Leonardo's heir."

"I wouldn't do that to you," said Angelo, reaching for her hand. "Tempting, though. All that money?" He laughed. "I don't give a good goddamn about money. Too much means trouble. I've got all I want."

She held his hand tightly. "I worry about you."

"Don't," said Angelo.

"Did Lily get here by herself?" asked Zoe.

"She smuggled herself aboard my car. I didn't find her until I got to the ferry parking area and she emerged. 'Surprise, Angelo!' She'd been on the floor of the back seat during the entire drive from New York to Woods Hole. A five-hour drive. Not a peep."

"You should have called her father. He's worried about her."

"I tried. My phone's not working. You know, the inn is fully booked. They're turning guests away."

"I was lucky to get a room when Rocco canceled."

"We could free up a guest room for the inn," said Angelo. "I have enough space for two."

Zoe laughed. "That's a lovely gesture. I'll move my things into your room and let the desk clerk know. He was a bit suspicious when I asked for your room number."

Amanda brought their drinks.

Zoe asked, "Has my friend left? The one with the scar who bought my drink?"

"He left about ten minutes after you did," said Amanda. "He was waiting for someone. He kept looking at his watch. I saw him look up as if he'd seen whoever he was waiting for, and then he left."

"Did you see who he was waiting for?" asked Zoe.

"I was busy and didn't notice."

After Amanda left, Zoe said, "All I know about Cosimo is he's Rocco's stepbrother. Does he have other brothers or sisters?"

Angelo picked up his beer glass and held it up for a moment before he took a drink. "Cosimo has a brother."

"You seem hesitant about him."

He set his glass down. "Cosimo is about the same age as Rocco, maybe a year or two younger. He has a brother named Caesar. About three years younger than Cosimo. Cosimo and Caesar were in a car accident a few years back. Rocco's car, Rocco driving. Caesar was badly injured." He ran his hand up and down the sides of his beer glass, leaving a moist trail. "Caesar was a teen at the time. No chance of his fathering children now."

"That's heavy," said Zoe.

"It's heavy, all right."

"That's how Cosimo got the scar?"

"Yes."

"And what happened to Rocco?"

"He was able to get out of the car. Not a scratch. Instead of getting help, he ran away from the wreck, hailed a cab, and went home. Cosimo's brother spent two months in the hospital. Rocco had been out partying before the wreck. After, he went home to bed."

"Cosimo has reason to despise him."

"Caesar has even more reason, but he'll never act on it." Angelo lifted his glass and wiped up the ring of condensation on the table with a napkin.

"I'm so sorry about that. I had no idea."

"If anything happens to Rocco, Cosimo and I are both willing suspects. I can get away with it. He probably can't."

Zoe finished her coffee; and Angelo, his beer. They left the pub and went past the dining room, where people were still eating, talking, laughing.

Upstairs, the chocolate cake and the pie were untouched.

"How was the steak?" asked Angelo.

"Thumbs up," Lily said. "Done just right."

"And the cake?"

"They gave me a huge piece. I can share it with you, if you'd like. I think my eyes were bigger than my stomach."

"You did pretty well," said Angelo, looking over the near empty tray. "I wouldn't mind taking a piece of your cake."

CHAPTER FOURTEEN

Red awoke, not sure where he was at first. He was on a bed, fully clothed, and he felt awful. He sat up slowly.

"It's alive!"

"Is that you, Elmer?" He turned his head slowly and squinted.

"None other." Elmer was sitting by the window and had set on the table what looked like a mortar and pestle. It was dark outside the window.

"What time is it?"

Elmer checked his phone. "Almost nine o'clock."

"Where am I?"

"You're sharing my hotel room. Temporarily."

"I must have had a good time." Red stood, gingerly at first.

"If you want to call it that. You can stay here tonight, but you've got to get out tomorrow morning, you understand?"

Red groaned. "I don't understand anything at the moment. The thought of moving anything . . ."

"Look, kid, I got work to do," said Elmer, "and it doesn't help, you hanging around stinking of the metabolic byproducts your body's producing after all the alcohol you swilled."

"I don't need a lecture. What are you doing with that?" Red indicated the mortar and pestle.

"It's none of your business."

"Just asking." Red went over to the small bathroom and came out with a cup of water. "Thirsty."

"I guess so."

"I guess I told you I work at the dog track. Where do you work?"

"At a college in the city," said Elmer.

"Teaching?"

"I'm a technician."

"What do you do?"

"Aren't you the nosy one," said Elmer. "What I do is I dust off the rock collections in the geology department. Any other questions?"

"No, seriously," said Red. "I mean geology. I had a rock collection once when I was a little kid."

"I have to deal with grownup idiots who

collect rocks. They come back from the field loaded down with rocks, and I have to find space for them. And the college doesn't have space." He jabbed a thumb at his chest. "Am I expected to generate it?"

Red leaned away from him. "Guess that's a sore subject."

"Damned right." Elmer bent down, took a beaker out of his suitcase, and set it on the table.

"You need a sturdy floor for rocks."

"You got it, kid. I have to find storage space that will support mega tons of rock. As you might imagine, not the fourth floor."

"What kinds of rock do they collect?"

"Ores, mostly. Everything from sandstone to rock that got formed down where the temperatures would melt the rock if the pressure from all the stuff above it didn't keep it from turning liquid."

"Like gold and silver ore, rocks like that?"

"Gold, silver, lead, zinc, copper — you name it. College where I work is just a community college, but their rock collection is one of the best in the state."

Red went back into the bathroom and came out with a refill on the water. "I feel awful."

"I don't want to hear your problems. I've got my own."

"Talk to me. That helps."

"Oh, for God's sake!" said Elmer.

"Like how do the metals get in the rocks?"

"That's a whole field of study. PhD stuff."

"Diamonds. I know they form way underground with heat and pressure. I know that much. Take gold. They knew how to mine gold thousands of years ago."

"Speaking of gold . . ." Elmer loosened up a bit. "You ever hear the story of Jason and the golden fleece?"

"Yeah, sure. Something to do with Greek mythology."

"Good to see you have some education," said Elmer. "Historians now think that in ancient times, miners would lay a sheepskin in a river that was carrying bits of gold washed out of rocks upstream, and the gold would stick to the sheepskin." Elmer waved a hand. "Voila! The golden fleece."

"Don't shout," said Red holding his head in both hands.

Elmer ignored him. "There's a mineral that forms during mine fires or burning coal seams."

"Yeah?"

"Other ways too, but that's one way. It's a pretty rare mineral, so it's not considered an ore. It's called arsenolite."

"From 'arson,' like burning mines?"

"It's supposed to have a sweet taste, but you'd better not taste it. Deadly poison. I don't think a tiny taste will kill you, but it's likely to make you sick. The name comes from 'arsenic,' like poison."

It was about two hours after Rocco left the jail. He'd gotten a ride right away and was dropped off at Mrs. Trumbull's, where he picked up his car.

Sergeant Smalley tailed him to Oak Bluffs. Night had fallen and the fog was still heavy. Rocco drove into the Camp Meeting Grounds, and there Smalley lost him.

Smalley slammed his fist on the steering wheel. The fool. Someone's out to get him, and they will. Whoever's got it in for him is most likely a pro. His only chance to stay alive is a couple of nights in jail. By then we should be able to sort things out.

He pulled out his mobile phone and punched in a number.

"Sheriff Norton here."

"Goddamn it, Grimsey, I lost him." Smalley was on his phone and driving on Seaview Avenue. "I'm heading back to Edgartown."

A long pause. "What are you saying?"

"Our friend, Rocco Bufano. He gave me the slip."

"How'd he do that?" asked the sheriff. "Where are you now?"

"I'm on my way to see you. I lost him about twenty minutes ago."

"Oh?"

"He drove into the Camp Meeting grounds and veered off into one of those outer circles. You know the roads in there. Nothing but paved paths. All one-way." Smalley glanced over to his left, where he could hear the surf beating against rocks at the base of the sea wall. "No way anyone could follow in this pea soup. It's a warren in there."

"You don't have to tell me," said the sheriff. "I didn't think he knew the Island well enough to head there."

Smalley tapped his horn and passed a slow-moving car.

"You on your cell?" asked the sheriff.

"I don't want to use the radio."

"Pull over."

Smalley passed Inkwell Beach, dutifully pulled off the road, and cut the engine. "He's here in Oak Bluffs, Grimsey. Somewhere."

"Why is he dodging us? We're trying to save the guy's life."

"He's dodging his would-be killer too," said Smalley.

"He never did tell us. Who wants him dead?"

"Take your pick," said Smalley.

"What do you know about him that we didn't uncover earlier? What are we dealing with?"

"His father is Leonardo Bufano. Bufano Industries."

"Yeah, there's that. He shouldn't have much to worry about. Bufano Towers? Bufano golf courses? Even if his old man hates him, he's not going to let someone bump off his son."

"From what I understand, Papa disinherited Sonny. So Rocco decided he'd have to marry money and picked Penny Arbuthnot, Victoria Trumbull's third cousin once removed."

The sheriff laughed. "She rates a free turkey at Christmas."

"I told him so. He canceled the wedding."

"I can understand his not wanting to stay here at the corrections facility," the sheriff said. "Good food, but the accommodations, well . . . not up to Bufano Towers." Another pause. "If he parked in the Campground, it'll be no big deal finding the car. You have someone watching it?"

"I don't have the manpower and he's not a suspect, so he doesn't rate a watchdog."

"No point in your heading here to Edgartown," said the sheriff. "Might as well go back to the barracks. It's closer to wherever he is."

"If he can lose us, I suppose he's alert and savvy enough to lose whoever else is after him," said Smalley, "but I doubt it." He started up the engine. "I've got a couple things to finish up at work." He glanced to his left before pulling away from the side of the road. Turned right onto Canonicus Avenue, past Naushon, Nashawena, and Pocasset Avenues. Canonicus changed into Uncas Avenue.

"I could get lost in this goddamned town myself," he muttered, "and I've lived on this Island all my life."

Rocco knew he was being followed. Probably the cops, but if it was someone else, he didn't want them following him. He didn't want the cops following him either, but at least they weren't threatening to kill him. He turned into the place they called the Campground, where he'd gotten lost the first day he was on the Island. The roads in that maze were all labeled avenues. Pawtucket Avenue, 4th Avenue. Yeah, sure. They were one-lane paved paths with grass sprouting in the middle. The whole place was made up of intersecting circles crowded with wooden houses the size of a kid's playhouse, painted every color that paint came in, jammed together so close you could reach a hand out your window and rap on the next-door neighbor's window. One lit match and the whole place would go up in flames.

He lost his tail after he made a few turns onto ever-smaller avenues. He kept going, turning onto one-way Commonwealth Avenue, then one-way Pawtucket Avenue, then one-way Allen Avenue, 4th Avenue, Rock Avenue, Chapel Lane — what determined how a path went from being called an avenue to being called a lane?

He was back where he started and totally confused.

He eventually found a place where two houses were separated enough so he could park between them. Locked his car and walked away. Heavy fog. Supposed to look for moss growing on the north side of trees. No trees. No moss. The sun had set long ago. Foghorns in the distance on Nantucket Sound. He'd walk toward the sound. On foot he could more or less hold a steady course through this maze, and eventually he found himself out on Circuit Avenue, the main drag of Oak Bluffs. Even the main drag ran in a circle. Everything ran in circles in this crazy town.

From Circuit Avenue he knew his bearings. Head toward the water, Nantucket Sound. Follow the road that skirted the Sound to the street where he'd rented a room in a rooming house, and crash. He was hungry, exhausted, and — he had to admit it — frightened.

His father wouldn't hire anyone to kill him; he was sure of that. But his father wouldn't hesitate to point out where he was staying — that is, if good old Dad knew where he was staying. Then there was the guy who'd loaned him a couple — a few — quite a few thousand bucks. Only nobody would kill for that. The characters at the dog races. Then there was Lily's father, Leonardo. He might have hired someone . . .

His head hurt. He ached all over. Maybe he was coming down with something.

He arrived at the shabby house where he'd seen the bed and breakfast sign and engaged a room. Went up the creaky wooden steps, opened the door with the glass panes that rattled — no key, of course — and started up the splintery wooden stairs.

The women who'd rented the room to him came out of a back room.

"Good evening, Mr. Smith. Did you have

a nice day?"

"Lovely, thank you, Mrs. Bailey."

"I'm so glad you did. There's so much to see and do on our fair Island."

"Yes, there is, Mrs. Bailey."

He could tell her what his real day had been like. Namely, hell. He'd canceled his wedding to the bride who'd claimed to be so rich but had nothing. He'd come from the jail, where the sheriff and the state cop wanted to incarcerate him. For his protection, they'd said. He'd seen the body they'd found hung in Victoria Trumbull's cellar. He knew who it was. It was a warning to him. He felt sick.

He'd have to get off this Island, and soon. But he had to get some sleep first. He was exhausted, wiped out. Find his car in the morning and take off.

He went up to his room, which was the size of a chicken coop. The ceiling sloped to a small window. The single bed took up most of the space. He sank onto it, grateful for a firm mattress. A big soft pillow. Clean sheets that smelled like fresh air. A down comforter. Sleep.

CHAPTER FIFTEEN

During the night the fog cleared, and the Island was treated to what Victoria Trumbull called a typical Vineyard day. Brilliant sunshine, a fluorescent blue sky, birds singing lustily, and leaves unfolding on trees that had been dead looking only a few days before.

Elizabeth had the morning off. She got up early and before breakfast went out to the vegetable garden with a basket to see what miracles had taken place since she'd last looked.

The air was filled with the scent of lilacs. Birds sang. Under the lilac bushes, stalks that had stood like dried sticks all winter had burst into blossom, each covered with dozens of tiny bouquets of white flowers. Elizabeth had always called the plants, which were a type of spirea, bridal wreath, but her grandmother insisted they were called widow's wreath.

"Bridal wreath is a more optimistic name," Elizabeth had said, trying to get her grandmother to see things her way. "That's what it's called in the seed catalogs."

"Widow's wreath is what my grandmother and her mother before her called it," said Victoria, her jaw set in that way that Elizabeth knew meant the end of the discussion.

So, in a way, they agreed to disagree. Elizabeth called it widow's wreath in her grandmother's presence.

Everything about gardening was miraculous. A seed, so small you could barely see it, would produce a kale plant from which you could harvest leaves well into the winter. Squash seeds the size of a little fingernail would grow into sprawling vines yielding enough squash to get them through the winter too.

She went to check the asparagus bed. Every year Arnie Fischer and his father before him had spread a load of manure on the bed, and every year the asparagus responded, sending up tender young stalks. And yes, new stalks had sprouted up everywhere she looked.

She went back to the house to get her grandmother. Today's harvest would require both of them.

Victoria was in the cookroom, typing her column for the *Island Enquirer.* She glanced up from her work.

"It's too beautiful a day to be inside," said Elizabeth. "The asparagus needs to be picked. Breakfast can wait."

"One more item and I'll be ready to go." Victoria typed rapidly, two gnarled forefingers hitting the keys, her thumb hitting the space bar. She finished, slung the carriage back, and pushed her typewriter aside.

They went out to the asparagus bed and worked quietly, Victoria down on her kneeler, Elizabeth bending over. They broke each stalk where it snapped easily, harvesting only the tender tips.

Song sparrows sang. Crows cawed, and both Victoria and Elizabeth looked up to see them chasing a red-tailed hawk. The hawk soared away, higher and higher, the crows after him.

McCavity, the cat, curled up beside Victoria and watched them work.

"You know, Gram," said Elizabeth after they'd been working for a while, "I've been thinking a lot about that body in the cellar."

"It raises some questions," agreed Victoria.

"A lot of creepy questions." Elizabeth pulled up a weed and threw it to one side.

"For instance, how did the killer know about our cellar? And how did he know we wouldn't be around to see or hear him? Was he spying on us? Is it someone we know? That's the creepiest thought of all — that it might be someone we know who hung that body in our cellar."

Victoria had picked the spears she was able to reach, and shifted her kneeler over a couple of feet to a fresh patch. "The police believe the victim was from off Island."

"What makes them think that?"

"For one thing, none of the Islanders who've seen the body can identify him." Victoria tossed a weed aside. "Then Sergeant Smalley asked if Rocco could identify the body. Rocco claimed the victim had been stalking him in New York." Victoria tossed aside another weed. "Rocco is the only person who seems to know anything at all about the victim. If the victim was from off Island, what was he doing here on the Island, and who hung him in our cellar, and why? And was he alive or dead when he was taken down to the cellar." She glanced over at McCavity, who'd pounced on the weed. "And how did the killer know that my cellar would be a place he could hang someone. How did he plan the time of his killing to correspond with a time when neither of us was home?"

"It must be connected to Rocco and Penny's wedding," said Elizabeth. "Rocco recognized the stalker, so the murder is linked to him. And to have the body in the cellar of where the reception is to take place can't be coincidental."

"According to Doc Jeffers, the victim was strangled before he was hung up," said Victoria. "He was killed with a garrote, a length of wire or cord the killer looped around his neck and drew tight."

Elizabeth stood up and stretched. She hefted her basket. "We must have four or five pounds of asparagus, and there's still at least that much more to harvest. At the rate it's growing, there will be more tomorrow."

She bent over again and got back to work. "Here's a key question: Assuming he was killed here on Island, where was he killed? On this property? Or killed somewhere else and brought here?"

Victoria, stiff from bending over, straightened her back. "Rigor mortis would set in at some point, and for a period of time the body would be difficult, if not impossible, to move. Decomposition would begin quite soon in this warm weather. So the killer had to take into account the time it would take to transport the body and dispose of it.

Once the body was in the cellar, decomposition would slow or stop." She got slowly to her feet, wincing. "Ouch!"

Elizabeth looked up with concern.

"I'm quite all right. I've just been kneeling too long. Let's process what we have."

"There's still a lot left to pick."

"We can do it later."

On the way back to the house, they stopped to admire the purple lilacs rising out of a froth of delicate white flowers, so massed they could have been a single large brushstroke.

"It didn't even register on me that these flowers are bridal wreath," said Elizabeth.

Victoria scowled.

Elizabeth continued. "Each flower is a miniature bouquet. Appropriate for Penny for a while. Poor Penny."

"I think Penny is well rid of him," said Victoria. "My grandmother insisted the flowers were widow's wreath."

"Of course," said Elizabeth. "Widow's wreath. That's what I meant to say."

They set their baskets down next to the kitchen sink.

"You know, Gram, wherever the deed was done, the killer would have to transport the body from there to here. Which seems to point to his being killed right here, on our property." Elizabeth emptied her basket into the sink and turned on the cold water. "When did Cousin Penny first tell you about her wedding and ask about holding the reception here?"

Victoria emptied her own basket and sat down. "It was about six weeks ago that she told me she was getting married. She asked me then if she might have the reception here."

"She'd met the guy only a few weeks before, hadn't she?"

"Probably six weeks or so before. It did seem a bit sudden. We should check our calendars for the past six weeks to see when we were both away from the house for an extended time. Something we'd planned that people would know about. The killer must have known that we would not be home."

"Before six weeks ago we had no idea Rocco existed and didn't know Cousin Penny all that well, so we can rule out any time before then."

"Let's have breakfast now and worry about the killer and the asparagus after we've eaten," said Victoria.

Smalley had just poured his morning's coffee at the state police barracks, when his phone rang. He looked at the caller's number. The groundskeeper for the Campground.

"Yo, Doug," he answered. "What's up?"

"You know Mrs. Curtain?"

"Sure. House with purple and pink trim on one of the outer circles of the Campground."

"She's the one. She just got back from off Island. Called to report a strange car, a blue BMW, in her parking spot, and she can't park her own car."

"How long has it been there?"

"She was off Island overnight. Said it couldn't have been there more than a day at most."

"Did she check the glove compartment for owner's papers?"

"The car's locked, so she couldn't. New York license plate." He gave Smalley the license number.

Rocco's car. He hadn't moved his car during the night. He was probably still on Island.

"Ring any bells with you, John?"

"He's a guy we were keeping an eye on," said Smalley.

"Troublemaker?"

"No. I was hoping to avoid trouble for him."

"I'm about to ask Kenny to tow it to the Park and Ride. Is that a problem for you?"

"Not at all. I'm glad to know where the car is now and where it's going. Park and Ride sounds good. If I hear from our car owner looking for his car, I'll tell him he owes the towing charge."

"Thanks, John."

After Smalley disconnected, he thought about calling Rocco, then remembered he didn't have his phone number. He would ask Mrs. Curtain to give him a call if Rocco showed up. He punched in her number, got the answering machine, and left a message.

Zoe was an early riser. Angelo was still asleep. She dressed quietly in her shorts and running shoes and ran a half mile along the beach, then back again, showered, and went for breakfast in a coffee shop she'd seen on Main Street. She sat at the counter.

"Nice morning," said the server, a young guy, high school age, late teens. "Coffee?"

"Please," said Zoe.

She could hear a police scanner behind the counter. A lot of crackling, a woman's voice with a lot of numbers, a man's voice with more numbers. Silence. More crackling.

"Here you are," said the server, sliding a heavy mug toward her along with a pitcher of cream and a bowl of sugar packets. "Would you like to order?"

"A scrambled egg and toast," said Zoe. "Is that a police scanner?"

"That?" he asked. "Just about everybody on the Island has a scanner. Way to keep up with the news as it's happening."

Zoe laughed. "I guess so. What's happening now?"

"Nothing much. The biggest excitement of the morning is they towed a car out of the Campground."

"That's supposed to be big news?"

He shrugged. "You know, nothing much happens around here. We gotta get our thrills somehow. Towing a car — and this car happened to be a BMW — out of the Campground is a big deal. How do you like your scrambled egg — runny or well done?"

"Not runny. In between. Does everyone have a scanner?"

"I'm guessing eighty percent of us do. Actually, news gets around even faster by a site on FaceBook called 'Islanders Know.' I mean, it tells the whole Island what you had for lunch yesterday."

"So the talk of the Island this morning will be about a car getting towed."

"Yeah. Well, you know, think of the aggravation of the poor guy whose car got towed. Walks back to get it, then what? Somehow he's got to find the police station, pay a fine. Imagine what it's like for him, all hot and sweaty, frustrated, trying to get his car from wherever they towed it, probably the Park and Ride, and he doesn't know where that is."

The server, a kid, really, swiped the counter in front of Zoe with a damp towel he'd had tucked into the top of his apron. He went on. "The guy probably got up in the morning, feeling all optimistic and happy, showered, shaved, maybe was singing in the shower. Put on a clean shirt. Now, two hours later, he looks like a homeless guy, sweaty and smelly, and he feels like one too. He has a boat reservation and he's late. If he's from off Island, he locked his car and the cops maybe broke a window . . ."

"Stop!" said Zoe, holding up a hand. "Are you still in high school?"

"A sophomore. This is my work-study job."

"You should study creative writing. You have a great future."

"Thanks," he said. "I better get your

213

order, or they'll be on my case. But that's what I'm aiming for. Creative writing."

After breakfast Elizabeth put the dishes in the dishwasher and stacked the seed catalogs Victoria had been studying on the chair next to her. She sat down across from Victoria, brought out her own calendar, and paged through it. "For the past six weeks, my schedule was full, but it's simpler than yours, I'm sure."

"I must say, the past month has been unusually busy," said Victoria. "The harbor must be getting ready for the season now."

Elizabeth was assistant dockmaster at the Oak Bluffs Harbor. She nodded. "Starting in early April it gets busy, cleaning up and stocking stuff after the winter. Setting moorings and getting ready for the Memorial Day rush." She looked up. "Everyone on the East Coast seems to have a boat. They all want to get out on the water. The past six weeks we worked overtime a lot. I took a couple of days off, but I worked a bunch of night shifts."

"Who had access to your schedule?"

"It's posted where anyone can see it."

"And my schedule," Victoria sighed. "I write up my planned forays in my column. Anyone who reads my column knows when

I'm going to be off Island."

Victoria rested her elbows on the table. "During the past six weeks, anyone could have had easy access to the cellar."

"You don't go down there much, do you?"

"Not often now," said Victoria. "Climbing down those stone steps is more of a chore than it used to be. Today was the first time I've gone down there for a long time. We had a freezer in the cellar, and I used to go down often. Daily."

"Whoever hung the body knew about the cellar and knew you were not likely to discover it."

Victoria thought a moment. "It also means the killer timed it so it would be found at the time of the wedding."

"Then the killer had to know about the reception. So he's either someone who knows us or someone who has been watching us for some time without our knowing it. Or one of the workers setting up for the wedding." Elizabeth thought for a moment. "Why choose our cellar to put a dead body?" She absently picked up one of the seed catalogs that was opened to a display of bright annuals. "And where were we when he did that?" She pushed the catalog aside.

Victoria got up from her seat and went

into the kitchen. "I'm sure the autopsy will answer many of our questions."

CHAPTER SIXTEEN

Penny adapted immediately to the brainless gofer job Mark had offered her. Early this morning the electrician had gotten two calls, one for one of the four weddings to be wired for electricity this coming weekend, the other for a future wedding. As the morning progressed, several more calls came in, and she set up wiring schedules for future weddings.

While discussing the minutiae of the electrical needs, Penny, based on her own experience at the Boston Boutique in contacting caterers, tent people, raw bar people, and clergy, realized she could offer billable advice to brides and their mothers. She could make a living on the Island, she was convinced.

She started to set up appointments to visit with the four brides Mark was dealing with and their mothers and grandmothers. In the future, if things worked out, she would be drinking a lot of sherry with Mark's customers. One of the four clients Mark had scheduled for this weekend was a Mrs. Curtain, whose granddaughter was to have a wedding in the Tabernacle, the great building in the center of the Wesleyan Grove Camp Meeting Ground. The reception was to be held at Mrs. Curtain's cottage, also in the Campground, and Mark would be doing the wiring for whatever she needed.

Penny set up a luncheon appointment with Mrs. Curtain for this noon. Ironically, this would be the day after her own wedding had been canceled.

She would happily kill Rocco, if it didn't seem so messy.

Dominic awoke to brilliant, dazzling, blinding sunlight and a headache. He had no idea where he was. He was in a bed. A hospital bed. He put his hand up to his forehead. There was a small adhesive patch there. A window let in fierce stabbing light that pierced his brain. If this was a hospital, he reasoned, there must be nurses. There must be a call button. He fumbled around the bed, every move shooting darts of pain into his head. He found a thin cable and followed it to the call button. With all his sickly strength, he pushed the button and fell back

218

onto the pillow, eyes tightly closed, his head throbbing.

The sound of squeaking shoes slammed into his poor brain.

"Good morning, Mr. Bufano!"

Tormenting him. Damned cheerful voice. Dominic groaned.

"I see we're awake. Hungry?"

Dominic put a hand up to his head.

"I'm Hope. How are you doing?"

"Am I alive?"

"I don't know. Are you?"

"Whatever I am, I wish I wasn't."

"That'll teach you. Are you hungry?"

"That light is killing me."

"What they call sunlight," said Nurse Hope. She rustled and squeaked over to the window. The blinds came down with the rattle of a broken racecar, and the light, blessedly, dimmed.

"Umpf," said Dominic.

"You're welcome. Tomato juice helps. And dry toast." He opened one eye. All he could decipher through the fuzziness and agony was that she was tall and slim, with long dark hair. "Someone will be by in a couple of minutes to check your vitals."

"Where am I?"

"Martha's Vineyard Hospital."

"Where?"

"Martha's Vineyard is an island off the coast of Massachusetts."

"Oh for Christ's sake," said Dominic.

"I don't know what you were drinking, but you probably broke a record of some kind."

"My forehead?"

"You fell out of bed and broke my Great-Aunt Victoria's chamber pot," said Nurse Hope. "An antique. It's a wonder you didn't break anything else."

Things were coming back a fragment at a time. "My brother's wedding."

"If your brother is Rocco Bufano, who was about to marry my cousin Penny, you can forget it."

Dominic tried to sit up. Pain shot along every nerve in his body. He slumped back on the pillow, putting a hand up to his head. "What?"

"He called it off. You won't have to go to the wedding."

"He *what*?"

"Canceled it."

Ouch! "Why?"

"He learned we Islanders may be famous, but we sure ain't rich."

"He's dead meat, then. I'm convinced someone's out to kill him."

"Calm down," said Nurse Hope. "You'll

recover." She patted his foot under the white cotton blanket. "Tomato juice and toast on the way." She left the room along with the agonizing sound of cloth swishing and shoes squealing on the linoleum floor. "Just let me die," murmured Dominic.

The state police cruiser pulled up to the west step. Sergeant Smalley, in full uniform, rapped on the side of the door and came into the kitchen. "Morning, Victoria, Elizabeth."

"Good morning, John," said Victoria. "You look quite dashing. Can we give you a cup of coffee?"

He patted his stomach. "Thanks, but I'm coffee'd out."

"Is there any news on the victim's identity?"

"Not yet," said Smalley. "That's why I'm here. To get your help."

"Of course. Anything I can do."

"I hope to locate someone who can identify our victim. Rocco invited his brother and three friends to the wedding. Do you have any idea where they might be staying? I'd like them to look at the body before we have to go through the process of obtaining DNA and dental records."

"Rocco wasn't much help, was he?"

"Yes and no. We're pretty sure he recognized the man, but he won't acknowledge it."

"He said it was someone who'd been stalking him, didn't he?"

"That stalker claim of his was off the wall. I don't believe it for a minute. He knows who it is. Since he's not forthcoming, it could be that one of those friends can help us. Worth trying."

"I have a list of Penny's wedding guests somewhere, and another of Rocco's. His list had only four people on it."

Scraps of paper and used envelopes were piled on the telephone table, and Victoria rummaged through them. Backs of envelopes and scraps had notes scrawled in Victoria's loopy handwriting.

"I'll have Dominic look at the body when he gets released from the hospital," said Smalley, shuffling through Victoria's notes.

"How much longer is he likely to be there?"

"He should be discharged this afternoon. Tomorrow at the latest. You've met him, I know. Have you met the others on Rocco's list?"

"I've met only Rocco and his brother." Victoria sorted through her papers. "I have no idea what Dominic is like ordinarily." A few scraps fluttered to the floor. Smalley picked them up.

"Here it is." Victoria selected a note written on the back of an electric bill. "Cosimo Esposito is staying in Oak Bluffs. At the Hotel on the Harbor. Cosimo is Rocco's stepbrother." She handed the note to Smalley. "I don't have any information on the others. And I have no idea where Dominic will stay when he's released from the hospital. I would imagine he'd stay with Rocco."

"Ah," said Smalley. "Where is Rocco staying?"

"At the Turkey Cove Inn, I believe."

"He's checked out."

"Then I don't know where he is. I met Rocco only that once, yesterday, when he came here to see about Dominic. He gave me his phone number."

"Let me copy that," said Smalley.

"Wouldn't you like to have a seat?" Victoria brushed potting soil off one of the gray painted chairs.

"No, no. Thanks, but I've got a full morning ahead of me. I won't be more than another minute or two. Help me get the timing straight. Rocco came to you because Dominic was here, passed out drunk in Penny's car. That was before Rocco and I went to the funeral home in hopes he could identify the body."

"Yes."

"Who called the ambulance for his brother?"

"I called," said Victoria. "It was quite a while after you and Rocco left. Dominic was asleep, or we thought he was. When he fell out of bed, we heard something break and were afraid he'd hurt himself. He'd cut his forehead. I haven't seen Rocco since you left with him."

Smalley nodded. "We drove from the funeral home to the Dairy Queen for something to eat, then to the sheriff's office. The three of us — Rocco, the sheriff, and I — we had a little talk. Rocco wouldn't give up his story about being stalked. He knows who the victim was, all right. At the funeral home he reacted strongly when he saw the body."

"Perhaps the shock of seeing a dead body?"

"Not at all. Not in the least likely." Smalley shook his head. "When Toby gave him the usual talk about how difficult it might be, seeing a dead body, Rocco said he'd seen plenty of dead bodies. Those were his words: 'plenty of dead bodies.' I'm a cop and I've been there for the deaths of friends, neighbors, and family, but I wouldn't say I've seen plenty of dead bodies."

"That's very strange," said Victoria.

"Yeah, it is. Well, he took one look at the body, and both Toby and I thought he was going to pass out. He wouldn't touch the smelling salts or sit, just wanted to get out of there."

"You'd think he'd want to cooperate. The victim's family should be told as soon as possible."

"When I pressed him, saying it was obvious he knew the victim, he came up with that stalking story."

"I wonder what he gains by not divulging the victim's name, if he knows it," said Victoria. "He was with you when Penny called saying Dominic was being taken to the hospital, wasn't he? That's when he suddenly canceled the wedding. What happened to make him change his mind?"

"We ordered food at the Dairy Queen and were eating in the cruiser in the parking lot. At least, I was. He didn't touch his food. I hoped to get him to talk about the victim. He kept changing the subject. Talked about his upcoming marriage to your wealthy cousin. 'Penny?' I said. 'If you're talking about Penny Arbuthnot, she's broke. Doesn't have a penny to her name.' I believe what I said was 'She doesn't have a pot to pee in.' You should have seen his face."

Victoria nodded. "Penny borrowed a great deal of money from her friends and family to put on this ridiculously extravagant wedding. So Rocco's reaction to the news that she was not as wealthy as he'd thought was to cancel the wedding."

"Right. Only a few minutes after I broke the bad news to him, Penny called. Dominic had been taken to the hospital. That's when he called off the wedding." Smalley took a notebook out of his shirt pocket. "Blamed it on Dominic's condition."

"Penny was under the impression that Rocco was heir to untold wealth, since his father is Giovanni Bufano, of the Bufano fortune," said Victoria. "But apparently Rocco is every bit as poor as Penny. For some reason, his father disowned him, and he seems to be seriously in debt."

"Funny." Smalley laughed. "I guess it's not funny for the two of them. But I can't help feeling it serves them both right." He slipped the paper with the names of Rocco's guests into his notebook and returned the notebook to his pocket. "It's possible that Cosimo, his stepbrother, may know where the other two on Rocco's list are staying. It's a place to start, anyway." He put on his hat. "Thanks, Victoria."

Smalley showed the names to the desk clerk at the Hotel on the Harbor, and he told Smalley that all three of the men he was looking for — Cosimo, Elmer, and Red — were staying there.

"You wouldn't happen to know where I might find them now, would you?" Smalley asked.

"They left for breakfast about an hour ago. They've discovered Linda Jean's. You might try there."

"Thanks, I will," said Smalley.

CHAPTER SEVENTEEN

About the same time Dominic was suffering from the mother of all hangovers, Bianca, who had booked a room at a bed and breakfast in Oak Bluffs, walked to Ocean Park, where she was to meet with Angelo.

Facing Nantucket Sound, the large open park was backed by a semicircle of quaint Victorian houses. She and Angelo had agreed to meet at the gazebo, still used for summer band concerts as it had been for more than a hundred years.

She knew where Rocco, the bastard, was staying.

Last night, a really foggy night, she saw him dart out of a sort of passageway on Circuit Avenue and followed him out of curiosity. Why was he acting so dodgy? Before he turned down one of the streets that headed toward the water, he looked around. Clearly, he didn't want anyone following him. She stayed hidden behind a group of tourists.

With the fog, it was easy to follow without being seen. But she stuck close, because it would be just as easy for him to lose her.

Every minute or so, a foghorn moaned somewhere in the Sound nearby. The noise was like a sick cow, only she'd never heard a sick cow moan.

Just this morning at Linda Jean's, someone was talking about the visitor from New York who told the Coast Guard she would pay to have them to turn off the foghorn at night because her sleep was being disturbed. Bianca felt sympathy for the woman.

The road ended near the Oak Bluffs ferry dock. Rocco turned right, the Sound on his left now, the park on his right. He stopped and bent down to tie his shoelaces. Checking behind him, that's what he was doing. She was sure he wore loafers that didn't have laces. He stood again and walked past the park. Then, quite suddenly, he ducked down a street with an unpronounceable name. He turned again, checking, before he went up the steps of a rundown house with a faded sign she couldn't quite read.

On this bright morning, she was to meet with Angelo and show him Rocco's hideout.

She strolled down one of the macadam

paths that led to the bandstand. To her right, a flock of Canada geese fed on the new grass. Beyond them a ferry, white against the deep blue of the Sound, was heading toward the Steamship Authority dock, which was within walking distance of the park. Several gulls flew overhead.

Now that the wedding was off, she was no longer feeling murderous toward Rocco. Furthermore, she'd learned that Rocco was broke, which made him lose his allure. But she couldn't let it go. He had to be taught a lesson.

The morning was so pure, the light so bright, the colors so vivid, the breeze so mild, her spirits lifted. She couldn't help feeling that everything was going her way. She watched gulls soaring overhead on outspread wings, floating on air currents high above her.

She would get Angelo to frighten Rocco. Maybe threaten him. Not kill him. Angelo would know how to handle a situation like this.

The park was deserted. Soon it would fill with dog walkers and kite flyers. No matter. They would have the privacy one gets in a crowd.

"Bianca."

She glanced toward the bandstand. Angelo

was striding toward her. Tall, slim, dark wavy hair, pale face.

"Where's your shadow this morning?" Bianca couldn't help asking.

"If you mean Lily, she's sleeping."

Bianca laughed. "What's that all about?"

"None of your business."

"What's her problem? She acts like a retard."

"She's my cousin, okay?" They were nearing a bench by the bandstand. "I don't want to talk about her."

"How'd you get here?"

"I rented a car."

Bianca laughed again. "What does Zoe think about your cousin?"

Angelo ignored her question. "Where is he?"

"Rocco?" she asked sweetly.

"Don't be cute."

"Okay." She got serious. "I want to talk business with you, Angelo."

"So?" He shrugged.

They reached the bench and Bianca sat. Angelo looked around, then sat next to her.

"Before I tell you where he is," said Bianca, "I want something from you."

"Oh for Christ's sake," said Angelo. "I don't have time for this. Where the hell is he?"

"Close by."

"Where?"

She folded her hands in her lap. "I know you're good at what you do, Angelo."

"What does that mean?"

She stood up and faced the Sound. "I want you to . . . warn someone."

"Someone like Rocco, right?"

"Well, yes."

"Where *is* Rocco?"

"Rocco and I were planning to get married."

"I know. Everybody knows."

"So when I get to the Island, I read in the paper he's getting married to some rich bitch." She turned and pointed to her chest. "What about me?"

"He's all yours. The wedding's off," said Angelo, smiling. "The rich bitch doesn't have a dime to her name. Same with Rocco. Not a dime to his name. Great match. Do you still want him?"

"No, I don't. I heard all about the poor boy. But I want him taught a lesson."

"So you come to me. Sit down, will you? You're making me nervous."

Bianca sat.

"You'll tell me where he is if I shoot out his kneecaps. Right?"

Bianca gazed out at the water and said

nothing. The ferry whistled and pulled away from the dock. A flock of seagulls followed.

"So, what do you want me to do?" asked Angelo.

Bianca shook her head.

"Women," muttered Angelo. "I'm wasting my time." He stood.

Bianca looked up. "Tell me something, will you, Angelo?"

"Now what?"

"Why were you at Mrs. Trumbull's?"

"Oh, for Christ's sake." He sat again. "I wanted to get some information on Rocco that I couldn't get any other way."

"I thought you didn't like Rocco."

"I don't."

"So why . . . ?" Bianca waited.

He said nothing.

"Oh. I see." She looked away.

A young boy, maybe six or seven, raced over to a place halfway between the bandstand and the road. The flock of Canada geese took flight, and she could hear the sound of their wings, their honking. The boy opened up a kite. An older man was with him, his father or uncle. And a scruffy dog, of course. Family scene. She couldn't quite tell from here, but the kite looked like a bird. A duck or a swan.

She turned back to Angelo. "How much

are they paying you?"

He placed his hand on his chest. "Some-one is paying me?"

Bianca said, "Angelo, I know how you make your living. You'd kill your grand-mother."

Angelo smiled. "I wouldn't kill Grand-mamma."

"Only because there's no money in it."

"True." He bent down and plucked a grass blade. "Nobody's hired me to kill Grandmamma." He glanced at her. "But back to Rocco." He made a slashing motion across his throat with the grass blade. "You don't want me to kill him. Just scare him."

"What do I owe you?"

He stood again and hiked up his trousers. "Show me where he is, and we'll call it even."

"You won't kill him, will you?" said Bianca.

Angelo smiled. "Not for you." He tossed the blade of grass aside. "I've got to get back to Lily. I don't like leaving her this long."

Cosimo, Elmer, and Red squeezed together into a booth at Linda Jean's, the restaurant across Circuit Avenue from the Tidal Rip bar. Cosimo sat on one side of the table, Red and Elmer on the other.

Linda Jean's, as usual, was bustling with breakfast eaters who knew this was the best place on the Island to be at this time of day.

"Man, I'm starved," said Red.

"Sounds like you've recovered," said Cosimo. "How's your head?

"Not too bad, long as I don't turn too quick."

"You did a job celebrating your birthday."

"I don't remember much after we got into Rocco's car."

"We retrieved your backpack and Elmer put you to bed in his room."

"Thanks, Elmer," said Red. "I appreciate that."

"Yeah," said Elmer.

The server, whose nametag read "Molly," was a matronly woman with graying hair pulled back in a bun. She brought mugs of coffee and dropped off three menus. "Be right back," she said. "Busy morning for this time of year."

Red examined the menu. "I'll take one of everything."

"Right," said Cosimo. The thin scar running down the side of his face was especially noticeable this morning. It ran from his hairline past his mouth, giving him a sinister expression, and ended at his chin. With his angular face, dark hair, and dark eyes, the scar actually enhanced his saturnine looks.

Molly, the server, returned with a pad and pencil. "What can I get you gentlemen? Will this be on one check?"

"We're doing Dutch," said Elmer, the one with short blond hair. He turned to Red. "I hope you brought your money."

"Yeah," said Red. "I did. I'll pay you back for letting me crash in your room last night."

"Are you ready to order yet?" asked Molly. "Or shall I give you another minute or so."

Cosimo checked the menu. "Two eggs, scrambled, sausage, toast. OJ."

"More coffee?"

"Please."

She took orders from the others and left.

Elmer turned to Red. "You have to get your own room from now on. It was okay for one night, but that's it."

"Sure," said Red.

"Last night at dinner, when you were otherwise engaged, we introduced ourselves," said Elmer. "Cosimo here is Rocco's stepbrother. Rocco and me, we're in a yacht club together, and he invited me to his wedding last minute." He opened one of the miniature tubs of half-and-half, poured it into his coffee, and stirred. "He thinks I'm a friend or something."

They watched the other diners for a while.

"Yacht club?" asked Red.

"City marina," answered Elmer.

"Do we have any plans for today?" asked Red.

"You go about your own business," said Cosimo. "I have things I've got to do."

Elmer too had things to do. He and Cosimo dodged the suggestion of meeting at the Tidal Rip later. They were quiet for a while after that.

Then Elmer said, "What's your connection with Rocco, Red?"

"Dogs," said Red.

"What do you mean, 'dogs'?" said Cosimo.

Red looked down. "I shouldn't have said anything."

"Anything about what?" said Elmer.

Molly returned to their table with a tray laden with plates. "For you, Red. I assume with that mop of hair they call you Red, right?"

Red nodded. "I don't even know my real name anymore."

"Here you are. Pancakes, two eggs, bacon, grits." She dealt out the rest of the food. "Scrambled eggs, sausage, and toast for you two."

After she left, Red reached for the syrup pitcher and poured syrup over his stack of pancakes.

"You trying to drown those or something?" asked Elmer. "What about dogs?"

Red wiped a finger under the pitcher's spout. "Dog track." He licked the syrup off his finger. "Racing."

"Dog tracks have been illegal for years," said Elmer.

"That's why I don't want to talk about it."

"There's one here? In Massachusetts?"

"A couple here in Mass."

"Go on, you can talk about it to us," said Elmer.

"There's a dog track near South Boston, where I come from. Cops know about it, but they leave it alone."

"You a gambler?" asked Elmer.

"Not me. When I was a kid, I used to go to the track with my old man. He was a gambler. He warned me about betting. Said it was an addiction. He lost a lot of money. I never got into it." Red picked up his fork and started in on his breakfast.

"You go see the dogs . . . because?" Elmer hadn't touched his food.

Red nodded. "I love those dogs. Greyhounds, you know. I get a charge out of watching them race. Beautiful animals." He pushed a mound of eggs onto his fork with his knife and got it safely to his mouth.

Elmer placed both forearms on the table. "If you're at the track so much, what do you do for a living?"

"I have a job at the track. After my old man died, I couldn't stay away. Guess that's a form of addiction he passed down to me."

"What kind of job do you have?"

"I care for the dogs. Clean cages and stuff." He set his utensils on his plate. "I mean, I love those dogs. They're sweet and gentle. And on the track, they're something to see. They can go forty, forty-five miles an hour."

Cosimo was silent. He ate steadily, watching Red the entire time as he talked.

"Yet you don't bet?" Elmer asked again.

"Too many guys go broke at the dog track."

"Including our friend, Rocco?"

Red stopped chewing and looked away. "I guess. I don't know anything about the betting part of it."

"How come you met up with Rocco?"

"He was at the track almost as much as me. Once in a while he comes by the kennels, watches me work. Your food's getting cold, you know."

At that, Elmer began to eat.

Cosimo set his fork down. "What happens

to the dogs when they don't perform as expected? They kill them?"

"They used to in the old days. When one of the dogs was past its prime, they euthanized him."

"What did they call old?" asked Elmer.

"Two or three."

"That's past its prime?" Elmer moved to one side so he could see Red better. "I got a mutt that's going on fourteen."

"They didn't know what to do with them when they slowed down."

"And now?"

"Well, they don't do that so much now. I mean, euthanizing them."

"Dog tracks are illegal. They shouldn't be racing dogs and killing them when they're no good for racing anymore."

"Greyhound Rescue Leagues put the dogs up for adoption."

Molly returned. "You boys all set?"

"That's all," said Cosimo. "Thank you."

"No problem." She dealt out three checks, one for each, and left.

"This place is a discovery," said Red, wiping his mouth.

Elmer continued to eat without speaking.

Red took a last swig of coffee and blotted his mouth on a napkin.

Cosimo, who'd been silent for most of the

dog conversation, said, "You involved with this dog-saving group?"

"Not exactly. But I had a couple of the dogs we saved."

"Had?" asked Elmer.

Red shook his head. "I don't want to talk about it."

Elmer pushed his plate away. "What do you say, Cosimo?"

"I'm out of this. I hate dogs." Cosimo picked up his check, looked at it, fished a twenty out of his wallet, and laid it and the check on the table. The others did the same.

Molly returned. "Everything okay?"

"Better than okay," said Red.

"I'll be right back with your change."

"Don't bother," said Cosimo.

As they were about to get up, a big cop in uniform entered, looked around, and came to their table.

"I'm looking for three guys, Cosimo, Elmer, and Red." He looked down at Red's hair. "Guess I've got the right guys."

"What have we done now?" asked Elmer.

"Nothing that I know of," said the cop. "My name's John Smalley, state police, and I need some help." He held out a hand to Cosimo. "I'm guessing I got Red right — are you Cosimo?"

"You've got it," said Cosimo, accepting

241

the hand and giving it a shake. "What do you need?"

Molly came by and picked up the checks and money. "Morning, John. These guys making trouble for you?" She turned to the three, who were still sitting. "Thank you. Come back again."

"Let's go," said Cosimo, sliding out from behind the table. "She needs the seating. Okay to talk outside, Sergeant?"

"We can sit in my cruiser. Parked outside."

"Handicapped space?" said Elmer.

"Where else?" answered Smalley.

They sat, three in back, Smalley in front.

Smalley turned to face them. "You know about the body at Mrs. Trumbull's, I assume. We haven't been able to identify him."

"You'd like us to take a look, then," said Cosimo. "I have no problem with that."

"Me either," said Elmer.

Red nodded. "I've never seen a dead body. Only my grandfather's closed casket."

"You've got time now?" asked Smalley.

"Sure, why not," said Elmer.

CHAPTER EIGHTEEN

Rocco awoke with sunlight streaming through the single window into his small room. A ray of sunlight touched the old bureau across from the foot of his bed, giving it an antique finish.

He rubbed his eyes, not knowing where he was at first. When it came back to him, he sat up with a jolt, hitting his head on the low ceiling that angled over his bed. He checked his phone. Still early.

He had to get off this Island, and right now.

Sunlight cast a shadow of the window on the floor by his bed. The shadow was of the wooden muntins that divided the window into six small panes, and when he looked down, he saw shadows of prison bars.

I've got to stop thinking like that, he thought. *I haven't done anything that would send me to prison.* But the thought of Sergeant Smalley and the sheriff suggesting they could hold him in the jail for — what, four days? He'd go crazy. He'd just plain go crazy.

I've got to get out of here, and soon, he thought. *I've got to get off this rock. They'll identify the body eventually. DNA. Teeth. Something. They'll charge me with impeding a murder investigation. They'll bring me in as a suspect. I'd better be far, far away before that happens. At the very least they'll imprison me for not identifying the body.*

He sat on the side of the small bed. A pretty good mattress. He'd had a decent night's sleep despite everything that happened yesterday. How had everything gone so wrong in such a short time?

After he'd checked out of the Turkey Cove Inn yesterday, he'd found this bed and breakfast. No one would find him here. When he booked the room, he'd left his overnight case with his bare essentials here. Most of his stuff — his clothing, his paperwork — was still in his car.

Did he dare get it? The clothes were expensive, bought to impress his wealthy bride. He couldn't afford to lose them or his papers.

He yawned and scratched his chest under his pajama shirt.

He'd have to find his way back into that

maze of the Campground and get it. Did he dare do that?

Dominic could get it for him. Was he still in the hospital? If they discharged him, he would have to find Dominic. He'd call and hope Dominic had his cell phone with him and that it was charged up. Then they'd meet somewhere and he'd get off the Island.

Was there anyone else he could trust? Not really.

There were the three guys he'd invited to the wedding, partly to have someone sitting on the groom's side of the church and partly because he owed all three, and what better way to pay them back than an invite to a Martha's Vineyard wedding? They actually owed him, come to think of it.

He didn't know Red well. The kid took care of greyhounds at the track, cleaned their cages and fed them. He owed Red something because of killing those two mangy dogs of his. To be fair, he shouldn't call racing greyhounds mangy, but Red acted like they were his kids, his babies. Anyway, inviting Red to the wedding was a way to pay him off. He'd promised to take care of all his expenses, transportation, hotel, meals, and all, after the wedding. Well, no wedding, so tough luck, kid. Not my fault the wedding is off. Damned bitch. At least Red got his first trip to Martha's Vineyard.

He crossed Red off as someone to call on for help.

He knew Elmer better than Red — a better class of guy. Elmer kept a boat at the yacht club in a slip next to his. They'd had a blowup because of Elmer's girlfriend. Elmer acted like she was the only woman in the world. All he, Rocco, had done was wave a couple hundred-dollar bills under her nose, invite her to a fancy restaurant, take her to a show, and she forgot Elmer. She was pretty boring, so Elmer could have her back. Nothing that couldn't be settled with money. He'd invited Elmer to the wedding, all expenses paid. Make things right between them. Well, damn that bitch Penny again.

He stood up and stretched. Touched his toes. No point in trying to touch the ceiling. At its highest, the slanted ceiling couldn't be more than seven feet high. He didn't need to exercise this morning anyway. Too much on his mind.

Cosimo, his stepbrother. That was a different kettle of fish. Where had that saying come from, anyway?

He and Cosimo hadn't spoken more than a few words since the accident. Wasn't his, Rocco's, fault. If his two stepbrothers hadn't

246

been with him, they wouldn't have been hurt. He'd made it up to Cosimo, been the first to make the gesture of reconciliation by inviting him to this grand Martha's Vineyard wedding and all. Already, it was paying off. After he accepted the invitation, Cosimo had been fairly civil to him.

And then he thought about his situation now, right now.

He slapped his leg. Shit!

Shit, shit. The whole thing was nothing but shit. That bitch Penny, pretending to be wealthy. Well, he'd fallen for her act, more fool him. Everything that was happening to him was her fault.

Then there was Caesar, Cosimo's brother. Those two stepbrothers of his. Dear God! He couldn't think about Caesar. Didn't want to think about the accident and what happened to Caesar. Cold sweat trickled down his back. That was reality. Caesar didn't need to accept that ride with him that evening. If he hadn't gone along, he wouldn't have been hurt.

Last evening after he left the sheriff's office, Smalley, the state cop, had followed him. He knew that. He'd gotten a ride to Victoria Trumbull's, where he'd left his car, and Smalley was on his tail from then on, into that maze of the Campground, where he'd lost him. It wouldn't take Smalley long to locate the car. Would he have a cop watching it to see when he returned? Probably not. Both Smalley and the sheriff told him, reassured him, that they were protecting him. You'll be safer in jail, they said. Sure.

They'd only questioned him about the identity of the body. They hadn't accused him of the murder. They had no reason to watch his car.

But that would change when they identified the body.

He had to be off this Island before then, and far, far away.

Everyone on this crazy Island seemed to have a scanner. The scanners would be buzzing about the state cop chasing someone unknown into the Campground last night. Between the Island's scanners, the cops, and the killer, they would find him.

Who was after him? Had to be a hired killer. It had to be. That was the only explanation for the mistaken identity, killing the wrong person, when he was the target. Someone hired the killer. And the killer was still on the Island and he, Rocco, was still the target.

The killer was not going to miss a second time.

Who had it in for him so bad he'd hired a hit man?

He sidled around the bed, avoiding the patch of sunlight with its prison bar shadows, and carried his toilet article kit down the hall to the shared bathroom. No sign of anyone having been there.

Who? That was the question. A hired killer. Who had hired him?

The killer had to be someone who didn't know him, or he wouldn't have hit the wrong guy.

How long did he have before they identified the body? It would take awhile. Sending for dental records. That would take time. And DNA. Used to take forever, but no more. Don't they have to match unknown DNA with something known? It would all buy time for him.

All he was certain of was that someone intended to kill him, and his only choice was to disappear.

But *who*?

The shower stall was small. He couldn't bend down to wash his feet. But it was clean and the water was hot, and there seemed to be plenty of it. He scrubbed himself, tried to wash off all the filth that had accumulated inside and out in less than twenty-four hours.

Back to who hired the killer. Someone at the dog track? Pretty shady characters there. He could see them as killers, at least most of them. He owed a lot of money, but it didn't warrant killing him. At least he didn't think so. They knew he was coming to Martha's Vineyard. He'd told them he was marrying a rich woman from Martha's Vineyard, and he'd pay up.

They wouldn't have heard yet about the way she'd misled him. All that expensive stuff she'd paid for — and more planned. Where did she get the money for tents and a raw bar if she was as broke as everyone said? You can't trust a woman.

The only other place where he owed big money was the yacht club. Well, the municipal marina. He'd run up a year's slip fees. Really sloppy management there. The city would confiscate his boat, not send a killer out after him.

The cops knew his car. The killer must know it too. The killer had done his homework, or someone had done it for him. He'd scouted out Mrs. Trumbull's cellar and knew he could hang a body, his body — he shuddered — where it would be found. The only mistake the killer made was to kill the wrong person.

Rocco shuddered again.

He got out of the shower and toweled himself dry on a big, but thin, towel and dressed in yesterday's clothes.

He'd have to go back to where he'd parked his BMW in the Campground. The owner of the house or a neighbor or whoever made the rounds had probably reported a stranger's car parked where it shouldn't be. The make, the model, the license plate. That would be all over the Island too. On everybody's scanner. On FaceBook. On the killer's iPad.

The killer would be waiting for him.

The aroma of coffee, frying bacon, and cinnamon drifted upstairs, and he went down to meet it. He hadn't had supper and he was hungry.

"Morning, Mr. Smith." Mrs. Bailey, his host at the bed and breakfast, greeted him at the foot of the stairs. She was a chubby, comfortable-looking woman with white hair and a pink face. She looked up at him. "Did you have a good night's sleep, Mr. Smith?"

"I certainly did, thank you, Mrs. Bailey."

"We have a nice day for you after yesterday's weather," she said. "I hope you're hungry. I've made a nice breakfast for you."

He assured her that he was famished.

She led the way into a small dining room, the table set with a single place setting on a neatly ironed place mat. A glass vase in the center of the table held a spray of lilacs.

"Am I your only guest?"

"It's early yet in the season. I'll be turning people away before long," she said. "I made some nice blueberry muffins for you."

"Thank you. My favorites."

He sat down and she bustled around, bringing a tray stacked with enough breakfast for three people.

"Is this your first visit to the Island?"

"Yes, it is."

"You didn't say how long you'll be staying, Mr. Smith."

"I'm not sure myself," said Rocco.

"It's no problem," said Mrs. Bailey. "Stay as long as you'd like. Not many visitors this time of year."

He nodded.

"We needed the rain," Mrs. Bailey went on, "but I'm sure it spoiled it for visitors. We don't want you to have a bad impression of our nice Island."

"Not at all, Mrs. Bailey." *Please go away, Mrs. Bailey,* he thought. *I've got to work something out. I have to think like a killer thinks, and if you say the word "nice" again . . .*

After Mrs. Bailey left, he dug into the eggs, the potatoes, the bacon. Drank the better-than-nice coffee.

If I stay here, he'll find me. He's paid to find me and he will.

Mrs. Bailey returned. "I like a man with a healthy appetite."

A last meal before the execution. He nodded, his mouth full of blueberry muffin, his mind on murder. His murder.

"Can I get you anything else?"

He blotted his mouth on a nicely ironed napkin and shook his head. When he'd finished chewing and swallowing, which he found hard to do with her watching over him, he thanked her and set the napkin neatly beside his plate.

"Do you plan on doing some sightseeing, Mr. Smith? I have some brochures I can let you have."

"No thank you, Mrs. Bailey. I'm really here on business." He realized right away that was a mistake. He knew what her next comment would be, and thought fast.

"What sort of business are you in, Mr. Smith?"

"Software development, Mrs. Bailey."

"That's nice," she said. "I don't know a thing about computers. I have a cell phone, but I don't even know how to use it. Perhaps you could . . . ?"

"If you'll excuse me." Rocco stood, bowed slightly, and went upstairs to get his things.

He left enough money to cover his night's lodging along with an extra twenty on the bureau, put his kit in his overnight bag, went downstairs — making sure Mrs. Bailey was out of sight — and left. He wanted to go where he could sit down and think about his next move. He couldn't do that with Mrs. Bailey hovering over him.

He had to decide on the risks of getting his car as opposed to getting the keys to Dominic, who could get the car for him. Or would it be smarter to leave the car behind?

No. He wasn't about to abandon his BMW. He had to get it.

There was a large open park with benches near the ferry dock. He could think without anyone bothering him, and he'd be able to see anyone coming from any direction. If he decided he had to leave now, right now, the ferry ticket office was a two-minute walk away.

CHAPTER NINETEEN

Dominic sat on the edge of the hospital bed, his feet dangling over the edge. He was feeling almost human. When Nurse Hope came into his room, he noticed that the tall, slender, dark-haired woman was extremely attractive.

"How are you feeling?" she asked.

"Ready to leave."

She took his temperature and blood pressure, then listened to his heart. He grinned. "What are you doing for dinner tonight?"

"Dinner date with my husband and three kids."

"Just thought I'd ask."

"One of my kids is a cop. Just thought I'd let you know." She checked the chart at the foot of the bed and wrote something on it. "The doc says you can go home now."

"Home is New York. I'm just visiting."

"You'd better stay off the booze."

"I'm quitting."

"That's what they all say. Do you have transportation to wherever you're staying?"

"I don't know where I'm staying. All I remember is being under a tree that was dripping water on me. An ancient woman tucked me into a bed. Last thing I recall is falling out of bed and breaking some antique china pot."

"You were at Victoria Trumbull's. She's my great-aunt."

"Mrs. Trumbull. That's the name." He slid off the high bed. "Where are my clothes?"

"How you're dressed now is how you arrived. No pants, no shoes."

"They must be at Mrs. Trumbull's."

"Can you call someone to bring your clothes?"

"My phone is in my pants pocket."

Hope sighed. "Call your brother on the hospital phone, then."

"I don't know his number. It's on my phone and my phone is in my pants pocket."

"I'll call my son." The irritation in her voice was obvious.

"The cop?"

"You have a problem with that?" Hope sounded more than annoyed.

"No, no," said Dominic, holding up a hand. "Sorry."

"He's off duty until noon. He can stop by

Auntie Vic's and pick up your clothes."

"I'd really appreciate that. When I have my wallet, I'll recompense him."

"That's not expected." She stepped out of the room and came back shortly. "He's here in Oak Bluffs. He'll pick you up in about ten minutes and take you to Auntie Vic's."

"Like this?" said Dominic, looking down at his black briefs. Emblazoned across the front in red was, "I'M JUST A LOVE MACHINE."

Hope glanced at his underwear. "We'll lend you a johnny coat. Don't want to shock Auntie Vic, although my guess is she's already seen it."

Ten minutes later, Dominic had showered and put what he had of clothing back on. Nurse Hope gave him a hospital robe, the kind that fastens in back, and he'd just finished tying it, when he heard a knock on the side of his door. He looked up and a huge, uniformed cop, six foot eight at least, ducked under the doorframe and strode into his room.

"You're . . . you're Nurse Hope's son?"

"Yes, sir." A deep voice to go with his size. "Are you ready to go?"

"Are you taking me to Mrs. Trumbull's?" Dominic had a lurking fear of landing in jail.

"Yes, sir."

"I'd appreciate that. Thank you."

"No problem."

Dominic slipped his feet into the throw-away paper slippers that Hope had given him and, feeling naked and vulnerable and somehow like a felon on his way to or from jail, followed the giant cop out of the hospital to the squad car that was parked outside.

Rocco descended the front steps of Mrs. Bailey's bed and breakfast slowly, a step at a time, looking both ways. The street was deserted. All of the little wooden houses on either side of Mrs. Bailey's and across the narrow one-way street were painted in pastel colors, like a child's picture book. Shades and combinations of pink and green and lavender and baby blue. Like candy. Not real. Gingerbread cottages. That's what they looked like, and that's what they were called.

Nothing seemed real. He paused briefly at the foot of her steps. His senses were alert to everything around him. He hadn't noticed before that the tiny garden in front of her house, which was painted a fading orange and yellow, was planted with matching orange and yellow flowers. Across the narrow street, her neighbors too had matched their gardens to their houses. Pink flowers in front of the pink house. Blue and lavender in front of that house. All unreal. Nothing was real. There was no killer after him.

But there was.

At the foot of the steps, he turned left toward the water. Today it was a brilliant optimistic blue, teasing him, unlike the gray of yesterday. A fishing vessel was heading up the Sound, away from him, toward the open sea and Nantucket. A flock of gulls, white specks seen from here, trailed after the boat. He could hear them from where he stood. The gentlest of breezes carried the scent of roses and honeysuckle. Rocco breathed it in, didn't try to identify the source, grateful to have a small pleasant distraction from the awfulness before him. The park was only a few short blocks. Every sense was alert. Scent, touch, sight, hearing.

The killer wouldn't attack him in the open. He hadn't used a gun on the victim in Mrs. Trumbull's cellar. His modus seemed to be close up and silent. Rocco shivered. Out in the open he would be safe.

He was approaching the park. He stopped, sheltered behind another painted house, hidden by its wooden porch with its carpenter's lace railing.

From there, he studied the park. A little kid was flying a kite. An elderly couple, the man on a walker, was strolling along one of the macadam paths. A flock of Canada geese took flight as they approached, flew in a wide circle, and returned, settling to graze, or whatever geese did. He stood there for a full ten minutes, studying every foot of the open park. The bandstand.

A couple was sitting on a bench under the bandstand. He looked more closely. They didn't seem to belong together. They looked familiar, both the man and the woman. He looked more closely. It took him a full half-minute to interpret what he was seeing.

His cousin Angelo. His hated, despised cousin Angelo. Actually, it wasn't he who hated Angelo. It was the other way around. Angelo hated him, but for no good reason that Rocco could come up with. Rocco just tried to avoid him. What in hell was he doing in a park in Oak Bluffs? What was he doing on Martha's Vineyard? Angelo hadn't been invited to his wedding.

There was no question at all, even from this distance, about the woman Angelo was with. It was Bianca, his former fiancée. His stomach lurched. Bianca and he had planned a September wedding. It was all set. The church, the priest, everything arranged. He'd never called the wedding with Bianca off. She was furious. So what? She'd get over it. And here she was. With Angelo. He'd seen Angelo's work. Angelo wouldn't hesitate to kill him. Would Bianca be so upset she'd have hired Angelo? With a temper like hers, he was glad that wedding was off. He'd now gotten out of two weddings he'd unwisely committed himself to. Something good was coming out of this. But Angelo's presence was more than bothersome.

Then he thought, perhaps Angelo is the hired killer.

No. Not possible. Angelo would never, ever have taken out the wrong victim, especially since he, Rocco, was the intended victim.

Had Angelo tracked him down to Mrs. Bailey's bed and breakfast? If so, how? It was possible that Bianca and Angelo had teamed up and planned to kill him. He could see, in a way, Bianca's reaction. Women got upset by stuff like calling off their wedding. But Angelo had not killed and hung anyone in Mrs. Trumbull's cellar. That was not his style.

Were two killers after him?

An awful thought.

He could walk over to them and confront them. Be interesting to see the looks on their faces. Imagine the conversation that would ensue. Walk up to them and say, "Hi, Angelo. Hi, Bianca. Are you here for the wedding? Sorry I didn't invite either of you, but glad you could make it anyway. By the way, the wedding's off."

Yeah, sure.

Would Bianca demand that he marry her now? Claim him again? Dumb thoughts. The park was out. He couldn't return to Mrs. Bailey and her nice bed and breakfast. To get to the ferry terminal, he'd have to walk past the park, in plain sight of Angelo and Bianca. That was out. His only option was to get back to his car.

Problem was, he wasn't sure he knew how to retrace his steps. Last night had been foggy, and he'd navigated his way to Mrs. Bailey's by the sound of the foghorn. Reversing direction would be a challenge.

He straightened his shoulders. Daylight made everything seem possible. Made the thought of his own death seem ridiculous.

Perhaps it was just as well he'd spotted Bianca and Angelo. Maybe Angelo was the hired killer. Therefore, Angelo sitting in the park talking to Bianca meant he could get to his car safely before they could act.

He turned back the way he'd come, but instead of going down Mrs. Bailey's unpronounceable street, he went down the next, equally unpronounceable street and headed toward the Campground, his BMW, and — he hoped — safety. Once he was in his car, he'd have all his belongings, clothing and papers. He'd drive to Vineyard Haven, get a reservation on the next ferry, and escape from this shitty rock.

He'd left Mrs. Bailey and her splendid breakfast later than he intended. He checked the time. After eleven. Mrs. Bailey's breakfast would hold him. Getting to his car meant safety.

At the park, Bianca was explaining to Angelo the location of the place where Rocco was staying.

"Just show me which house it is, then leave me alone. I'll take over. Knowing Rocco, he's probably still in bed."

"I want him taught a lesson, is all," said Bianca, "I mean, don't rough him up too bad."

"Don't worry," said Angelo. "I'll be gentle. Let's go."

They walked the few blocks to the street Rocco had turned onto the night before. A couple of cars passed them, heading in the direction of Edgartown. They turned onto the street where the bed and breakfast was located, and Bianca pointed it out. A house with orange and yellow trim that needed a fresh coat of paint. The wooden steps were scuffed. On the porch, a yellow wicker table held a pitcher and two glasses, and next to it were two yellow rocking chairs. Paint was flaking off both table and chairs.

"Lo, how the mighty have fallen," said Angelo. "We part company here."

"Make sure he gets it that the message is from me," said Bianca.

"I'll do that," said Angelo.

He went up the worn steps and crossed the bare wood floor of the porch. The tops of the windows and door terminated in Gothic arches. The house was decorated with fancy cutout wooden gingerbread, or carpenters' lace, he'd heard it called. He wasn't sure what you'd call this kind of architecture. It looked like a combination of styles — church, wooden tent, and Victorian, all mixed together.

He looked for a doorbell, but there wasn't one, so he knocked. Gently, because it looked as though a powerful rap would break the door down.

A white haired, pink-cheeked woman answered.

"Good morning." Angelo figured that Rocco hadn't used his real name. "I hope I'm not disturbing you this early."

"Not at all," said Mrs. Bailey. "Come in, won't you? Are you looking for a nice place to stay?"

"Actually, I was looking for a cousin of mine who's staying here. Is he in?"

"Oh yes, indeed. Mr. Smith. What a nice man. In software development, he said. Won't you come in? He's finished breakfast and is upstairs." She started for the stairs, but turned. "Where are my manners! I'm Mrs. Bailey. Would you care for a blueberry muffin and a nice cup of coffee while I get him?"

Angelo had not had breakfast and said he'd be delighted. He settled into a worn, comfortable, overstuffed chair in the small front room. Mrs. Bailey brought him a cup of coffee and a still warm blueberry muffin.

"I won't be a moment," she said, starting up the stairs.

Angelo heard her knock. He heard her say, "Mr. Smith? You have a visitor." Heard her knock again. "Mr. Smith?" Heard her open the door and heard silence. She came back downstairs. "I'm sorry, he seems to have stepped out."

"Has he checked out?" asked Angelo.

"Well, no, he didn't check out, but he did leave some money and his things are gone."

Angelo stood.

"Please, Mr. . . . er . . ."

"Smith," said Angelo. "He and I are both Smiths."

"Of course, Mr. Smith. Please finish your coffee."

"Thank you, but I'll see if I can catch up with him," said Angelo. "I'll take this nice muffin with me, if I may."

"Yes, yes, of course. I hope you'll come again. Perhaps my Mr. Smith plans to return and hasn't really left."

"Perhaps you're right," said Angelo.

CHAPTER TWENTY

A police car pulled up to Victoria's west step, and she was pleasantly surprised when her great-grandnephew, Ben, eased out of the driver's seat, so handsome in his uniform.

He opened the back door, and a man Victoria didn't at first recognize stepped out. He was dressed in a hospital gown and had paper slippers on his feet. Then she realized who he was. Dominic.

"Aunt Victoria, my mom asked me to bring this man to you. I believe his clothes are here."

Dominic, clutching the back of his gown to cover the black underpants, said, "I'm sorry for all the trouble I've put you through, Mrs. Trumbull. Now it looks as though you haven't got rid of me."

"Come in," said Victoria. "Your clothes are dry."

The cop was getting back into the cruiser.

"Can't you stay, Ben? It's not yet eleven."

"No, ma'am. I have to be at work at noon. I like to be early."

Dominic turned, still clutching the back of the loose gown. "Thank you. You can't imagine how much I appreciate your bringing me here."

"No problem," said Ben.

"I'd like to pay you something."

"No, sir. Line of duty." He slammed the door shut and took off.

"I guess I made a fool of myself," said Dominic, following Victoria into the house.

"Well," said Victoria, "yes, you did."

"Thank you for your hospitality."

Victoria said nothing else. She escorted him to the downstairs bedroom, where the bed was made and his clothes were folded on top of the coverlet. She left him alone.

He'd just put on his pants, when his phone began to vibrate. He pulled it out and checked the number. Rocco.

He pressed the answer button. "What's up?"

"Hey, Dom, good to hear your voice. How're you doing?"

"I'm alive," said Dominic. "What do you want?"

"I was on my way to pick up my car, but I wonder if you'd do me a favor."

"Depends," said Dominic.

"It's a long story, but I parked my car in the Campground last night, and I don't want to pick it up myself. Would you get it and meet me somewhere?"

"You're asking me to do you a favor?"

"Come on, Dom. Bygones are bygones. You like driving my BMW."

"You better tell me where and when, because my phone is about to die, and I don't have my charger with me."

Rocco was quiet for a moment. "Pick up the car at the Campground, and I'll meet you at the bed and breakfast where I stayed last night. Let's say, around twelve-thirty." He explained where Mrs. Bailey's place was.

"I have to take a cab to get wherever. You'll have to tell me where in the Campground you left the car."

"Not sure I know myself, but it's on the side of the Campground away from the water, and it's near a house with cutout pink hearts all over the porch. Pretty distinctive. You can't miss it."

"I can't promise you anything, but I'll try. If I can recharge the phone, I'll give you a call."

After he disconnected, he rejoined Victoria in the kitchen, where she was putting a handful of asparagus spears in a bowl of water.

"For my lunch," said Victoria. "Straight out of the garden." She looked him up and down. "You look quite respectable."

"Again, my apologies," said Dominic. He handed Victoria the hospital gown and the slippers. "I learned the nurse is your grand-niece. If you see her, would you mind returning these to her?"

"Of course," said Victoria. "I heard you on the phone. Was that your brother?"

"Rocco, yes."

"I believe the police are trying to locate him. Do you know where he is?"

"What's he done?"

"Nothing that I know of," said Victoria. "I believe they simply want to ask him more about the body he said he wasn't able to identify."

"He wants me to pick up his car, but you know, I don't have a key to the car. What does he expect me to do?" Dominic waved an arm in a theatrical gesture. "That's his problem. I'll check on his BMW in case he left the keys in the car, but I doubt if he did."

"Did he tell you where he's staying?" asked Victoria.

"He gave me the address of a place he

stayed last night. I suppose it won't hurt to give you that information." He described the yellow and orange gingerbread cottage.

"I know the cottage," said Victoria. "It belongs to Patience Bailey, and has been in her family since it was built. Thank you. I'll let Sergeant Smalley know."

"You don't know where my overnight case might be, do you, Mrs. Trumbull?"

"I never saw a suitcase," said Victoria. "Did you leave it in your hotel before you came here?"

"I don't think I checked into my hotel. The last I remember is meeting someone on the ferry who was coming to the wedding, and we stopped at a couple of bars in Oak Bluffs and had a few drinks."

"Quite a few," said Victoria. "Did you leave your suitcase in one of the bars?"

"I don't know." Dominic ran a hand over his head, ruffled his uncombed hair, and ran the hand down his forehead, past his eyes, nose, unshaven cheeks, then dropped it to his side. "It's all a blank."

Victoria was beginning to feel sorry for this young man. "Don't worry — we'll locate it."

"Perhaps someone stole it."

"Unlikely."

"If it shows up, would you mind giving

271

me a call? My phone is about to go dead, but I can probably pick up another call or so before it dies."

"Of course," said Victoria, and wrote down his phone number. "Where will you be staying?"

"I made a reservation at the Turkey Cove Inn, where most of the wedding guests are booked. I hope they've held my room for me."

"You were found in Penny's car. Why don't you look there? Perhaps whoever brought you here left your suitcase as well."

"Good idea."

He came back a few minutes later, smiling and carrying his suitcase. "That's a relief. Guess I have everything I need now. I have my phone charger, and it's just a matter of plugging it in somewhere."

"I don't know whether you've heard," said Victoria. "Your brother canceled the wedding."

"They told me at the hospital. I was supposed to be best man. I'm surprised that the wedding is off. Rocco was telling everyone what a great catch he had, his bride from Martha's Vineyard and all."

"I'm sure the news is a shock to you," said Victoria. "I suppose you haven't had a chance to make plans for the next few days.

Do you have a car of your own on Island?"

"I don't own a car. Don't need one in the city. I flew to Boston, took the bus to Woods Hole, and then the ferry. I planned to stay for a few days, so I'll be here tonight and tomorrow at least. I'd better call a cab, get out of your hair."

Victoria gave him the number for Obed's Cab, and while they were waiting, they conversed.

"Have you been to Martha's Vineyard before?" she asked.

"Never," said Dominic. "I feel as if I haven't been here yet. Yesterday is a blur."

"I understand," said Victoria. "Ordinarily, a wedding is a good occasion to visit the Island. Are you close to your brother?"

"Hardly. Rocco and I haven't had a lot to do with each other since he walked away from a horrible accident a couple of years ago."

"An automobile accident?" asked Victoria. "What happened."

"He'd been drinking. Was driving too fast and cut a corner too close and flipped the car. It rolled down an embankment and wrapped around a tree."

"Good heavens. And he walked away from it?"

"He wasn't hurt. Not a scratch. But our

two stepbrothers, Cosimo and Caesar, were seriously hurt. Caesar almost died. He was in the back seat, and the lower half of his body was crushed. They saved his legs. He can walk okay. He was in the hospital for a couple of months. Cosimo was in the front seat and got cut by glass. You saw the scar on his face?"

"I haven't met Cosimo."

"He was nice looking. Classic Italian. Dark hair, dark eyes, pale face, straight nose. The scar pulls at his eyes and mouth, and now he looks creepy."

"He must feel terribly bitter," said Victoria.

"He never liked Rocco when he and Caesar lived with us, and now, well . . ."

"Yet Rocco invited him to his wedding."

"Rocco thinks everyone loves him. He doesn't think he did anything wrong. He was smart enough to save his own neck. It was their fault they couldn't get out of the car. What was he supposed to do? That's how he thinks."

"And Cosimo accepted the invitation."

"Mrs. Trumbull, I know Cosimo. He was my stepbrother for ten years, after all. Knowing Cosimo, he's ready to send Rocco to the farm. He doesn't care about the wedding. Believe me, that's how he thinks."

"You mean, kill him? Surely that can't be true." She looked out the window. "Here's your taxi."

Dominic went to the door. "You've got to remember, Mrs. Trumbull, we are Italian through and through. It's a matter of honor to Cosimo. And to me."

CHAPTER TWENTY-ONE

Smalley called Toby at the funeral home to make sure he was there, and then drove Cosimo, Elmer, and Red directly to it. Toby met them at the back entrance.

"I'm going to ask you to go in one at a time," said Smalley. "Start with you, Red. Then you won't have too long a time to anticipate and a longer time to recover."

"Thanks a lot," said Red. "Let's go."

Toby gave his talk about the discomfort of viewing the deceased. Red looked at the corpse with more composure than anyone expected, and shook his head. "Not even slightly familiar. Sorry."

Elmer was next. "Nope. Don't know him."

Cosimo went in last. Toby turned down the sheet that covered the victim's face. Cosimo stared. He looked up at Toby and down at the dead face again. Then at Smalley. And then his eyes rolled up so only the whites showed, and he fainted.

Smalley hadn't expected that. He was close enough, though, to catch Cosimo and keep him from falling. Toby whisked a chair under him and brought out smelling salts. Toby glanced at Smalley who glanced back.

Cosimo came to. His eyes were watering.

"I'm sorry," said Smalley. "We didn't mean to shock you like that. Are you okay?"

"Yes," Cosimo said. "No." He bent his head down between his knees.

Toby held the smelling salts under his nose. Cosimo pushed them away.

Smalley said, "You know him."

Cosimo looked up. Tears streamed down his cheeks. "My brother. My kid brother." He bowed his head. "Caesar!" He got to his feet. Stood, unsteady at first. Planted his feet apart. Looked up beyond Smalley.

He turned to Toby. "How did he die?"

"He was garroted," said Toby. "Probably with a length of wire."

"That bastard. I'll kill him for you, Caesar." He spoke to the shriveled body on the steel table. "I swear to God, I will. I came here on purpose to kill him for you, little brother. I saw you suffer for what he did to you. I'll avenge you. I will. Oh God! My God!"

Smalley drove them back to their hotel, Cosimo, Elmer, and Red. No one spoke. When he dropped them off, he told Cosimo to stay in the cruiser. "I want to talk to you," he said

Cosimo, wiped out, sat.

Smalley stood outside with the door open. He leaned a hand on the top of the cruiser and bent down so he was talking only to Cosimo. "I'll take care of notifying anyone you want told," he said. "Also, I want you to know that I heard you identify your brother. But I didn't hear anything else you said. You identified your brother, that was all. You understand?"

Cosimo nodded.

"Can I do anything for you? Anything at all?"

"No," said Cosimo.

"I'm sorry," said Smalley. "I know that's not enough." He pushed away from the vehicle and stood back so Cosimo could get out.

"Thanks," said Cosimo.

"Please, guy, don't do anything rash."

"Yeah," said Cosimo. He eased himself out of the cruiser and Smalley slammed the door behind him. He walked to the hotel steps, Smalley watching. Went up, one step at a time. Into the hotel and the door closed behind him.

"Someone is going to kill Rocco, and I hope it's not him," said Smalley, getting back into the driver's seat. He fastened his seat belt and headed back to the barracks.

Sarah Germaine was sitting on the porch at Alley's Store, eating an Eskimo Bar. It wasn't noon yet. Joe, the plumber, was driving by on his way to a job in Chilmark and saw her there. He continued past the church to where Music Street ended, made a wide U-turn, and parked in Alley's parking lot. He went up the steps and onto the porch.

"What are you doing here this time of day?"

Sarah wiped her mouth on a paper napkin. "I had to do an errand for the tribe in Vineyard Haven."

"That your lunch?" he said, pointing to the ice cream bar.

"Dessert," said Sarah. "Where are you heading?"

"Blocked toilet up to Chilmark."

"I'd hate your job." Sarah ate the final shreds of chocolate coating, folded the wrapper into a neat square, and tossed it into the trash container.

"Yeah, well I don't have to answer to a bunch of wild-eyed idiots who don't know what the hell they're doing and take it all out on you."

"It's not so bad," said Sarah. "I get a regular paycheck, I've got my own office, a spectacular view, and I don't have to peer into people's toilets."

Joe glanced over at the parking lot. "Well, look who's coming."

Linc's pickup pulled into a spot, and he came up onto the porch. "I see the gang's all here. What's up?"

"I heard on the scanner they'll be towing a BMW parked illegally in the Campground," said Joe. "Gotta get it out because it's blocking the owner's access."

"Not exactly newsworthy," said Sarah. "So what?"

"A BMW getting towed is newsworthy. You don't hear that often. You wanna guess who it belongs to?"

"C'mon, Joe. I've got to get back to work. Unlike some people." Sarah checked her phone.

"Guess I better not keep you." Joe stepped away from the post.

"Stop! Okay, whose car?"

Joe leaned back against the porch support again. "The groom's."

"Groom? You mean Mrs. Trumbull's cousin's groom's car?"

"Yup, Rocco Bufano."

"Wonder what that means." Sarah sat back and punched a finger at her phone's keyboard. "I'm logging onto Islanders Know. Stub your toe and it's on Islanders Know."

"What's that?" asked Joe.

"FaceBook," said Linc. "Everybody's on FaceBook now, and everybody follows Islanders Know."

"Never heard of it."

"You're the only one on the Island who hasn't," said Linc.

Sarah said, "It's almost as good as the way news spread in my grandmother's day. We'll know when Rocco shows up to get his car."

"Him leaving it in the Campground was a stupid thing to do," said Joe. "Of course they're going to tow it."

"That's his problem. He deserves it, abandoning Penny what's-her-name like that," said Sarah. "Why did he leave it there in the first place?"

"He was trying to ditch the cops who were following him, and he had the smarts to know you can lose anyone in that labyrinth."

" 'Labyrinth,' Joe? You swallow the dictionary?"

"Labyrinth, and he probably figured there's a minotaur lurking in there ready to devour him."

Linc laughed.

"Wow. I'm impressed." Sarah sat back. "Well, I've got news for you too. You know the body in her cellar?"

"Mrs. Trumbull's cellar, I presume?"

"How many bodies in whose cellars do we find how often?"

"Point taken," said Joe. "What about it?"

"He's been identified."

"Just now?" asked Linc.

"Maybe an hour ago?"

"Anyone we know?" asked Joe.

"Not exactly. Turns out, it's the brother of the groom's stepbrother."

"Say what?" said Joe.

"Rocco Bufano — the groom — had two stepbrothers. This was one of them. The other brother identified him at the funeral home."

"What other brother? The groom's or the stepbrother's?"

Sarah sighed. "I know you're not bright, Joe. Let me explain it to you again."

Joe, who'd been chewing on Red Man, spit off into the ragweed that had established itself next to the porch. "Please do." He wiped his mouth on his sleeve.

"Mr. Bufano, Rocco's father, Bufano Industries?"

"Yeah, yeah. Mega-millions."

"Billions," said Sarah. "He has these two

sons, Rocco and Dominic."

"The drunk who ended up under Mrs. Trumbull's tree."

"You got it, you smart man. That's one son. Well, Mr. Bufano married a second wife who had two sons. I can't think of their names, but there are two of them."

"Cosimo and Caesar," said Joe.

Sarah opened her eyes wide. "How did you know that?"

"I get around. Peering into toilets and such. Go on."

"The state police sergeant —"

"Smalley," said Joe. "I'm good at names."

"I know who Sergeant Smalley is," said Sarah. "Well, Sergeant Smalley asked all the people Rocco invited to the wedding to look at the body, see if they knew who it was. Cosimo took one look and passed out. It's Caesar, his kid brother."

"Wasn't he supposed to be in the wedding?" asked Linc.

"You mean, like best man? No. He'd been badly — and I mean badly — injured in a car accident that was all Rocco's fault, and he refused to have anything to do with Rocco after that."

"Rocco's a real popular guy, it seems," said Joe.

"Everybody's mad at him. His ex-fiancée

is ready to kill him. She was having their wedding invitations printed while Rocco was proposing to Penny. I've got to get back to work before noon." Sarah looked at her phone. "Then, of course, there's his brother, Dominic the drunk, who wouldn't mind getting his older brother out of the way."

"Where do you get all this stuff?" asked Joe.

"I've got my sources," replied Sarah, looking smug.

"You'd think billions could be spread around," said Linc. "Seems like he'd end up rich without offing his brother."

"I wouldn't know. I gotta go." Sarah started to get up.

"I've got a bit of news," said Linc. "Shall I save it for this afternoon?"

Sarah sat back. "Go ahead, Linc. Shoot."

"Picked up a couple from Mrs. Trumbull's last night and dropped them off at the end of the Edgartown Road."

"Not the happy couple, I gather," said Joe.

"I don't know who they were. She didn't seem all that tightly wound, but hard to know."

"Was she the one with the magenta and blue hair? Big glasses?" asked Sarah.

Linc nodded. "He said they were going shopping. She didn't say a thing. That is, he wouldn't let her say a thing. After I let them off, about twenty minutes later I was driving up North Water Street, and they were on the porch of the Turkey Cove Inn, just opening the door."

"So?" said Joe.

"If I had the money to stay at the Turkey Cove Inn, I wouldn't be hitchhiking."

"Maybe they left their Rolls Royce on the mainland because they couldn't get a reservation on the ferry," said Sarah.

"People who stay at the Turkey Cove Inn get ferry reservations back in February," said Linc. "Or they use taxis."

"Maybe they were just having drinks at the pub," said Sarah.

"They were staying there," said Linc. "I could tell."

"I really gotta go," said Sarah. "See you later."

"Alligator," said Joe. "After a while, . . ."

". . . crocodile," said Linc.

Cosimo went into the empty dining room. He sat at a table by the window and looked out at nothing. He saw nothing, heard nothing, felt nothing.

Charles, the server, came in a bit later to vacuum the dining room and set up for lunch. He saw Cosimo sitting there. A half hour later, he was still there, same position.

"Hey, man, you need anything?" Charles asked.

Cosimo looked up at him, his face blank.

"I'm bringing you a cup of coffee. I don't know what happened, but hang in there, man." A few minutes later he was back with coffee. Strong, fresh coffee with cream and three sugars. Cosimo accepted the mug. Charles left, and when he came back a few minutes later, Cosimo had taken only a few sips.

"Can I get you something to eat? A muffin or something? On the house."

Cosimo shook his head. "Thanks for the coffee."

CHAPTER TWENTY-TWO

Angelo checked the time. He'd left Lily for far too long. He walked quickly back to where he'd left the rental car and headed toward Edgartown. State Beach was on his left, stretching for a couple of miles, a curved sweep that cradled the best swimming on the Island. Even now, late morning on a cool May day, there were wind surfers out there. He saw an old guy, probably in his sixties, wade out into the tropical blue water that must be arctic cold. The guy ducked in, swam a couple of strokes, and waded back out into the warm sun.

Pink and white wild beach roses were blooming in the long border that stretched the entire length of State Beach between the road and a bicycle path. A swarm of bicyclists was coming toward him, dressed alike: helmets, goggles, spandex.

He was feeling increasingly uneasy about Lily. He'd let his concern for her slip out of his mind while he and Bianca met. He looked down quickly at the passenger seat, where a canvas bag held a length of wire coiled up like a kid's jump rope, with both ends twisted into loops, the loops padded with adhesive tape.

It will be quick. Rocco will turn his back on me. I'll toss the wire over his head and pull it tight. Rocco will feel something at his throat. Put his hands up. Doesn't know what's happening. Too late.

But Lily too knows all about garrotes and how they work. Probably knows exactly how to use it, better than I do. If she kills him, she'll be caught, and she'll brag to the cops that she did it and how she did it. But if I do it first, they won't catch me.

I've got to find her.

His foot pressed down harder on the accelerator. I should never have left her this long.

He reached Edgartown and was on Main Street. He passed the Dairy Queen, passed the jail, turned onto North Water Street, reached the inn, and parked in front. Up the stairs to the porch, two at a time, into the lobby. Through the front door. A quick nod in response to the concierge, up the stairs to the second floor, two at a time, practically running down the hall, slip the key card into the slot, open the door.

"Lily?"

No answer.

"Lily, you here?"

Check the bathroom. Check under the bed. Not here. I should never have left her. Where would she go? Would she know where Rocco is? On his drive here from the Oak Bluffs park, he hadn't passed her walking. How would she go about finding Rocco? How would a ten-year-old think?

Mrs. Trumbull's. She'd go there first.

Back to the car. Damn the one-way streets. He wound his way first right, then left, found himself where he'd started. *Calm down,* he told himself. *Go slow.* Past that house with black shutters. All the houses were painted white with black shutters. All had white fences out front, covered with roses about to bloom. His shoulders ached. At last he found the Edgartown Road. He knew where he was and he could speed up. He reached Victoria Trumbull's, dashed up the steps, burst through the kitchen door without bothering to knock. Mrs. Trumbull was standing there, facing him.

"Good morning, Angelo. I'm glad to see your ankle has recovered."

"Mrs. Trumbull. My apologies. I was a fool. I owe you an explanation," said Angelo.

"I have to find Lily. Is she here?"

Victoria stepped aside and there was Lily, sitting at the table, a mug of hot chocolate in front of her.

"Hi, Angelo," said Lily. "Where did you get the car?"

Angelo slumped into the captain's chair, and the chair groaned. "I was worried about you, Lily."

"But where did you get the car?"

"I rented it. Thank God you came to Mrs. Trumbull's."

"She knows I'm an expert on weapons and asked me all about them," said Lily. "She had marshmallows for the hot chocolate."

Victoria sat down. "I notice you've lost your Italian accent, as well, Angelo."

"A thousand apologies, Mrs. Trumbull. I thought I was being clever, and I was wrong. I thought I had a good reason, and I was wrong there too. Please accept my apology."

"Accepted," said Victoria. "Zoe came by last night and explained the situation to me. Lily is quite astonishing." She turned to Lily. "I was interested in everything you told me about weapons."

"How long has Lily been here?"

"You can talk to me, Angelo. I'm not deaf. I've been here more than an hour. I told

Mrs. Trumbull all about how I plan to kill Rocco, and she was interested. She asked me how I would do it. And we talked about murder weapons they used in the twelfth century."

Angelo looked from Lily to Victoria.

"I understand how she feels about Rocco," said Victoria.

Lily said, "I thought a garrote would be the best way to kill him. It would be easy for me to handle. It doesn't take much strength, and he would never expect it of me."

Angelo continued to say nothing.

"I agree with Lily that a garrote would be an appropriate weapon." said Victoria. "I also said this wasn't the best time. Saturday, the day the wedding was scheduled, would be more symbolic."

"Mrs. Trumbull." said Angelo. "Lily," he said, turning to her, "I've begged you not to talk. You must learn to keep quiet."

"But Angelo, Mrs. Trumbull understands — truly she does. She promised to help me."

Angelo turned from Lily to Victoria, his mouth slightly open.

"The water is still hot," said Victoria. "Would you like to join us with hot chocolate?"

"She has graham crackers to go with it," said Lily.

Elmer found Cosimo in the dining room, his shoulders hunched, his hands around a mug of cold coffee.

"C'mon Coz, let's go over to Linda Jean's and get a fresh cup of coffee," said Elmer.

Cosimo shook his head.

"You've got to get moving," said Elmer. "Can't just sit here. Keep your strength up."

"What for?" said Cosimo.

"You're depressing everyone around you."

"Go to hell," said Cosimo.

"At least get out of the dining room. You're taking up a table. They're going to be serving lunch in a couple hours. You're scaring away lunch guests. Come on. Red and I are going back to Linda Jean's."

"Go ahead."

"You're a selfish son of a bitch, you know." Elmer placed his hands on the table and leaned over, his face almost touching Cosimo's. "You stuck me with that kid, and now it's your turn. I didn't know him any better than you did. The least you can do is take some of the babysitting off my shoulders. I can't take much more of his whining."

Cosimo looked up. "Rocco killed my brother."

"Rocco didn't kill Caesar. Whoever was hired to kill Rocco killed Caesar. Stop feeling sorry for yourself. Get up off your fat ass."

Cosimo looked down into his mug. A dark line had formed around the edge of his cold coffee.

Elmer moved his face closer to Cosimo's, and Cosimo moved back. "You're not the only one who wants him dead, you know. There's Red. Rocco killed Red's dogs. Killed them in front of Red. I know you hate dogs, but those dogs were the kid's family. Red's got an antique Luger from the First World War. His great-grandfather's."

"Does it still work?" Cosimo looked up.

"Who knows? He's been cleaning and oiling it. He got a box of bullets for a Luger. And me? The love of my life. Madeline. My first love. The only woman I ever loved. We'd known each other since we were high school kids. He steals her from me. Throws around money he doesn't have. Tosses her away when he sees some new woman. She doesn't want me anymore." Elmer stood. "I don't have the guts to stick a knife in him or choke him to death, but it will be easy to drop arsenic in his scotch. I wish I had the guts to strangle him." Elmer jammed his hands into his pockets and leaned down again. "Come on. Get up, you goddamned baby."

Cosimo got slowly to his feet.

"We're going for coffee — you, Red, and me. Come on. I'll pay."

"I've got something I have to do around noon."

"So do I. We got time."

As they left the dining room, Charles gave Elmer a thumbs-up.

Elmer and Red seated themselves across from a silent Cosimo at Linda Jean's.

"You guys must love this place." Molly had stopped by their table at Linda Jean's. "We're not serving lunch for another couple of hours."

"Can we get some coffee? Our pal here" — Elmer nodded at Cosimo — "needs a bracer."

Molly looked at Cosimo, then looked over the tables toward the kitchen. "We haven't cleaned out the coffee urn from breakfast. What's in there would raise the dead. If you can stand it, you can have it on the house."

"That's the ticket," said Elmer.

Molly left and returned a minute later with three mugs of dark sludge. "Macaroni and cheese is the noon special, in case you survive the coffee."

"Thanks," said Elmer. "We appreciate it."

"Is everything okay? He okay?" A nod at Cosimo.

"Everything's fine," said Elmer.

When they'd drunk as much of the bitter black coffee as they could stand, Elmer left a five-dollar tip, and they walked back along Circuit Avenue to the hotel. Shopkeepers were sweeping the sidewalk in front of stores and watering plants in boxes out front.

Shop windows were full of beachwear, souvenir T-shirts, towels, hats. Everything that had a surface on which to paint or embroider something, sported the distinctive triangular shape of Martha's Vineyard.

Cosimo kept turning and looking behind them.

"How much longer are you sticking around, Cosimo?" asked Red.

Cosimo didn't answer.

"You, Elmer?"

"I don't know."

"Cosimo feeling antsy or something?" asked Red.

"Leave him alone," said Elmer.

"You know, Rocco invited me here for an all-expenses paid trip," said Red, "and I don't have enough money for bus fare home."

"We're all stuck," said Elmer. "I told Cosimo about your great-grandfather's Luger."

"I read up on how to use it," said Red.

"Does the gun work?" asked Elmer.

"I cleaned it."

"Yeah, I've been watching you clean it. Have you tried shooting it yet, or are you scared to?"

"All I need to do is point it at his head and pull the trigger."

Elmer said, "You better practice with it first. A gun like that must be a hundred years old."

"Made in 1908," said Red.

"Strangle him with a piece of wire works better than an antique gun," said Elmer. "Also, it takes longer for him to die."

"Yeah?"

"We passed a hardware store," said Elmer. "What say we go back and get them to cut us some pieces of nice heavy wire and a half dozen handles. When he shows up dead, who are they going to blame?"

Cosimo smiled, the first time since he'd seen his dead brother.

They continued to walk.

"How come you keep looking back, Coz?" said Red.

"Shut up, Red," said Elmer.

"Just making conversation," said Red.

"Well just cut it out," said Elmer. "Cosimo doesn't feel like conversation."

Red asked abruptly, "How'd you get that scar, Coz?"

"Auto accident."

"What are you looking for?" asked Red.

Cosimo didn't respond.

They continued to walk.

"About the accident. What happened?" asked Red.

"None of your business," snapped Cosimo.

"Whoops. Sorry. I guess I pushed the wrong button."

"Lit the wrong fuse, is more like it," said Elmer.

When they left Linda Jean's, Cosimo had a prickly feeling that someone was following him, and he kept looking behind him to catch a fleeting shadow, someone suddenly ducking into a store, someone looking too casually into a store window.

Nothing.

And then, a couple of blocks before they were to turn onto Lake Avenue, where the hotel was, he glanced behind him again.

"How come you're so spooked?" asked Red. "What are you looking for?"

Cosimo said, "You go on. There's something I want to get." He cut away from them and went back up Circuit Avenue, walking fast.

"What's his problem?" asked Red.

"He's gone kind of nuts after seeing his brother like that," said Elmer. "Cut him some slack."

They watched Cosimo get as far as the entrance into the Campground, turn into it, and disappear from sight.

"Where's he going now?" asked Red.

"Got no idea whatsoever," replied Elmer. "When we get back to the hotel, how about you make arrangements for your own room. I've got something I need to tend to before noon."

"So do I," said Red.

"Do you have anything left from the three hundred bucks you had yesterday?"

"Yeah. Enough."

"Okay, then. See you about," said Elmer.

Chapter Twenty-Three

With Red off somewhere getting his own room, Elmer opened his suitcase and took out a few more items to go with the mortar and pestle and the small beaker he'd put on the table earlier.

Damn that Red. He was behind schedule, what with Red being there. He unfolded a large sheet of white paper he'd had in the suitcase and covered the table with it, moving the beaker and mortar and pestle on top of it. He next brought out a package of empty gelatin capsules. Two hundred and fifty for seven bucks, and he needed only one. Maybe two for backup. Three for super backup. Two hundred and forty-seven left over. Maybe somebody else could use them.

He pulled on a face mask, tucking the elastic loops around his ears. He'd picked up the mask at his doctor's office, thinking it might come in handy sometime. He pulled on disposable gloves. Nitrile gloves, not the cheap plastic ones. More expensive, but better to be well protected.

Then he lifted out a small, heavy object. It was in a quart-size plastic bag and was wrapped in layers of newspaper. He unwrapped it carefully. A rock, about the size of a cell phone, encrusted with octagonal, whitish crystals about a quarter inch on a side. Trying to prevent obvious damage to the specimen, he knocked off two of the crystals into his mortar. Before he did anything else, he rewrapped the rock in its newspaper and plastic bag layers, and returned it to his suitcase.

The rock was from the geology lab. It had come from a mine in France, and it was a rare specimen of arsenolite. The specimen that he'd taken from the lab was labeled, "Extremely poisonous! Do not taste!" Tasting, he knew, was one way of identifying minerals.

He zipped up the suitcase and got to work, smashing and grinding the three crystals into a fine powder. He then poured the powder into the small beaker, which had a pouring spout that would minimize spillage when he filled the gel capsules.

He messed up the first couple of capsules but finally got the hang of filling and capping them. He put the filled capsules in a breath mint tin. Some powder was left over. He wasn't sure what to do with it, and decided to fill up as many capsules as there was powder. He was filling the last of three more capsules when he heard Red's voice downstairs, talking with someone. He whipped off the mask and gloves and shoved them into the wastebasket. He'd worry about them later. He kept repeating to himself, *Don't get sloppy. Remember to be careful with this stuff.*

He didn't want to be here when Red came back to pick up his belongings and ask questions he didn't want to answer. He slipped out and left by the back stairs.

On the seventh floor of the Shirt Factory, Giovanni's phone rang. He picked up the receiver. "Don Giovanni speaking."

"Leonardo here, Giovanni."

"Yes, yes. What news?"

"The victim mistakenly identified as Rocco has been identified."

"You sound concerned, Leonardo. Is it someone we know?"

"Unfortunately. It was your stepson."

"My stepson? Cosimo?"

"Caesar."

"That can't be!"

"It is so. My helper mistook him for your son."

"Not Caesar! Caesar is my chosen. He's my heir. The papers are signed."

"It's too late now," said Leonardo.

"Making him my heir was the least I could do for him. Rocco destroyed him. Please, tell me it's not true."

"I wish I could. I felt you should be told."

"Does Cosimo know?"

"Cosimo identified his brother's body at the mortuary."

"My God," said Giovanni. "I would not wish this on him. Cosimo was a difficult boy, but he doesn't deserve this."

"Does his mother still live?"

"No. She passed away several years ago. I loved her. Very much. But I was no good for her. She left me."

"My condolences," said Leonardo.

"We've had enough violence in our lives, Leonardo. Let this rest. Can you make your peace with what was done to your Lily?"

There was a long silence at the other end. Then, "You're right, Giovanni. I will call off my helper. His mistake can never be corrected. I will take care of him. He will never make a mistake again."

"We've been on the phone too long, Giovanni. I hear your clock. It sounds as though it is getting ready to strike the hour."

"May Lily stay with you for a couple of hours, Mrs. Trumbull?" asked Angelo. "I have something I need to do around noon."

"Angelo, I'm not deaf, like I keep telling you," said Lily. "Ask me if I *want* to stay here."

"My apologies, Lily," said Angelo.

"Yes, I *would* like to stay."

"We'd be delighted to have you here as long as you'd care to stay," said Victoria.

Lily smiled. "Shall I, like, bring the mattress down again?"

"I think we can wait for that," said Victoria.

"I'll be back late this afternoon," said Angelo. He drove away.

Lily and Elizabeth harvested the last of the day's asparagus. Then Elizabeth left for work, and Lily and Victoria washed, cut, steamed, and packed the tender spears. Lily carried the quart bags, more than a dozen of them, to the freezer in the woodshed.

Victoria settled Lily at the cookroom table with the stack of garden catalogs and headed out to the garden to weed.

She paused at the door. "Will you be all right while I'm gone, Lily? There's cranberry juice in the icebox, and you know where the graham crackers are."

"I love seed catalogs," said Lily. "Everything looks good enough to eat. I'd order a hundred dollars' worth of seeds if I had a garden."

"I understand you live in a penthouse in New York. I should think you could have a garden there."

"My father would let me do that," said Lily. "I like that. I'll tell him I want a garden."

"You're welcome to cut out pages from the catalogs of things you'd like to grow." Victoria stepped back inside, reached for the scissors she kept in a box on top of the refrigerator, and gave them to Lily.

Lily smiled and ran her fingers along the sharp blades.

"When I come back from the garden," said Victoria, "I'll get you some paper, tape, and paste so you can make a book of flowers and vegetables you'd like for your garden."

Lily looked up from a colorful page of dahlias. "Where are you going now?"

"Out to pull up weeds, and then I'll take them to the compost heap."

"How long will you be gone?"

"Not more than an hour," said Victoria. "Would you like to join me in weeding?"

"No, thank you," said Lily. "I'll work on my garden plans."

Red paid for a single room and went up to Elmer's room to gather up his things. Elmer wasn't there, but he'd apparently been working at some kind of project at the table by the window. The small glass beaker he'd seen earlier now had remains of powder in it, and next to it were a couple of crushed gel capsules.

What you don't know about people, thought Red. *Didn't know he was into drugs. That's one thing I'm staying away from. Glad I decided to get my own room.*

He moved his own belongings into his room and then went down to the dining room. It was still too early for lunch, not even eleven, and the dining room was empty except for Charles, who was sitting by himself at a table near the kitchen, playing a game on his laptop. He looked up as Red approached.

"Have you seen the other two guys who are with me?" Red asked.

"Not since Scarface was in here this morning, moping about."

"We had coffee together on Circuit Avenue, and then those two disappeared."

"Can't help you," said Charles. "What's

his problem? He was so down I thought he was going to end it all."

Red wasn't sure how much to say. It was going to come out sooner or later. He might as well be the one to break the news. "His brother died."

"That's too bad," said Charles. "What did he die of?"

"He was strangled," said Red, getting more confident in his role as messenger.

Charles set down his iPad. "Was it some kind of freak accident?"

"No," said Red. "He was murdered."

Charles opened his mouth and said nothing. Opened his eyes wide.

"You heard about the body in Victoria Trumbull's cellar?"

"Was that his brother?"

Red nodded. "His kid brother." A flush of pleasure engulfed him. He was the bearer of news. He was being listened to with respect.

"No kidding," said Charles, pushing his iPad away from him, solitaire forgotten.

"They were close, his brother and him. Hit him hard."

"What was his brother doing in Mrs. Trumbull's cellar?"

"That's what we're investigating now," said Red, taking on the investigative responsibility. "Probably where my buddies are now."

"I've never been this close to a murder investigation before," said Charles. "Did you know his brother?"

"Not well," said Red, who'd never met Caesar and didn't know he existed until yesterday. "Well, I better get busy."

"Let me know what you find out, will you?"

"Don't know how much I can divulge," said Red. "But sure. Be seeing you."

Red left the dining room with a confident step. *Wonder where the other two disappeared to.*

Bolstered by his new feeling of confidence, Red went back up to his room and took out his great-grandfather's souvenir Luger from the First World War. It looked pretty efficient, with that long sleek barrel and the grip that sloped back. He'd ordered ammunition on the Internet the week before he turned twenty-one, faked his birthday by a couple of weeks. He opened the box. The bullets looked more like jewelry than something lethal. A shiny brass bottom and a copper-colored slug.

He needed to practice, since he'd never shot anything before. He decided to practice on the beach. He just needed to know the gun worked. Then he would find Rocco and kill him. For his greyhounds. Red felt his face flush. He loaded eight bullets into the magazine and stuck the Luger into his backpack.

He left the hotel and walked up the street past the Flying Horses. He continued until he came to the Steamship Authority wharf. He turned left, where a line of cars was parked. The beach was about six or eight feet below the road, so he continued until he found a set of steps leading down onto it.

He had figured out how to attach the magazine to the pistol. Pretty simple, actually. He took the gun out of his backpack, and then his hands started to shake. Suddenly, he was terrified. This gun was designed to kill. It was lethal. He'd loaded it with eight bullets. It could kill someone. *Well, dummy, that's what I plan to do.* Could he hold this against Rocco's head and pull the trigger? The gun was a semiautomatic. If he pulled the trigger now, would all eight bullets shoot out? Would he have to reload it before he . . . ? Could he really kill anyone? *The gun is more than a hundred years old. My great-grandfather got it as a souvenir, and I don't know whether he ever shot it. Lugers are supposed to be great guns.*

But suppose it backfires. It could kill me. He lifted the gun, sighted along the long barrel, and couldn't bring himself to pull the trigger.

"What do you have there?" asked a male voice.

Red turned. A uniformed cop.

Red felt his face flush again. "It's a gun."

"I can tell," said the cop. "Let's have it." The cop was behind him. Maybe the cop thought he would shoot him.

"It's my great-grandfather's," Red said, his voice shaking. "A souvenir from the World War. I . . . I . . . I just wanted to see if it works."

The cop reached around and slipped the Luger out of Red's shaking hand. "May I see your permit?" The cop held out the hand that wasn't holding Red's gun.

"A . . . a . . . a permit?" said Red.

"Why don't you come with me to the station and we'll talk about it," said the cop. "My cruiser's right up there. I'll carry your gun for now, if you don't mind."

Red nodded.

"Do you have ammunition in your backpack?"

"Y–Yes," said Red.

"I'll just carry that for you too," said the cop.

Red handed the backpack over.

CHAPTER TWENTY-FOUR

Victoria liked the feel of good earth on her hands and wouldn't wear garden gloves unless there were blackberry vines with wicked thorns that needed to be pulled out. She would weed as much as she could, standing or bending over. It had become difficult to get down on her knees and even more difficult to get up again. She could dig out the weeds with a long-handled hoe and separate them from the soil with a rake.

Mint was up. She picked a bunch to put in tonight's salad and in Elizabeth's and her cranberry juice and rum this evening. Song sparrows had nested in the birdhouse she'd put up for bluebirds. The bluebirds hadn't come, but the music of the song sparrows made up for it.

She hoed three rows — the beets, the lettuce, and the Swiss chard — then raked up the weeds and dropped them into her basket. When the basket was full, she put it in the garden cart and wheeled the cart to the compost heap, where she emptied out the weeds. Three guinea hens gathered around, waiting to dig in the compost to see if she'd brought them some insects or juicy worms.

She was so absorbed in the pleasure of the garden that time passed more quickly than she'd expected, and it was almost two hours before she finally returned to Lily.

The garden catalogs probably kept her as entertained as they would me, Victoria thought. *I could spend an entire afternoon imagining how this flower or that vegetable would look in the garden, and then how lovely in a vase on the dining room table with a dish of steamed vegetables ready to be served.*

She walked slowly back to the house. *I overdid it as usual,* she thought. A hot bath with lavender and rosemary bath salts would take care of the aches before they occurred.

"Hello, Lily," she called out. She wiped her feet on the mat in front of the door and came into the kitchen. "I've got some mint you're welcome to take back to the hotel."

No answer.

Victoria went into the cookroom. The wastebasket was brimming over with cutout pages, and on the table a stack of pictures, neatly cut from the catalogs, were pushed off to one side.

"Lily?" Victoria called.

In the kitchen there was no evidence of snacks eaten or juice poured. She looked out the kitchen door to the east and the fishpond, but no sign of Lily. She went to the woodshed, which she'd turned into a sort of solarium where her plants kept her company during the winter, where she had the freezer, and where she kept her tools in a small bureau.

Her pliers were on top of the bureau, and the top drawer was partly open. That was the drawer where she kept packing tape, duct tape, garden string, clothesline, and picture wire. A new package of picture wire had been opened, and what seemed like quite a long length had been cut off. Presumably cut with the pliers that were on top of the chest.

Lily had explained to her how a garrote could be made out of a length of wire or sash cord or whatever was handy. Handles at both ends, if you had handles; or if not, you could twist the ends of the wire or rope around so you had loops that you could secure with tape or wire, and if you had time and material, you could pad the loop so you wouldn't hurt your hands when you pulled the wire tight around somebody's neck.

Victoria hurried back to the cookroom and punched in the number for the state police.

The uniformed cop drove Red, his Luger, and his backpack to the state police barracks. He parked behind the Victorian building, and they went in through a side door.

"What are you going to do with me?" asked Red.

"First of all, sir," said the cop, "I'll just ask you a few questions, if that's all right with you."

"Sure, yes. Sure. Anything," said Red.

"Do you have a permit for the gun?"

"N–No, I don't. I didn't know I needed a permit. I mean, it's an antique."

"Yes, sir, you do need a permit. Do you know if the gun is registered?"

"I don't know. My dad's grandfather got it as a souvenir in the World War. The First World War. I don't think anyone registered it. I didn't know that was necessary."

"Yes, sir. Guns must be registered."

"What do I do? Can you register it for me and give me a permit?"

"We can start the process, sir, but it will take time. In the meantime, we'll keep your weapon safe here. Along with the ammunition."

"Am I under arrest, then?" asked Red.

"No, sir. I'll get your name and contact information and notify you when the gun is registered. At that time you can apply for a permit to carry the gun."

"You mean, I can go?"

"When we get your information, yes, sir. Do you have a driver's license? We can start with that. Also we might as well take your fingerprints while we're at it."

"Fingerprints?" said Red.

"Yes, sir. It's pretty easy these days, not messy ink all over your fingers like it used to be."

If he refused to be fingerprinted, he'd be suspected of something. If his fingerprints were on record . . .

Red produced his license and gave him the information needed. The officer filled out forms and fingerprinted him.

"See? Not a big deal," said the cop. "I'll give you a receipt that certifies we are holding your property until you can legally possess it. I'll remove the ammunition from your backpack and then you can go." He emptied the backpack onto the desk. Besides the box of bullets, Red's underwear, shirt, and sweater, there was a coil of wire.

The cop put everything back, including the wire, and made no comment.

Red shifted from one foot to the other, sure that he was about to be arrested on the basis of the wire.

The officer gave him his backpack and filled out a receipt for the Luger and the ammunition. Red still stood, shifting nervously.

After an uncomfortable silence, the officer said, "Just curious, sir, what were you planning to do with the Luger?"

"I wanted to learn how to shoot it," said Red, looking down at his feet.

"You don't want to practice there on the beach. It's too close to people. There's a shooting range here on the Island. When all your papers are in order for possession of the firearm, we'll be glad to help you get connected with the range people."

"Well, thank you," said Red. "I'm just here for a couple of days. I live outside Boston."

"You've got a good excuse to return to the Island, then. Your Luger is a beautiful gun." He picked it up from the desk, where he'd laid it on top of a cloth when they came into the building. "It may be an antique, but Lugers have a reputation for accuracy. They're deadly." He set the gun back down reverently. "Looks like someone's been taking care of it, polishing it like that. They made them to last back in those days. Do you need a ride back to where I picked you up?"

"No, no. I'm fine," said Red. "But thank you, Officer . . . ?"

"Adams. Tim Adams." They shook hands.

Red escaped, walked on wobbly legs down the steps and headed back to the hotel. The exchange at the police station had drained him of any thought of murder. His name, date of birth, Social Security number. His fingerprints . . .

When he passed a trash barrel, he removed the coil of wire from his backpack and threw it away. He walked another ten steps, turned around, returned to the trash barrel, and retrieved his wire. Put it in his backpack and continued on his way.

Smalley was there before Victoria had time to consider what her next step should be. She was standing by the kitchen sink, gazing out at the fishpond, when he arrived. He took off his hat and tucked it under his arm.

"I was on my way here when I got your call," he said.

"Please sit, John."

"Don't have time. Let me know what's

going on."

Victoria, herself, sat and told Smalley how Lily had explained to her the making of a garrote and how an uncomfortable length of wire was now missing.

"Does she know where Rocco is?"

"I have no idea."

"News used to travel on the ether," said Smalley. "Everyone on this Island got the news before we did. Never could figure out how. Now it's the Internet. I'll have Tim look out for her." He tugged his phone out of his pocket, punched in a number, and told Tim about the need to find Lily and keep her away from Rocco. "And call Mrs. Curtain. I don't have her number here. Tell her to watch for Rocco. He's bound to show up to get his car. He'll have quite a shock when it's missing." He disconnected and put the phone back in his pocket.

"Where is his car now?" asked Victoria.

"We had it towed to the Park and Ride lot. Rocco will have to pay towing fees plus a fine."

"It was foolish of him to leave it in the Camp Meeting Grounds," said Victoria. "Why there?"

"From his perspective it was a smart thing to do. He was avoiding me, probably because he didn't want me to know where he's staying. And he knows someone is out to get him. So he must have figured he would lose me or another tail, if there was one, then walk to wherever he's holed up, and pick up his car later."

Smalley put his hat back on. "The fog was thick last night. Rocco must have figured chances were, no one would see him. Made a good cover." He headed for the door but turned. "He gave me quite a ride for my money. Impossible to follow that BMW of his in the Campground. In the fog. We'd have found the car sooner or later, but fortunately, Mrs. Curtain called to report a car parked in her spot. He didn't count on blocking the owner's car from parking, and her calling the cops. I've got to get back to the barracks."

"I suppose everyone on the Island with a scanner, including whoever is after him, has heard about an expensive car being towed out of the Campground."

"Not just a scanner," said Smalley, hand resting on the doorknob. "Scanners are old news. Now it's FaceBook. There's a site called 'Islanders Know' that's like a gossip column. Like the old days when some elderly woman would hear a noise and twitch her curtain aside and see someone visiting a lady friend, and the whole neighborhood hears about it in real time."

"Some things never change," said Victoria.

CHAPTER TWENTY-FIVE

At the Hotel on the Harbor, Janice, a marine geology intern at the Woods Hole Oceanographic Institution, was earning money to support herself during the summer by cleaning rooms. She was new at the job. She was straightening out Elmer's room, conscientiously trying not to disturb his things while vacuuming, dusting, and making his bed. She worked methodically, bathroom first, then the two beds, then straightening out things on the table. Vacuuming she'd do last.

When she got to the table, she wasn't sure at first what she was seeing. She was accustomed to lab ware, since a lot of her work at Woods Hole involved chemicals. But here on the table was a mortar and pestle, a small chemical beaker with a trace of white powder in it, and beside the beaker, several broken gel capsules. There was a dusting of white powder on the table. Should she clean it up, clean around it, or leave it alone?

Her first thought was perhaps the guest was preparing his medicine. Her next thought was, drugs.

But would a drug dealer or user leave everything out in the open like this? She didn't think so.

This was something she didn't want to deal with. She'd better bring this to the attention of the manager.

She went downstairs and found Charles, who was, as usual, playing a game of Free Cell on his iPad.

"Where's Mr. Wesley?" asked Janice.

"The manager? He's playing golf at Farm Neck. Why do you need him?"

Janice explained about the powder. "Do you know anything about drugs, Charles?"

Charles smiled. "Enough."

"Room twenty-three, well, the guest left something suspicious on the table. You want to take a look at it?"

"What do you mean by 'suspicious'?"

"It's like a mini chemical lab with a mortar and pestle, a beaker, a couple of crushed gelatin capsules, and a dusting of white powder on the table. I didn't want to clean it up and find out it was somebody's expensive heart medicine or some kind of drug setup."

"I'll take a look," said Charles.

They went upstairs to Room 23, and Charles opened the door. They went over to the table, and he tapped his little finger in the powder and sniffed it, then touched it to his tongue.

"I don't think that's a smart thing to do," said Janice. "Suppose it's a poison of some kind?"

"Slightly sweet, slightly caustic. Rules out a couple of things. It's not flour or sugar."

"And arsenic doesn't have a taste."

"How do you know?" asked Charles.

"Inorganic chemistry," replied Janice. "Arsenic trioxide is how arsenic usually comes. It's a white powder, and it's odorless and tasteless. Highly poisonous. So this can't be arsenic trioxide."

"I love a smart woman," said Charles.

"But you know something," said Janice. "I think you better wash your mouth out, quick."

"Okay." He went into the bathroom and returned seconds later, wiping his mouth on a paper towel.

"I started to say there's a mineral called arsenolite that's white and that's supposed to have a sweetish, corrosive taste, and it is wicked poisonous. We have a specimen in our geology lab at the university with warning labels all over it. It's not real common, but there you are. You don't have to ingest much to kill you. Maybe you've already tasted a lethal dose, if it's arsenolite."

"Thanks a lot," said Charles. "Bring on the antidote."

"I don't think there is an antidote. It's supposed to be a painful death. I wouldn't know. Headache, stomach cramps —"

"Enough already!"

"Maybe our guest is planning to murder somebody."

"You're beginning to get me worried," said Charles.

"Maybe there's a lab on the Island that could analyze this." Janice looked at the dusting of powder on the table.

Charles straightened his shoulders. "You know, the chances of this being arsenic is like zero. I'd feel like a fool making a big deal out of a guest grinding up his pain medicine."

"I haven't emptied the trash, yet," said Janice. "Maybe he threw out the packaging."

"How would you get hold of arsenic?"

"Lab supplier. Lumberyards use it as a wood preservative, or at least they used to. College geology department."

Janice rummaged through the trash and

found a pair of nitrile gloves and a surgical face mask.

"What did he need gloves for?" asked Charles. "And a mask?"

"Not for his medicine, that's for sure," said Janice. "Better to be safe than sorry. I'm taking a sample of this to the police. They'll know what to do with it."

She fished an envelope out of the trash. Using a folded sheet of paper, she carefully scraped a quarter-teaspoonful of the powder into the envelope. "I don't think our guest will miss it if he comes back and it's something innocuous. Tell Mr. Wesley where I am, if he returns from golf while I'm gone."

She drove to the police barracks, which wasn't far from the hospital, parked behind the building, and pressed the button that seemed to be the way to summon someone.

A tall, gangly cop opened the door and smiled when he saw her. "I was expecting someone else, this red-headed kid, to return, and you're a pleasant change. Can I help you?"

Janice suddenly had cold feet. "I have this powder I couldn't identify . . ." She stopped, feeling foolish.

"Come on in. I'm Trooper Tim Adams." He held the door for her.

"Janice Swinburne. I clean rooms at the

hotel, and I found this powder in a guest room, and I guess my imagination ran wild, and I talked myself into thinking it might be arsenic."

"Easy enough to check," said Trooper Tim.

"Will you send it to a lab?"

"No need to do that. If you think it might be arsenic, we've got an arsenic test kit here somewhere. Just dying to use it." He laughed at his joke. "Seriously, it's supposed to give pretty accurate results, and I'm glad to have the opportunity to try it." He went into a back room and returned with a box. "This still has five tests. We've never used it."

"How long does it take?" asked Janice. "I can come back tomorrow."

He checked the directions on the box. "It says twelve minutes."

"Guess I'll stay." She gave him the envelope and he put half of her powder in water and went through the steps. "Last step is we put a strip on the top and put the cap on and wait ten minutes." He set the timer on his phone. "It's supposed to detect as little as two parts per billion."

"Billion?" repeated Janice. "Two parts per billion? That's incredible. Salt in seawater is thirty-five parts per thousand. A thousand thousands is a million, and a thousand millions is a billion. I mean, wow!"

He shrugged. "Can I get you a cup of coffee?"

"I'd love that," said Janice. "I feel silly coming to you like this."

"Ms. Swinburne —"

"Janice."

"Well, yeah. Okay. Janice. We should have practiced with this test kit here at the barracks, so you can think of how you're helping train the state police."

For the final ten minutes, they talked. Janice, about her internship at Woods Hole; Tim, about his always wanting to be a cop.

The alarm on his watch went off. "You hold the color chart. We'll compare the shade of color on the strip with the colors on the chart. The yellow end is two parts per billion; the brown end is two hundred and forty parts per billion. There's a range, so we can be pretty accurate." Tim undid the cap and took out the paper strip. There was a circle of color on the center of the strip, and the color was a dark, rich brown.

"No need to compare it with the chart," said Tim. "It's off the chart. You called it, all right. Must be close to straight arsenic."

Janice gasped. "Charles! He tasted it."

"How much?"

"A couple of grains. He washed his mouth out."

"Who's Charles?"

"He works at the hotel."

"From what I know, it won't kill him. At most it might make him sick, but I doubt it."

After Tim cleaned up and put away the test kit, Janice, who'd watched silently until he was finished, said, "Now what?"

"You mean, should we move in and arrest your guest?"

"Something like that, I guess."

"Afraid we can't do that. He probably has a perfectly innocent reason, other than murder, for putting arsenic into gel capsules."

"When you put it that way, it sounds highly suspicious," said Janice. "What do you suggest we do?"

"Let's assume we believe it's a suspected crime-to-be. We would need a warrant to search his room and confiscate his arsenic. And how would we justify suspecting that the powder the housekeeper, you, brought us to be analyzed was suspect? We have a right to privacy, you know. You had no right to seize his powder."

"But he's obviously planning to kill someone," said Janice.

"How often have you heard someone say, 'I could kill that guy,' and he probably doesn't mean it at the time, but he for sure won't carry it out."

Janice shook her head.

"Who knows how many million say it — like ten million, fifty million — for every one who actually does it."

Janice was unconvinced.

"It's my duty as a cop to protect all our rights, you know. Your right to privacy is a biggie." He looked at her. Light brown hair, cut short, with streaks of sun-touched blond. Brown eyes. High cheekbones. "Can I buy you a drink at the Tidal Rip when I get off duty later?"

She checked him. Light brown, sun-bleached hair, cut very short. Brown eyes. Nice smile.

"Lovely," she said. "Maybe I'll have figured out how to trap him by then."

Janice drove back to the hotel. Charles was working on yet another game of Free Cell on his iPad. The tables were set for lunch, and she could smell meatloaf cooking.

"Meatloaf seems to be the staple around here." She lifted her nose and sniffed with appreciation. She hadn't thought about it before, but now she realized she hadn't met the cook in the couple of weeks she'd worked here. "Smells divine. Where's the chef?"

Charles poked a finger at his chest. "I'm it."

"You're the chef?"

"Temporarily. Our French chef is temporarily incarcerated in the House of Corrections. Lucky jailbirds."

"Do you cook all the items on the menu?"

"Only meatloaf," said Charles. "That's all I know how to cook."

"What if a diner asks for the bouillabaisse?"

"I tell them the meatloaf really is better."

"Save me some for lunch, will you? I have to finish upstairs." She turned to go.

"Wait! I don't want to embarrass you, but did you take the suspected arsenic to the police station?"

"I did."

"What happened?"

"I've got a date for tonight."

He lifted his eyebrows. "And you, an intelligent woman?"

"Nothing better seemed to be coming along."

"I suppose he said of the powder, 'Don't bother your pretty little head — it's talcum powder,' so you giggled and said yes to the date."

"You're revolting. Did you know there are arsenic test kits?"

"No!" Charles did a pretend shock.

"Tim tested it and he was very meticulous about it."

"Tim, eh?" said Charles. "On familiar terms with a cop."

"The test kit could identify two parts per billion of arsenic."

"Yeah, well there's trace arsenic in everything," said Charles. "Rice, brussels sprouts, kale, tuna fish, chicken —"

"This was off-the-scale straight arsenic."

Charles's jaw dropped. "You're shitting me! That powder really is arsenic? Truly?"

"Tim doesn't intend to arrest him, and we have a murderer staying with us."

"Bring me some more of the powder, and I'll dust our guest's meatloaf with it," said Charles.

"Tell him you did and see what he does." Janice turned to go back upstairs. "I have to finish vacuuming his room. I won't touch his arsenic. I hope he's not a serial killer."

Chapter Twenty-Six

Lily had tired of the seed catalogs and decided to go back to the inn. She walked to the end of Victoria's drive. She let a couple of cars pass, and when she saw a pickup truck approaching, held out a thumb the way Angelo had. The truck stopped. The driver reached over and opened the passenger door.

"Fancy seeing you again. I'm Linc and I know you're Lily. Where are you heading today, Lily?"

"The same place."

Linc told her to fasten her seat belt, and after she did, he took off. "Near Cannonball Park."

"Yes. Do you know about cannons?"

"Not much," said Linc. "Your friend didn't give you a chance to talk yesterday."

"He tells me I talk too much," said Lily. "He has to remind me to keep quiet."

"Now you can say whatever you want,"

said Linc. "Were you here for the wedding?"

"No!" said Lily.

Linc glanced over at her. "No?" he asked.

"I hate Rocco."

"Yeah? How come?"

"He's a bad man."

"Who? Rocco what's-his-name?" said Linc.

"Do you know him?"

"No, I don't. But it sounds as though I wouldn't like him."

"Nobody likes him, and I hate him."

They passed the hostel and were quiet until the airport.

"You told us the Navy built the airport," said Lily.

"Right. The Navy was here during the Second World War."

"Navy Seals have a lot of weapons."

"Sure do," said Linc.

"I mean besides handguns, assault rifles, sniper rifles, and submachine guns, they have a lot of other weapons."

Linc glanced over at her. She was sitting quietly with her hands folded in her lap.

"Did you know, they have bayonets, toma-hawks, and daggers? Knives. I can name them, like combat knives and mission knives."

"Hey," said Linc, "where do you get all

this from?"

"It's really interesting," said Lily. "You told me I can say whatever I want."

"True," said Linc.

"Well, I can tell you all about the M4 and the MK 18. That's a close-quarters battle receiver —"

"Stop!" said Linc.

Lily looked hurt. "I can tell you about twelfth-century weapons instead. Mrs. Trumbull was interested in that. There's halberds, lances, and battle axes, and I can tell you all about them."

Linc said nothing but gripped the wheel tightly.

"Have you heard of a guisarme? That's twelfth century. They have curved blades that can really slice people up. You see pictures of them all the time."

Lincoln gripped the wheel still more tightly. His knuckles were white. "We're getting close to where you saw the windmill."

"Did you know that up until the 1970s the garrote was how they executed people in Spain, instead of hanging them? That's not long ago. They used crusher garrotes, not cutter garrotes, which are like cheese cutters that can cut through veins and muscle and decapitate —"

"Stop! Lily, I don't like war and weapons.

I don't like talk about executions. I don't want to hear any more. I've got a weak stomach."

"Mrs. Trumbull was interested in my telling her about murder weapons." Lily sounded hurt. "Angelo is always telling me to stop talking."

"Angelo's right."

Lily was quiet until they reached the end of the Edgartown Road, and Lincoln pulled over to the side.

"Do you know where you're heading?" he asked.

"Yes, thank you for the ride. It was nice talking to you."

Lily got out. Lincoln drove off, shaking his head.

Lily retraced the route she and Angelo had taken the day before to the Turkey Cove Inn. The desk clerk gave her the card key, and she went upstairs to her room. Once inside, she sat on the edge of the nicely made-up bed, picked up the leather-bound menu, called room service, and ordered a filet mignon well done, a hot dog, strawberry shortcake, and chocolate ice cream.

Angelo checked the time. Almost eleven. He'd left Lily in the care of Victoria Trumbull, and his errand should be done by dinnertime, when he'd pick her up.

He was grateful to Mrs. Trumbull and felt sheepish about the stupid plot he'd concocted to stay at her house. Now that he'd met her, he realized he probably could have explained the situation to her, strange as it might seem, and simply asked her if they might stay. She would probably have accepted the explanation and invited them to stay. He'd lied to her. Now she must think little of him, since he'd lied.

Someone on the ferry had introduced him to a great resource, a real-time gossip site on FaceBook called Islanders Know. It was supposed to be just for Islanders, but the stranger had given him her password. This morning he learned that a blue BMW with New York plates had been towed from the Campground and taken to the Park and Ride lot in Vineyard Haven.

Rocco's car. He would never abandon that car. Never, even knowing his life was in danger. Rocco would never believe his life was in danger. Angelo patted the bag on the seat next to him.

He drove up the steep hill to the Park and Ride lot to what seemed like the top of the Island. A big water tower loomed in the background to his left, and close by was a shelter for people to wait for the shuttle bus. To his right was a veritable sea of cars. Hundreds of them, baking in the late morning sun, glittering in varied colors like gems on strings, the parking lot a strange neck for such a necklace. Neck. He patted the bag again. And no one around. Not a soul. Just row after row of cars. Where were all the people?

If the cops stored cars at the Park and Ride, they'd probably be off to the back of the lot, so he drove down one of the lanes, between two solid masses of parked cars, to the end, where there were a dozen cars isolated from the rest. Sure enough, there was the electric-blue BMW. No point in waiting by the car. He could stake out close to the shelter, if he could find a spot. He'd see Rocco coming, however he came, whether by cab or police escort or — unlikely — by foot.

Shortly after Smalley left Victoria, a white car pulled up under the Norway maple, and Zoe Harrington got out.

"I hope you're here about poetry," Victoria greeted her. "Not something distressing."

"Not distressing exactly, but not about poetry. I wish it were."

337

"How can I help you, if it's not poetry?" asked Victoria. "Is it about Lily?"

"Yes."

"Come in," said Victoria. "Let me get you some tea or hot chocolate. There may even be coffee leftover from this morning."

"Tea sounds good. Herbal, if you have it."

"I do. All kinds," said Victoria, putting the kettle on. "Tell me what's concerning you about Lily." She sat.

"Early this morning," said Zoe, "I was in a diner and heard that a blue BMW with New York license plates was towed out of the Campground. At the time I laughed. I thought it was funny that a car being towed out of the Campground was even worth mentioning." She looked around the kitchen, at the wide wooden floorboards and the colored glass bottles and plants on shelves in the windows. "But when I thought about it, I realized it must be pretty unusual for a stranger to park there. I mean, the place is like a park or a museum, with hidden entrances." She moved a pile of newspapers from a chair to the table and sat down. "Then I got to wondering. The car's description fits Rocco's car. A blue BMW with New York plates." She glanced over at Victoria. "Does anyone know where Rocco is?"

"I don't even know who would know," said Victoria. The kettle whistled, and she got up and went about the tea-making process. "Would you like honey?"

"Yes, please."

Victoria brewed her own Earl Grey and sat across from Zoe.

"As you know, Mrs. Trumbull, Lily's father, Dottore Caruso, wanted me to locate Lily and keep an eye on her to make sure she didn't carry out her determination to hunt down and kill Rocco. I did find her and kept an eye on her for a few hours. Then she disappeared. You have no idea what a relief it was to me when I heard that Angelo found her here."

"She was here until about two hours ago," said Victoria. "She was cutting out pictures in seed catalogs while I went out to the garden. When I came back, she was gone.

"Sergeant Smalley of the state police came right away and left a few minutes before you arrived. He understands the situation with Lily's ten-year-old mentality coupled with an extraordinary knowledge of murder weapons."

"Did she say anything to you before she left, Mrs. Trumbull?"

"No." Victoria shook her head. "When I went out to the garden she was happily cutting out pictures of flowers and vegetables. I was in the garden longer than I meant to be, close to two hours, and when I returned she was gone."

"We've got to find her, Mrs. Trumbull. If she were to kill Rocco . . ." Zoe closed her eyes. "If she were convicted of killing him, she'd be incarcerated, either as an adult or as mentally challenged, they'd call it, which would mean being locked up in a mental institution. Either way, I shudder at what life would be like for her. And for her father. She's his only child, you know."

"You knew Angelo was here earlier?"

"Yes. He called me when he found Lily. Where is he now?" Zoe looked around as though hoping he might appear.

"He left before I went out to the garden, so that would be a little less than three hours ago."

"Do you know where he went?"

"He didn't say, and I didn't think to ask. He said simply that he had a job to do and he'd be back later."

"Not exactly helpful, is it."

"No, unless he put two and two together after hearing about the car being towed."

"I can't imagine where he might have heard about it. Towing a car is not exactly world-shaking news, even here."

"I learned from Sergeant Smalley there's another way we Islanders can get news. Many of us have scanners, but he told me there's an even more efficient grapevine called 'Islanders Know.' It's on FaceBook, something I know nothing about."

"I do," said Zoe, taking her phone out of her shoulder bag and punching in a series of numbers. She looked up. "What did you say the name is?"

"Islanders Know," said Victoria.

"Got it," said Zoe. "But it won't let me log on unless I verify that I'm an Islander."

"You can use my name," said Victoria. "It's time I learned something about social media."

Rocco's overnight case was light, the morning was bright, and he'd seen Angelo and Bianca in the park before they saw him, in time to avoid them. Now that he'd decided to get his car, he felt that maybe things weren't as bad as they'd seemed last night.

Last night he'd been convinced that Angelo intended to kill him. Since Angelo was sitting in the park with Bianca, the fiancée he, Rocco, was trying to avoid, that constituted two major problems he didn't have to worry about. He knew where those two were, out in the open, not lurking behind him.

He pushed to the back of his mind the niggling feeling that perhaps there was a killer at large other than Angelo. Finding his car in the maze of the Campground was his only concern right now. He checked his pocket to reassure himself that his car keys were there.

He took the street that paralleled Mrs. Bailey's so he wouldn't have to go past her bed and breakfast. The street ended and he turned right onto Circuit Avenue, familiar territory.

Was it just yesterday that he, Cosimo, Elmer, and Red had celebrated his upcoming marriage with single malt scotch, all they cared to drink, and where he'd left a tip of a hundred and fifty bucks? They'd hit every bar on the street yesterday afternoon looking for Dominic. Seemed like a thousand years ago that he was on top of the world. About to marry a reasonably presentable rich woman who would make all his problems go away.

Dominic drunk, as usual, at Mrs. Trumbull's. The embarrassment of his brother's behavior. Everything had gone downhill from there.

He hadn't anticipated what was coming when Sergeant Smalley asked, politely, if he would mind going to the funeral home to see if he could identify a body. He'd been so cocksure of himself. "Glad to help, Sergeant. No problem. Seen plenty of dead bodies before."

The mortician gave him a lecture about how difficult it might be to view a dead body. No problem. And then he pulled back the sheet. Rocco realized instantly that the person lying there was a case of mistaken identity. He, Rocco, was the person meant to be lying on that mortuary table.

The polite police sergeant's eyes had looked right through him, cold and unbelieving. That same sergeant had told him the woman he was about to marry was penniless. Broke. She must have figured that he, Rocco, was rich. I mean, Bufano Industries, and all.

His father had disowned him. Disinherited him. Did it all legally. Nothing Rocco could do would break that ironbound decision. How could his father even think of disowning him? What had he done that was so terrible? He could name a half-dozen guys who'd done worse than he ever had. He'd been his old man's heir. The elder son. Set to take over Bufano Industries, in line to inherit his father's billions. Dominic wasn't even in the running, what with his drinking problem.

He passed a couple of houses, a place called Good Dog Goods, a church. Circuit Avenue went from being a two-way street to being one-way. A couple of cars passed, heading away from him.

A billion dollars was a lot, and his old man had two or three billion. How many millions were in a billion anyway? Couldn't his father have spared him a couple of million? Wouldn't have made a dent in the billions he had. To his father, a couple of million would be like the pennies you don't want filling up your pockets.

He passed the stationery store with the giant yellow pencil over the door and stood on the curb, waiting for a break in the line of cars. How many cities or towns, for that matter, could boast a main drag that was one-way, one-lane?

A car stopped and flashed its lights at him. He waved thanks and crossed.

Once he picked up his car, he'd drive to Vineyard Haven, get lunch at the Black Dog, get on the ferry, and be on his way back to New York, where he'd be safe again. No one was after him there.

The more he thought about it, the more he was convinced the mess he was in was all Penny's fault, the way she had lied to him. Maybe not lied, but certainly misled.

A lot of people in town. The sidewalk was crowded. He stepped off into the street to avoid a group of three kids coming toward him, laughing and talking, eating ice cream cones, not even noticing him. He passed a couple of shops he remembered from yesterday. Looked in the windows. He absorbed the sounds around him. People laughing and talking, cars moving, doors opening and shutting. And he smelled popcorn, molasses, hot dogs, peanuts, ginger, pizza, all mingled together. He considered picking up a T-shirt to take back to the city. Suddenly everything felt normal, as if he'd woken up from a bad dream to reality.

Then he realized that this pleasant reality was concealing a nightmare, and he'd better get on the road without delay. Angelo and Bianca weren't going to sit there all day. Angelo was going to kill him. When he said that to himself, it seemed unreal. How could he be alive, smelling flowers and food one minute, and the next — poof! Like that. Be gone? It wasn't possible. He would never die. He couldn't imagine his nonexistence, and he certainly couldn't imagine the means by which that might happen.

He could buy a souvenir T-shirt on the

Internet, probably cheaper than buying it here.

Somewhere along Circuit Avenue, he'd need to make a left turn between buildings to get into the Campground. Last night he'd come out through a wide place between two shops. And there it was, like he'd remembered. Maybe the rest of the route to his car would be just as easy. He was at least halfway there.

He turned away from the bustle and sounds and smells of Circuit Avenue, with its tourists and sun, into the gap between the two buildings and stepped into another world, one of silence and shadow.

CHAPTER TWENTY-SEVEN

Cosimo had seen Rocco duck into the passageway from Circuit Avenue into the Campground. He walked quickly, hoping not to attract too much attention, reached the entrance to the walkway between two shops, one painted green, the other yellow. He turned right and walked through time to a place that was a total contrast to the noisy clamor of Circuit Avenue.

A road that was really no more than a paved path curved away from him in what seemed to be a circle. Small gingerbread houses painted in every imaginable color lined the circle. Ahead of him was a large building that seemed to consist of several tiers ending in a dome topped with a huge cross. The silence after the noisy clamor of Circuit Avenue was eerie.

He looked both left and right. No sign of Rocco. Which way would he have turned? People tend to turn right, so taking a chance, he followed the road to his right. Where were the people? No children, no barking dogs, only silence broken by the occasional breeze rustling leaves on trees that arched high above him, and his softer than soft footsteps on the macadam.

How could Rocco have disappeared so quickly and so completely? Smaller paved paths branched off the circle. He followed one that ended in another circle and came out where he'd started. There were other paths. Did they all lead to circles? Following each of them would lead him farther and farther astray, and he would never find Rocco. This was a fool's errand.

Rocco must have gone down one of the numerous branching-off side avenues. To find him, Cosimo would have to go down each one.

He wandered around in the Campground. After a half hour, he found his way back to the circle, which wasn't a circle, but a teardrop shape. At the point of the teardrop, he suddenly found himself out of the Campground, on a wide road with cars. There was a dumpster on the corner, and he emptied stuff out of his pockets into it, including a length of tightly coiled wire. He turned onto the road, and there was the harbor, facing him. He wasn't sure how this had come about, but he felt as though he'd been spun about and spit out from some magic place. One more right turn, and he was back at the hotel.

He shook his head in bemusement at the way he'd gone into the center of the labyrinth and come out the other side into normality.

Was anything that had happened back there real?

He stopped to look at the harbor. Yesterday had been so foggy, he hadn't realized how many boats were tied up. He turned back to the hotel and went up the steps and into the dining room.

Charles looked up from his iPad. "Hey, arisen from the dead. You look a lot better than you did a while back."

"I took a walk through the Campground," said Cosimo.

"Surprised you didn't get lost. Most people do." He closed his iPad and stood up. "Meatloaf is the special today. Will you be having lunch with us?"

"I don't know. Have you seen the other two who're with me?"

"The one you call Red had a run-in with the cops."

"What happened with the police?"

"They confiscated his great-grandfather's gun."

"How did that happen?"

"Seems you're supposed to have a permit, which he didn't have, and the gun was supposed to be registered, which it wasn't."

"Did they arrest him?"

"No, the cop was real nice. Got his name and address and family history all the way back to the Conquerors, fingerprinted him, and said they'd process the permit and registration for him as a courtesy and they'd let him know when he could come back and get his gun."

"Where is he now?"

"He said he was going to explore the Campground to burn off the adrenaline."

"And the other guy, Elmer?"

"I don't know where he is."

"Why the frown?" asked Cosimo.

Charles turned away.

"What's the problem?"

"Janice, the girl who cleans —"

"Woman," said Cosimo.

"Yeah, well, whatever. It's a long story. Janice was cleaning his room and . . . oh well." He turned back to the table where he'd left his iPad. He picked up a laundered napkin from a stack and started to fold it.

" 'Oh well' what?" said Cosimo, alarmed.

"I shouldn't have said anything. I don't want to get her in trouble."

"Come out with it," said Cosimo.

Charles tossed the half-folded napkin back on the table. "Don't look at me like that. I didn't do anything."

Cosimo stared at him.

"Okay!" Charles held up a hand. "She saw what she thought was drug paraphernalia, and since the manager is out at Farm Neck, playing golf, she asked me to take a look."

"What kind of drug paraphernalia?"

Charles squirmed. "There was a white paper on the table and a chemical beaker with white powder in it, a mortar and pestle, and a couple of broken gel capsules, like he was trying to fill them with the powder."

"So? He could be fixing his medicine."

"Could have been, but it wasn't."

"Stop dragging this out. What happened next?"

"Janice insisted on taking a sample of the stuff to the cops. She had it in her head that it was arsenic."

"Yeah, yeah. Sure. Guests are always filling capsules with arsenic."

"The cop was really nice."

"The same cop who was nice to Red, I suppose."

"I think there's only one on duty there

351

this time of day."

"Okay. A nice cop."

"Believe it or not, they have an arsenic test kit at the police station, and he tested it, and sure enough — arsenic."

"Arsenic?" asked Cosimo. "Arsenic?" he said again, louder. "You're joking."

"Cross my heart, hope to die," said Charles, blessing himself.

"Where's Elmer now?"

"Best guess, he's going to put arsenic in someone's coffee."

"Jee-zus," said Cosimo. "You're not funny, you know. Red with a gun, Elmer with poison."

"What do you have?" At Cosimo's look, Charles said, "Just kidding, honest." He held up his hands as if to ward him off. "I didn't mean anything."

Angelo found a parking spot between a white pickup and a silver Suzuki and pulled into it. From where he sat, he could see anyone or any vehicle coming up to the Park and Ride. While he waited, he fiddled with the FaceBook site Victoria Trumbull had informed him about, Islanders Know.

As she'd told him, the site buzzed with local news. Someone had an antique gun the police confiscated because it wasn't registered. Someone's chicken had stowed away in someone's car. Someone got picked up for a taillight out. Someone's BMW got towed from the Campground.

He had a mild sense of belonging to this community, knowing whose BMW that was.

Then a light went off in his mind. Rocco would go back to the Campground to pick up his car. It would take him some time to work out what happened and where the car was. One thing Angelo was sure of, and that was that Rocco would never leave this Island without his precious BMW.

Angelo pulled away from the Park and Ride and headed to the Campground. Since his car was a rental, no one would recognize it or him. He had some idea of the layout of the Campground, and the chatty Islanders Know site had given him a pretty good idea of where the owner could go to find his car.

Well, Rocco would have a surprise. He, Angelo, would be waiting.

Thank God, Lily was safe with Victoria Trumbull. That was a worry off his mind. He didn't think Lily would know how to find Rocco, but on the other hand, her mind had strange ways of working that often bordered on genius. A ten-year-old genius. Mozart wrote genius music when he was younger than Lily's mental age. Maybe Mozart had been an autistic savant.

As soon as he stepped from Circuit Avenue into the Campground, Rocco found himself surrounded with little gingerbread houses painted, like Mrs. Bailey's, in pastel colors, with matching flowers in their tiny front yards. Tall trees, the tallest he'd seen on the Island, loomed over him. He faced an enormous dark building in the center of a circle. In the fog last night, he hadn't noticed it. He paused, trying to recall which direction he'd come from, left or right, and decided left.

Narrow paths branched off from the paved road he was on, wide enough for only two people walking side by side, yet they had signs labeling them avenues. Pease Avenue. Fisk Avenue.

It was the silence of this place of little pastel houses and tall trees that got to him. There were no people walking or sitting on porches. No cars. No children screaming for ice cream. No bicycles weaving their way past him. Only silence. He looked up and caught only a small patch of that great blue sky that had arched over him before he'd turned into the Campground. The avenue he was on circled the tall building in the middle. He walked past the houses, one after another, all alike except for their color schemes, and he realized he'd walked around the circle and had come back to where he'd started. He would need to turn off somewhere and walk down one of the still narrower avenues, but which, he had no idea. His first foray put him in another circle, smaller than the first. He circled that and returned to the first. Nothing looked like the landmarks he'd seen last night.

All he'd had to navigate by last night was the moan of the foghorn on the Sound. Even if it were foggy now, it wouldn't help him. There was no one around he could ask for directions. Even if there were, how would he describe the house where he'd parked? Would he say it was a house with a parking place next to it? Almost all the houses seemed to have parking places next to them. Hadn't seemed that way last night. He couldn't recall what color the house was. It had been just a shape in the fog.

A mental image that he didn't want to recall came back to him. The mortuary. That body on that table in the mortuary. That person who was meant to be him. It was unreal to think someone wanted to kill him. He walked faster and began to sweat, although the day was cool. He went down one avenue after another, returning to the main circle, increasingly frustrated, until finally he saw something familiar. The porch balusters on one of the houses were decorated with sawed-out wooden hearts painted pink. He'd noticed that house last night. A house with wooden hearts. He stopped and wiped his forehead. A sign above the door of the house said "1839." He didn't know whether that was a year or the house number. But the heart porch gave him a burst of hope, and he soldiered on, one false start after another until at last he knew he was on the right avenue. His car would be on his left, two or three houses along.

He reached the house. He knew it was the right house. He recognized a big flat square stone by the parking space. A car was parked there, but it wasn't his car. Had he come to the wrong place after all? His car was missing. Where was it? Had it been towed? If so, where to?

Now he was concerned about the time. It was close to noon. How long would it take him to find his car, and should he do that, or should he get off the Island while he could? Walk back to the park and the ferry dock and hope that Angelo was gone by now.

He thought again about Angelo. He

thought about the body hung in Victoria Trumbull's cellar. That wasn't Angelo's work. Angelo would kill and leave. He wouldn't send a message like that, a message that said clearly, "You are next." Angelo wouldn't have killed the wrong person.

Should he assume his car had been towed to a storage lot, and go to the police and find out where? He had no transportation now to get to the police station. Sergeant Smalley now seemed like a distant refuge.

He should simply knock on the door and ask the person inside what had happened to his car, and offer apologies for having inconvenienced him.

He went up onto the small porch and knocked. A car was there, but no person answered his knock. He knocked again, tried to peer through the stained glass of the front door, but could see nothing inside.

He was sweating again, standing on the porch, this time a cold sweat that smelled of fear. He would have to walk back the way he'd come. This time he would book a passenger ticket. No one could trace him that way. Leave his car here, wherever it was. The killer would assume he was still on the Island. He'd get Dominic to pick up the BMW later.

He heard heavy footsteps. Relief washed

over him. The owner was returning and would help him.

He turned but saw no one.

"Hello?" he said. "Hello! Anybody there?"

He turned the other way, and saw a sudden movement. "Hello, I can't see you, but are you the —"

Suddenly a line or cord was thrown over his head and pulled tight against his neck by strong hands. It didn't register on him at first what it was. He reached his hands up to push it away, whatever it was, and was about to turn to see who was behind him. He heard someone breathe. Heavy breathing. He felt hot breath on the back of his neck. He put his hand between the cord or whatever and tried to pull it away from his throat, but it was getting tighter and tighter, and his fingers were caught between his throat and the cord.

He thought, *What's happening?* and he thought, *Who'd do this to me?* and he thought, *This isn't funny,* and he was dizzy and dizzier, and he couldn't breathe and he choked, and he thought, *This can't be the end,* and he knew this was the end, and he didn't feel it when he fell off the porch, rolled down the steps, and into the purple and pink flowers that matched the trim on the house.

CHAPTER TWENTY-EIGHT

Mrs. Curtain, who owned the purple and pink house, walked home from a pleasant luncheon she'd had with a delightful young woman, Penny Arbuthnot. The woman was assisting the electrician who was wiring the house for her granddaughter's wedding reception. They had dined at the Hotel on the Harbor, where they'd had delicious meatloaf and had drunk most of a bottle of red wine.

The young woman, in addition to helping the electrician, was a bridal consultant, and Mrs. Curtain would most certainly recommend her to friends, who had a seemingly endless supply of daughters and granddaughters about to get married.

After lunch, Mrs. Curtain did some shopping on Circuit Avenue and found paper napkins to go with the purple and pink decor of her Campground gingerbread house.

She always loved the approach to her house. It had been in her family for generations and had absorbed the joys those generations had found in the small cottage.

Her first reaction upon seeing a man sprawled out in her petunias was aggravation. A man lying there had crushed her flowers. And the reception coming up in a few days. Another drunk. She would call the groundskeeper to get rid of him, and then she would need to replant the bed of crushed petunias.

When she looked more closely, her second reaction was to cover her mouth with her hand, rush inside, and call 911.

In the Shirt Factory's seventh-floor penthouse apartment, Giovanni went to his kitchen and prepared himself an afternoon snack: cheese, grapes, and a glass of red wine. His cook had prepared a light supper for him and left it in the refrigerator for him to warm up later. His needs were modest.

Such a tragedy about Caesar. He mourned his loss. A fine young man, an example for his two sons, even though Caesar had been the youngest. When he saw how his own sons were turning out, self-absorbed Rocco, who understood nothing but his own desires, and Dominic, who loved the bottle, he had named Caesar his heir. Only his lawyers knew.

Rocco had taken advantage of his cousin Lily, physically twenty years old, mentally only ten. Rocco had impregnated her. When he'd learned she had taken no precautions against pregnancy, didn't understand what was happening to her body, Rocco had taken her to a side-street abortion clinic.

His own son had done that.

Had Rocco consulted with him, his father, Giovanni would have been upset, of course. Furious. But he would have ensured that Lily was seen by the very best physician in a sanitary setting, not by a backyard butcher.

With Caesar's death, there was no more need for killing. He couldn't stomach any more violence. He and Leonardo were in accord on that, and Leonardo had called off the hired killer.

Giovanni was left with two failed sons. Rocco and Dominic. He'd disinherited Rocco. With Caesar, his favorite stepson, gone, would Dominic be the one to inherit his billions? Dominic, who would attempt to drink it up? He would have to do something to forestall that. He'd never gotten along with his other stepson, Cosimo, and Cosimo detested him, he knew. Could that rend be repaired?

Something to think about. Cosimo as his heir.

The phone rang and he answered. "Don Giovanni here."

"Leonardo here, my friend. Bad news, I'm afraid."

"Let me sit before you tell me anything more."

"It has to do with your son Rocco."

"As I've told you, I have no son Rocco. What about this person by that name?"

"He's dead."

Silence.

"Are you there, Giovanni?"

"Yes. I am not sure I heard you."

"Rocco is dead. He was killed sometime around noon today."

Giovanni took a deep breath. "Please. Details."

"He was found lying dead in the front garden of a woman who lives in Oak Bluffs, in an area known as Wesleyan Grove, or simply the Campground."

"You said he was killed."

"Garroted. Yes."

"By your helper?"

"I have not heard from my helper."

"Here is something we wished for. Then we wished for it not to be. Now it has happened, and I feel great sorrow."

"I am sorry, Giovanni. We may wish for things to be undone, but —"

"I know, Leonardo. I need to think. We will talk tomorrow."

Sergeant Smalley and the Oak Bluffs ambulance arrived at the same time. Doc Jeffers showed up shortly after on his Harley, small blue lights flashing across the visor of his helmet.

"What have we got here?" The doc bent down to the body in Mrs. Curtain's petunia bed.

Smalley couldn't see the face of the man sprawled out in the flowerbed, but he knew who it was. And he had an even sicker feeling that he knew what had happened to him.

Doc Jeffers got to his feet. "Dead, all right. Seems to have been strangled with wire or thin cord. The autopsy will confirm cause of death."

"Crime scene, Tim," Smalley said to the trooper standing by. "You know the drill."

"Yes, sir. Seal off the avenue."

"Right."

The commotion had brought out the few residents who were in the Campground this time of year.

"Been an accident, folks. Please step away," said Smalley.

Tim was at work unrolling crime scene tape.

"I should have anticipated this," said Smalley, half to himself. "The stupid guy. He wouldn't believe this was going to happen to him." He looked around for Tim. "Make sure the area you seal off includes the house, the avenue in front of the house, and an area around the house. And," he added, "when you finish there, get the forensics people here."

"There's only one of me," muttered Tim, adding under his breath, "and furthermore, I have a date tonight and I intend to keep it."

Zoe returned to the Turkey Cove Inn, hoping that Lily had also returned. She stopped at the desk.

"Has the young woman staying with us come back to the hotel?"

"Yes, ma'am, she did come in and picked up her key, but I saw her go out some time ago."

"How long ago was that?"

"More than an hour. It wasn't yet noon."

"Thank you. I'll take our key."

"Certainly, ma'am."

Zoe went up to the second floor and knocked on Lily's door, hoping she had come in unseen by the desk clerk. But there was no answer. She tried to think what Lily would do. Would she know about Rocco's car being in the Campground? It was difficult to know how Lily's mind worked. So bright in some odd ways, so childish in most. Could she figure out where Rocco was and then how to get there? Was there any point in driving around, hoping to find Lily? Lily knew how to hitchhike and would wait for a white pickup before sticking out her thumb.

First things first. Zoe decided to get something to eat, since it was well past noon and she was starving. She went down to the pub and seated herself at the same table where she and Angelo had talked last night. The same server, Amanda, greeted her, and she ordered a cup of clam chowder.

"Chow-duh coming up, ma'am. That's how they pronounce it here."

"Do you work both lunch and dinner?" Zoe asked.

"Lunch, afternoon, dinner, and evening," said Amanda with a smile.

"Kind of a heavy schedule, isn't it?"

"It's not bad. I'm saving up for tuition this fall."

"Where are you going to school?"

"Boston University. Majoring in English

lit." She tucked her order pad into her apron pocket. "I'll have your chowder in just a couple of minutes."

Zoe had her head down, checking her email on her phone while finishing her chowder, when someone slipped into the chair next to her.

She looked up and the start of a frown turned to pleasure. "Angelo. Am I glad to see you. We've lost Lily again. She returned here from Mrs. Trumbull's, but she left again."

"So I heard from the desk clerk."

Amanda came to their table. "Would you care for something, sir?"

"How's the chowder, Zoe?"

"Better than excellent."

He looked up at Amanda. "Chowder it is, then."

"Cup or bowl, sir?"

"A bowl, definitely. And a Sam Adams draft."

Amanda picked up Zoe's cup. "Can I get you anything else, ma'am?"

"I'm all set, thanks."

After she left, Zoe said, "I planned to go on a quest to find Lily when I finished lunch, but I haven't a clue as to where to start."

"I do. Let's start at Cannonball Park and go from there."

Cosimo was about to go up to his room, when Red came downstairs. They stood in the lobby near the registration desk. The only hotel person around was Charles, who was bustling around in the dining room where three or four tables were occupied by people conversing as they finished lunch.

"Where've you been?" asked Red.

"Around," said Cosimo.

"You had lunch yet?"

Cosimo asked, "Where's Elmer?"

"Probably drugged out on some beach somewhere."

"What do you mean by that?"

"He had some kind of drug paraphernalia in the room. I saw it when I went to get my belongings out. I've got my own room now, you know."

"Glad to hear that. What kind of drug paraphernalia did he have?"

"Like a mortar and pestle and some gel capsules. I didn't know he was a druggie. He doesn't seem the type."

"So he was grinding something up and putting it into capsules?"

Red shrugged. "I guess. That's what it looked like."

"Do you know where Elmer is now?"

"No idea. You had lunch yet?" Red asked again.

"You go ahead. Smells like meatloaf is the special for today."

Janice, the geologist/housekeeper, decided to be straightforward in this business about the arsenic. Confront Elmer. She also decided she'd better confront him when there were witnesses around, in case things turned violent.

She would make sure Charles was somewhere close, and she would call Trooper Tim if things got ugly.

She finished making up the rooms and came downstairs. Charles was clearing tables and chatting with a few diners still hanging around. Two guys, one tall and skinny and handsome in a gloomy way, the other a redhead, were standing by the registration desk, which, as usual, had no one there.

"Would you like to register?" she asked. "I can help you, if you'd like."

"We're already registered," said the taller one.

She suddenly felt uneasy. "Is one of you Elmer?"

"I'm Red and he's Cosimo," said the

redhead. "We're waiting for Elmer. I mean, I guess we are." He glanced up uncertainly at the other guy.

"Did you have a message for Elmer?" asked the guy named Cosimo.

"I'm the housekeeper, and I had a question about cleaning his room."

"I've been staying in his room," said Red. "I just this morning got my own room. Maybe I can answer your question."

Janice was now perplexed. Perhaps Red was the arsenic person, not Elmer. Perhaps Red was the one she should confront. Seconds passed. She made her decision: don't confront either until she knew more.

"If I can't be of any assistance, I'll go on about my business," she said.

"Nice to meet you," said Red. "What did you say your name is?"

"I didn't say, but it's Janice."

CHAPTER TWENTY-NINE

Red and Cosimo left, and Janice went into the dining room to disrupt Charles's game.

He looked up. "What's happening?"

"Did you know that a guy named Red was staying in Elmer's room?"

"I didn't. Is that a problem?"

"Red — obvious, what with his hair — just told me he's been staying in Elmer's room."

"So?" said Charles.

"Well, I don't know whether it was Red or Elmer who was grinding up the arsenolite." Janice began to chew on the side of her thumb.

"You wash your hands after touching that stuff?" asked Charles.

"Oops. You're right." She dropped her hand to her side. "Actually, I did wash my hands. How are you feeling? Symptoms of arsenic poisoning take a while to show up."

"What kind of symptoms?"

"Headache and stomach ache, like the flu or food poisoning. But when the symptoms show up, it's too late."

"Why are you telling me this?" asked Charles. "Don't you have work to do?"

"I have to decide whether to clean the table in his room or not. Or empty the trash. Could be evidence."

Someone was coming up the front steps. The door opened, and a chubby man with short blonde hair came in. He looked around, and when he saw Janice, he came over to her.

"Are you the housekeeper?"

"Yes, sir. Can I help you?"

"I left kind of a mess on the table in my room, and I wanted to make sure no one touched it."

"Well," said Janice, hedging to gain time, "well, I didn't know whether to clean it up or not, so I didn't do anything. The rest of your room, though, it's clean, sir."

"Thanks." He started to leave, then turned back. "I was grinding up a rock sample for some work I'm doing."

"Really," said Janice, not sure what to think. "What kind of rock?"

Elmer hesitated. "Not the whole rock, just a couple of crystals. From a rock specimen from France."

Curiouser and curiouser, thought Janice. "Are you a geologist?"

"Not quite. I work in a geology lab."

"Working on your degree?" asked Janice.

"One of these days," said Elmer. "Well, I better get back upstairs and put my lab equipment away."

"What are you going to do with the powder you ground up?" asked Janice.

"I'm putting it in capsules."

"It must be a pretty dangerous mineral if you have to use gloves and a face mask."

Elmer flushed and turned to go. "Don't want to breathe in rock dust, you know."

"Especially if it might be some kind of poison or something," said Janice.

He turned back. "Yeah. Sure. Of course. If it was poison. You just don't want to breathe in any kind of rock dust," he said. "Black lung disease, only not from coal."

Janice was beginning to enjoy this, watching this little man squirm. "You know, Charles, over there" — she nodded to where Charles was hunched over his Free Cell game — "he tasted it to see if it was flour or sugar or something that I should just clean up."

Elmer paled. "He . . . what?"

"He said it had a sharp, sweet taste. Maybe a seasoning he can use in the dining hall." She smiled. "What's the matter?"

"How much did he ingest?"

"I wouldn't know. He may have taken some away to use in the kitchen. He didn't think you'd mind, since I was just going to clean it up. He said it would add a nice flavor to his meatloaf."

"Oh my God!" said Elmer. "He can't do that. You've got to stop him!"

"He's already cooked the meatloaf. It smells great."

"Oh my God," Elmer said again, this time more like a prayer. "The mineral I ground up is —"

"Arsenolite?" asked Janice sweetly.

"Who are you?"

"I'm a geologist disguised as a charlady."

"How much did he eat?"

"He touched his pinkie to it and tasted a few grains. I made him wash his mouth out." She assumed a look of great concern. "Do you think he'll die?"

"I don't know. I don't know how powerful arsenolite is. It said on the sample, 'Do Not Taste; Extremely Poisonous.' "

"You snuck a specimen of arsenolite out of the geology lab — you know, it's a pretty rare mineral. How did you get away with it?"

"I run the lab," said Elmer, stretching the

truth a bit.

"So you ground up a couple of crystals. Who are you planning to kill?"

"How much did he put in the meatloaf?"

"If he put in a teaspoonful, and the meatloaf serves about twenty . . ." said Janice.

The delightful aroma of baking meatloaf, tonight's special, wafted toward the foyer, where Janice and Elmer stood.

Elmer pushed his way past her and confronted Charles. "The meatloaf. You'll have to destroy it!" said Elmer. "In a safe manner. You can't just throw it out."

"What are you talking about, sir?" asked Charles, getting to his feet.

"If you throw it out, someone's pet may eat it. Or a homeless person."

"Why would I throw it out, sir?"

"Your housekeeper said you seasoned it with the powder on the table in my room. It's arsenic."

"I know the powder is arsenic. No way would I put it in my meatloaf. I'm not a mass murderer!" Charles raised his voice to a shout.

"You knew it was . . . arsenic?" Elmer said softly.

"She took a sample to the cops, and they tested it. Arsenic." He lowered his voice. "Mind telling me . . . us, I guess . . ."

Janice had joined them. "Mr. Rudge — you are Mr. Rudge?"

Elmer nodded.

"Who were you planning to kill?"

Elmer said nothing.

"I mean, from the look of it, you filled a bunch of capsules with arsenic. Any one of the capsules would take out two or three people if they're sharing the coffee you dropped the capsule in."

"It's a long story. Is the meatloaf okay? It smells good."

"If you're asking did I poison it, no, I didn't," said Charles. "And thank you. It's my specialty. I'm cook until the chef gets out of jail."

"You'd better take the specimen back to the geology lab before someone misses it," said Janice. "Did you damage the specimen?"

"I was careful, just a couple of small crystals around the edge."

"Also, I'd appreciate it if you cleaned up your stuff so I don't have to touch it. Gather it up and we'll dispose of it in the hazmat place at the dump."

"Will the police be coming to arrest me?"

"They told me it's none of my business what you do in the privacy of your room. But I'd like to know who you're planning to kill so I can warn them. Then the cops can arrest you."

"I was hoping to eliminate one miserable excuse for a human being. But I guess I've missed my chance."

"If he's that bad, let someone else do it," said Charles. "That's called delegation."

Angelo's rental car was parked in front of the inn. He and Zoe drove down one-way streets, one after another, until they found their way onto Main Street. Cannonball Park was a lush green triangle bounded by Main Street, Cooke Street, and the Edgartown Road. They circled the park before they found a place to park, then walked back to it. Sure enough, there was a cannon and mounds of cannonballs held together with cement to keep people from taking souvenirs. It didn't take long to find Lily, sitting on a bench in the shade of a great obelisk that honored the Island's Civil War dead.

"Hello, Lily," said Angelo. "We were looking for you and thought you might be here."

"This is a nice park. I think that cannon is a twelve-pound Napoleon, but I can't tell for sure. I asked that man over there" — she pointed to a man reading the *Wall Street*

Journal on another bench — "but he didn't know."

"Did you have a good time at Mrs. Trumbull's?" asked Zoe.

"My father is going to make a garden for me on the penthouse roof," said Lily, "and I was cutting out flowers and vegetables to grow in my garden."

"Where did you go when you left Mrs. Trumbull's?" asked Angelo.

"Linc gave me a ride to the Cannonball Park, and I walked to the hotel and ordered lunch."

"Good for you. What did you order?"

"Steak and ice cream."

"Then where did you go?"

"I didn't see Linc, but a nice lady drove me to the Campground, which is where I wanted to go."

Zoe held her breath.

Angelo said, "Why did you want to go to the Campground?"

"Rocco was there, and I hate Rocco. I had my garrote with me. See?" She held up the homemade garrote she had made using Victoria Trumbull's picture wire. She'd made a loop at each end and secured it with packing tape. Then she had padded the loops with more tape.

"How did you know he was there?"

377

"I heard someone talking about a blue BMW in the Campground. I knew that was his, and they told me how to get there."

"Did you find him?" asked Angelo.

"Yes," said Lily, with a downcast expression.

"And . . . ?" said Angelo.

"He was already dead, but I killed him again. He was on the ground, so I killed him. I wanted to kill him. I wanted to see how good my garrote was. I made it myself, you know."

"So you didn't kill him." Angelo was not sure what he'd heard.

"Yes. I killed him," said Lily. "He was on the ground. Garrotes are extremely efficient. The Spaniards used them as a more humane way to execute people than by hanging them."

"Was he already on the ground?"

"Yes, so I killed him, and I'm glad I did."

That evening it was cool. A bank of low cloud had moved off, exposing a high screen of clouds and lower ones, some lacy, some elongated. Sunset would be spectacular this evening.

Victoria pushed her typewriter aside and moved her chair around so she could watch the changing colors from the cookroom window, a display she never tired of.

"Mind if I join you?"

She turned at the sound of her grand-daughter's voice. "You're home early to-night. Just in time to see the sunset."

Elizabeth was wearing her harbor uniform: tan slacks and a white short-sleeved shirt with an arm patch that read "Oak Bluffs Harbor."

She moved the stack of seed catalogs from a chair and sat down next to her grand-mother where she too could watch the sun-set.

Victoria turned to the window. "Another minute or two, and the colors will flare up."

"The harbor has been so busy I haven't had time to think. Has anything happened with our investigation?"

Victoria explained. Cosimo had identified his brother as the man hung in the cellar, and Rocco had been found dead in Mrs. Curtain's petunia bed.

Elizabeth stood. "I'm getting us both drinks. Cranberry juice and rum?"

"Lovely," said Victoria.

The thin clouds that partly covered the setting sun suddenly turned gold. The long cloud streamers flamed with reds and pinks.

Elizabeth brought their drinks, and they sat quietly, watching the display and sipping their drinks, neither wanting to discuss the day's events.

"When the sun sets, I realize how little time it takes for it to rise, travel across the zenith, and set," said Victoria. "I marvel at how swiftly our world is spinning, yet we humans and trees and buildings don't fly off into dark space."

"A thousand miles an hour," said Elizabeth.

The colors spread and the sky turned a brilliant rose-red. The colors brightened, then faded. The lacy clouds dissipated, and the long streamers turned a deep purple. A first star appeared.

"Venus," said Victoria. "As children, we always called Venus the evening star and wished on it. Somehow a planet doesn't convey the magic of a star."

CHAPTER THIRTY

The following morning Victoria got a call from Smalley. "Mrs. Trumbull, I'd like to talk to you. Your cousin's planned wedding appears to be the focal point of the two murders. Would you mind coming to the barracks, where we can discuss this? I'll pick you up."

Victoria agreed.

At the state police barracks, she was seated at the head of the conference room table. Smalley sat on her left.

When Tim, the trooper, passed by the door Smalley called out to him.

"Sir?" asked Tim.

"I'd like you to sit in on this."

"Good morning, Tim," said Victoria.

"Morning, Mrs. T. Want me to take notes, Sarge?"

"Not at this point. This is an informal meeting. First, though, how about bringing us some coffee." He turned to Victoria.

"Tim had some interesting exchanges yesterday that may or may not be pertinent to our discussion this morning."

Tim returned shortly, carrying a tray with a pot of coffee. He poured a mug for each and then joined them, sitting on Victoria's right and across from Smalley.

"Here's what we know, Mrs. Trumbull." Smalley straightened the lined yellow pad and pencil that were in front of him and cleared his throat. "Rocco, the second victim, was in serious financial trouble, both at an illegal dog track and at the municipal marina. There may be other creditors we don't know about. If he was involved in something else, drug trafficking, for example, they wouldn't hesitate to kill him. His father disinherited him for reasons we don't know, so he was essentially broke. I gathered he was marrying your cousin because he thought she was wealthy, and when he found out otherwise, he broke off the engagement."

"I know very little about Rocco and anything related to him," said Victoria.

"I realize that," said Smalley. "I'd like to go over everything you do know: his contacts, any loose talk, gossip — anything. Since you're a deputy, you know the drill about how important anything and everything can be." He picked up his pencil, and Victoria waited to see what the first line of his doodle would be. "And since you're more or less unofficial, you have certain 'freedoms,' I might say, that I, for instance, don't have." He drew a wiggly line across the bottom third of the page.

Tim nodded at Smalley's notepad and said to Victoria, "I collect his doodles, you know. I have eight framed, and I gave the rest to the Thrift Shop for the Chicken Alley Art Sale."

Smalley set down his pencil and folded his arms. "I heard that, Tim. We're talking business now." He turned to Victoria. "Mrs. Trumbull, I'd like you to speak with the people who've had close contact with the victim. Casually, informally. There are five or six of them. Speak to Cosimo, the brother of the man found in your cellar." He stopped and added cream and sugar to his coffee and stirred it. "He's understandably upset. I was with him when he identified the victim as Caesar, his brother."

"That must have been a devastating experience for Cosimo. His own brother."

They were silent for a few moments.

Victoria said, "I'm sure you'd like me to tell you what I can about Rocco's brother, Dominic, and the couple who showed up at

383

my house, Angelo and Lily. I know nothing about the two men who were wedding guest friends of Rocco's."

"I'd like you to talk to them, especially." Smalley picked up his pencil again and drew what looked like spiky grass blades sprouting from the wiggly line.

Tim nodded at the sketch in progress and said to Victoria, "One of them sold for two hundred and fifty bucks."

Smalley laid down his pencil again. "Victoria?"

Victoria thought for a while, holding her mug close to her face, so the fragrant steam could rise to her nose. "I'll tell you now everything I can, and I might as well start with Penny, the bride."

She took a sip of coffee and set the mug down. "Penny is a distant cousin of mine, so although I've known her since she was a child, we're not close. Her engagement to Rocco was a surprise to me, and I was even more surprised when she asked if she might hold the reception on my property." She looked down at the yellow pad in front of her. "I said yes, of course, thinking it was likely going to be a modest affair."

She looked up at Smalley. "Penny is what is known as 'financially challenged.' I knew she had to be careful about expenses. I was flabbergasted when I realized she intended the reception to be a 'Vineyard wedding extravaganza' " — Victoria made quote marks in the air — "costing thousands of dollars, far, far more than she could afford."

Smalley drew vertical lines above the grass. Tim watched.

Victoria continued. "It became clear, almost immediately, that she expected her groom, the son of Giovanni Bufano of Bufano Industries, to be her savior. She hoped to impress him by all the wedding trappings, suggesting that she too came from wealth."

"How much time was there between Penny's request for you to host the reception and the discovery of the body in the cellar?" asked Smalley.

"I would say about six weeks. Mark Johnson, the electrician, discovered the body on Wednesday, the day before yesterday and three days before the wedding was scheduled."

"By then, had most of the wedding guests arrived?"

"I wouldn't know. Penny invited two hundred and expected more than that to attend the reception. The church, of course, holds only a hundred fifty."

"Do you know where the guests are staying?" asked Smalley.

"I believe most had booked rooms at the Turkey Cove Inn. Since the inn is in Edgartown, I was unlikely to see most of them until the reception."

"I checked the inn, and it's fully booked," said Tim. "The manager said it's unusual for this time of year, but there was a group attending a memorial service for the deceased pastor of their church, and about a hundred guests for the Bufano–Arbuthnot wedding."

"Anything else we need to know about Penny?" asked Smalley.

"As you can imagine, she was upset when he called off the wedding. She still believed he was incredibly wealthy, and she had incurred, in vain, enormous debts that she will have to repay."

"Did she threaten him when he backed out?"

"She said what one would expect her to say along with tears and hysterics: 'I could kill him!' But when she learned that he was every bit as impoverished as she was, her mood changed dramatically. She has now accepted a job as assistant to the electrician."

"The guy who found the body," said Tim.

"She's turned her job as electrician's assistant into a bridal consultancy business."

"That was a quick turnaround," said Smalley. "Based on her experience in setting up her own wedding, I assume."

"That's about all I can tell you about the bride." She watched Smalley sketch horizontal lines across the vertical ones. He seemed unaware that he was drawing. Victoria took another sip of coffee.

"After Penny, the next person of significance to appear at my house was Dominic, the groom's brother, whom I met under less than favorable circumstances."

Tim laughed. "I guess so."

"He was quite intoxicated," Victoria continued. "Someone had driven him to my property and deposited him and his suitcase in Penny's car, where Penny found him, passed out." Victoria set her mug down. "Penny called Rocco to let him know his brother's condition. Rocco arrived, and he and Mark, the electrician, carried Dominic to my downstairs bedroom." She glanced at Smalley. "I believe it was about that time that you asked Rocco to go with you to the funeral home to see if he could identify the body that was in my cellar."

"Yes," said Smalley. He set his pencil down again. "When we were at the funeral home, it was clear that Rocco knew who the victim was. It was also clear he was not going to identify him."

"Why was he so unwilling to identify the victim as his stepbrother, Caesar?" asked Victoria. "You'd think he'd want his father and stepbrother to know as soon as possible. The identification was bound to be made eventually."

"I wondered about that. Given his actions in the past, such as walking away from a near-fatal automobile accident without a twinge of remorse, I believe his reaction to seeing the body of his stepbrother was similar. What happened to his stepbrother was only of concern to him because he recognized it as a failed attempt on his life. His world didn't extend beyond him and his own concerns. No one else existed."

Smalley sketched some more before he continued. "He gave us a strange song and dance about the victim stalking him, which we didn't believe. What we did believe was Rocco's conviction that he was meant to be that dead body lying on the mortuary table."

"It must have been a horrifying experience for him."

"Yes and no. He was clearly shocked. More by the fact that he believed he was the intended victim than by the fact that the victim was his stepbrother."

"I saw Rocco for only a short time between getting his brother, Dominic, out from under the dripping tree and into a dry bed, and when you showed up to take him to the funeral home. When he arrived, he was driving a bright blue BMW that was so low to the ground he had trouble getting out."

"That blue BMW has been a dead giveaway," said Tim.

"When you called, John, three of us were in the kitchen chatting — Rocco, Penny, and I. That was the first and only time I saw Rocco.

"After you and he left, Dominic fell out of bed and cut his forehead. We called the Tri-Town Ambulance, they took him to the hospital, and I didn't see Dominic again until he was discharged the following day, yesterday." Victoria sat back and folded her arms over her chest. "He came to pick up his clothes and to apologize. He was wearing only a hospital gown and paper slippers."

Tim laughed.

Victoria said, "The Chilmark police officer who delivered him was my great-grandnephew, Ben."

"He's known as the Gentle Giant," said Tim.

"Did Dominic say anything that might

shed light on our investigation or on his thinking?" asked Smalley.

"Well, yes," said Victoria. "He did." She sat forward and folded her hands on the table. "Dominic apologized graciously to me and offered to pay my great-grandnephew, the police officer, who refused the offer.

"He then went into the bedroom where I'd laid out his dried clothing, and while he was dressing, he got a call on his cell phone from someone who turned out to be his brother, Rocco. At one point his voice was quite loud, and I heard him say with some impatience, 'Tell me where in the Campground you left the car,' and 'I can't promise.'

"When Dominic appeared, dressed, I asked him if that was his brother, Rocco, on the phone. He confirmed that it was. Rocco had asked him to pick up his car from the Campground and deliver it to the bed and breakfast where his brother had stayed. Rocco gave him a description of the house, which I recognized as belonging to Mrs. Emma Bailey, a friend of mine."

Victoria reached for her coffee and finished it. "Dominic told me he couldn't pick up Rocco's BMW, as he didn't have a key to it. He went to Penny's car and found his suitcase, which had been left there when he was dropped off."

Tim got up and refilled her mug.

"Thank you," said Victoria.

"I don't suppose he opened the suitcase in your presence," said Smalley. "Interesting to see what he had in there besides clothes."

"No, he didn't. I think he wanted to get out of my hair as quickly as he could. He told me he didn't own a car, that he had booked a room at the Turkey Cove Inn and hoped they had kept it for him, and he called a cab to take him there."

"Do you know which cab he ordered?"

"Obed's Cab."

"Tim, check to see where Obed dropped him off."

"Now?"

"Yes, and then come back here."

Tim left.

"While we were waiting for Obed to show up, I asked him if he was close to his brother. He said, 'Hardly,' and told me he'd had little to do with his brother after Rocco was responsible for that serious accident involving Caesar and Cosimo. Instead of helping, or even summoning help, Rocco walked away from the wreck and the two injured young men."

Tim returned. "Turkey Cove Inn, Sarge."

"Thanks."

Victoria continued. "Caesar and Cosimo's mother was married to Giovanni Bufano for about ten years, so the two were Rocco and Dominic's stepbrothers."

"Interesting," said Smalley. "I hadn't picked up on that. No love lost between the two sets of brothers, I gather. Why did Rocco invite them to his wedding, and why did they accept, any idea?"

"Rocco was quite narcissistic, as I understand it. He thought everyone loved him. He had no idea how much he was hurting others. Their thoughts and feelings didn't concern him. He wanted a showing of some sort at his wedding, since most of the people Penny invited were her connections, not his. He asked his brother, Dominic, to be his best man and invited his stepbrother Cosimo to be one of the groomsmen, but not Caesar, the one badly and permanently hurt in the accident."

"Did Dominic say anything further?"

"Yes. As the cab was pulling up, Dominic told me in a decidedly offhand way that Cosimo intended to send Rocco 'to the farm,' which I interpreted as an idle death threat. When I expressed distaste at the very idea, he added, 'We are Italians, Mrs. Trumbull. It's a matter of honor to Cosimo and me.' "

"Wow," said Tim.

Smalley went back to his doodling. "Tell me about the visit from Angelo Federico and Lily Caruso."

"Quite extraordinary," said Victoria.

"Extraordinary in what way?"

"They arrived clearly putting on some kind of act. Lily came to my door. I believe you've met her, slim, almost anorexic, magenta and blue hair, glasses with large black frames."

Smalley nodded.

"She told me that her cousin, Angelo, who was limping up my drive, had injured his ankle, and they'd like to stay with me until he was able to walk better. She also said they were both cousins of Rocco's and were here for the wedding. My efforts to have him sent to the hospital didn't work.

"The whole situation, including his injured ankle, was obviously faked. I was curious to know what was going on, and I was intrigued by the two of them." Victoria took a sip of her coffee. "But when Penny, the bride, heard that a man named Angelo, who claimed to be Rocco's cousin, had arrived, she swore that Angelo hated Rocco and that Rocco didn't want to have anything to do with Angelo. Penny was adamant about my sending the two away. She insisted that

Rocco would never have invited Angelo to his wedding."

"Let me get this relationship straight," said Smalley. "Rocco, Angelo, and Lily are cousins from three branches of the family, right?"

"Yes. The three are probably third or fourth cousins," said Victoria.

"Leave it to a Vineyarder to figure out someone's genealogy," said Tim.

"Fourth cousins would have a common great-great-great-grandfather," said Smalley.

"That's right," said Victoria. "Now, this is what I've learned about Angelo and Lily. Angelo is extremely protective of her. She's in her twenties and has a form of autism that gives her the mental age of a ten-year old. She is what is called an autistic savant, a condition that used to be called idiot savant."

Smalley nodded. "An autistic savant is a developmentally disabled person with prodigious knowledge of some narrow field way beyond what a normal person can know. Interesting. Very interesting. And her specialty is . . . ?"

"Weapons," said Victoria. "Through the ages."

"Oh my God." Smalley tossed his pencil down. "Did Lily have anything against

Rocco?"

"Yes. Mind you, this is a ten-year-old in a woman's body. Rocco took advantage of her, impregnated her, arranged for an abortion by a backyard practitioner, and the abortion was botched. I learned this from Zoe Harrington, a woman sent to the Vineyard by Lily's father to find Lily."

"Twists and turns," said Tim.

"Unbelievable twists and turns, certainly," said Victoria. "Lily has repeatedly threatened to kill Rocco. She has the knowledge and ability to do so. She was closely supervised at home. However, when she heard that Rocco was getting married here on the Vineyard and that Angelo intended to come here, she managed to get away from her minders and hid under the back seat of Angelo's car." She took another sip of coffee and set the mug down. "Zoe, the woman sent to find Lily, and Angelo are close personal friends."

"Interesting," said Smalley again, sketching.

"Lily and I spent part of yesterday morning together. It was an interesting experience, talking with a near genius about weaponry, and seeing her as a twenty-year-old woman acting and talking like a ten-year-old child."

"The study of autistic savants is a new field," said Smalley. "A lot we don't know about the brain and its workings."

"Lily explained to me how she planned to kill Rocco. I was fascinated by the detailed plan she had concocted and the description of the weapon she intended to use, and exactly how she would use it. She had taken into consideration her strength in her choice of weapons."

"A garrote, of course," said Smalley.

Victoria nodded. "I knew it was unlikely that I could dissuade her, so I suggested that she put off killing him until Saturday, the day of the wedding. I told her that would be more symbolic. I'm not sure she understood the concept of 'symbolic.' I hoped that would stall her temporarily and buy time for others to encourage Rocco to leave the Island immediately. I suspected he was planning to leave but might not have realized the need for urgency."

"How long did Lily stay with you?"

"Unfortunately, not long. I went out to the garden and left her alone to ponder over seed catalogs and cut out pictures that appealed to her. I was sure that would keep her occupied while I was gone. Time got away from me." She glanced up. "I'm a gardener, after all. I should have recognized that. I spent more time away than I should have. When Lily tired of the catalogs, she left."

Smalley leaned back and bowed his head. He was quiet for several long moments. He looked up. "Does this mean we know who our killer is?"

"I wish I could say no. All I can say is, I don't know. Her father's concern is that if she succeeds in killing Rocco, she will be tried and convicted. Like any ten-year-old, she would brag about the killing and proudly tell, in detail, how she did it. There's no way to stop her from talking. She may brag about killing him whether she did or not. She would imagine that her plans had succeeded. Her father is convinced she could never survive incarceration, whether as an adult in an adult facility, or as a mentally challenged person in a mental institution."

"None of this is on the record," said Smalley. "I don't want to take her in as a person of interest. Not yet, anyway. Not until there's no other option." He stood. "Let's take a break, and then Tim can tell you about his experiences yesterday."

Chapter Thirty-One

When they reassembled around the conference table, Smalley said to Tim, "The floor is all yours. I'd like you to tell Mrs. Trumbull what happened yesterday."

Tim shifted around to a comfortable position and straightened the papers that were in front of him. "Yesterday morning I was making my rounds in the cruiser. Not strictly my job, you know, Mrs. Trumbull, but I like to see what's happening around my community. I'm a state trooper." He looked at Victoria, who nodded.

"I usually go up Lake Avenue to the Steamship Authority, then turn left onto Seaview to where it ends at the harbor. If the paper boat is in, I schmooze with the skipper, maybe talk to the harbormaster, then retrace the route.

"Well yesterday morning, I saw this young redheaded guy down on the beach pointing what looked like a real gun out to sea, so I pulled in next to the steps down to the beach and came up behind him carefully, so as not to startle him, and quietly said something like, 'What do you have there?' He turned around, looking scared. I must have frightened him."

Smalley sketched flowers on the horizontal and vertical lines that had become a fence.

"I asked if he had a permit," Tim continued. "He didn't know what I was talking about. He said the gun was an antique Luger, as if that meant it wasn't a real weapon, so I asked if it was registered, and he said he didn't know. It was a souvenir from the First World War, he said. So I invited him to come with me to the barracks where we could talk about permits and registration. He said okay. I told him I would carry the gun for him and the knapsack that he said had ammo in it.

"He was all shook up. He was sure I was going to arrest him. We went to the barracks, and he told me he'd never shot a gun and just wanted to see if his great-grandfather's antique Luger worked. He kept saying 'antique' like that would excuse everything.

"I said we'd take good care of the antique gun — I emphasized the 'antique' — would check on its provenance and register it, and look into getting him a permit to carry. I got all his personal information, name, date of birth, social security number — the rest. I fingerprinted him. I said when he came back to pick up the gun and permit, we'd help him get in touch with the gun club here so he could practice."

"All proper," said Smalley. "You handled that well."

"Thank you, sir."

"Tell Mrs. Trumbull about checking his backpack."

"Yeah, sure. Almost forgot. I asked him — he called himself Red, naturally — I asked Red if he had ammunition to go with the gun. He said he did and opened his backpack to take it out. In doing so, a coil of wire dropped out. It looked to be about three or four feet in length and seemed to have handles at the ends."

"A garrote," said Victoria.

"Exactly," said Smalley.

"One of Rocco's friends is called Red."

"Exactly," said Smalley again. "Now, Tim, tell Mrs. Trumbull about your second visitor."

"This woman named Janice came in. She's an intern at the Oceanographic in Woods Hole. Marine geology is her field. Well, she's working as a housekeeper at the hotel. She brought in a sample of white powder, maybe a quarter of a teaspoonful, that she'd seen in a guest's room, and she was wondering if it could be arsenic. She was kind of embarrassed because she thought that was ridiculous for a guest to have arsenic in his room, and I guess she was afraid I'd think she was crazy or something." Tim paused.

"Well, it just so happens that some time ago one of the water resources groups here on the Island presented us with a kit for testing water for arsenic content, accurate to two parts per billion. The safe standard of arsenic in drinking water is ten parts per billion, so it's pretty sensitive. We dissolved about half her sample in water and ran it through the test, which takes about ten minutes. We both expected it to be negative. But when the test came through, the results went off the scale."

"What sort of scale was it?" Victoria asked Tim.

"Like a color comparison. The yellow end of the scale means pretty weak, the brown end of the scale means strong. It's supposed to take a couple seconds to register, but this went *whammo*! Hit the darkest brown on the scale instantly. Straight arsenic.

"She wanted me to go arrest the guy. I

401

said that's not what's done. You need a warrant to search his belongings, and you need to have a good reason to get that warrant, and — you know, I said all the rest. Well, she wasn't real happy about it. The guy was filling capsules with the white powder, and she figured he's a mass murderer or something."

"Did you get the name of the guest?" asked Victoria.

"Yeah. Elmer Rudge."

Victoria looked at Smalley. "Coincidences do occur, but . . ."

Smalley said, "I thought you should know about this. You haven't met any of the three, Cosimo, Elmer, or Red, have you?"

"No, not yet."

"I'd like you to talk to them," said Smalley. "In some ways the two murders look suspiciously like a mob hit to me. Both Mr. Caruso and Mr. Giovanni have known mob connections. If so, the feds need to be involved. They seem like they were done by a hired killer. Someone familiar with a garrote. If so, we may never be able to name the killer or the person who hired him."

"I can't help but think it's a family problem, not mob related," said Victoria. "But in any case, we'd like to be able to clear all the others who were quite open about their antipathy to Rocco."

"Precisely," said Smalley.

Victoria called Angelo. "I'd like to talk with you and Zoe, if you're available."

"When would you like us?"

"Any time. Now would be fine."

"I assume Lily is included," said Angelo.

"Certainly. You've found her?"

"We did. In Cannonball Park. That's where we are now."

"Of course. A logical spot," said Victoria. "I can offer you a glass of wine and graham crackers."

"Sounds like a deal. We'll be there shortly."

When they arrived, Lily immediately started talking. "I found Cannonball Park right away. It has cannons and cannonballs, which, of course is why it's named that. The cannon is from the Civil War and, I believe, is a Napoleon twelve-pounder."

"It had just been made into a park when I was a child," said Victoria. "Come in, all of you. I'm always happy to see that Angelo's ankle has recovered."

"Mrs. Trumbull, that's an embarrassment. Please," said Angelo.

"You deserve a bit of teasing," said Zoe.

"I've laid out wine and crackers in the parlor," said Victoria.

She sat in the wing chair under the picture of her grandfather and his brothers, all sea captains. Lily and Zoe sat on the couch, and Angelo poured wine for all three before he sat in the throne chair.

"Sergeant Smalley wanted me to ask you a few questions, and since this is informal, your answers won't go into any record," Victoria said, by way of introduction. "I met earlier today with Sergeant Smalley at the state police barracks, and we are just as puzzled as ever about the two killings. Perhaps you can shed some light."

"We'll do whatever we can," said Angelo.

"You know Rocco is dead, don't you, Mrs. Trumbull?" said Lily.

"Yes, I'd heard."

"I hated him, so I killed him."

Zoe and Angelo froze and sat like stone.

"How did you kill him?" asked Victoria.

"With the garrote I made from your wire, of course. Did you notice?"

"Yes, I did," said Victoria. "That was clever of you. Where was Rocco when you killed him?"

"He was on the ground, already dead, but I killed him."

Victoria glanced at Angelo, who was stone-faced. She glanced at Zoe, who was looking down at her hands.

"Did you kill the man who was in my cellar?" asked Victoria.

"No, of course not. I didn't hate him."

"How did you learn where Rocco was?"

"A nice woman at the hotel told me."

"What did she say?"

"She said she saw on FaceBook that a blue BMW was towed out of the Campground. I knew right away that was Rocco's car. I know his car."

"Then what did you do?"

"I asked her where the Campground was, and she told me. And she told me where the car was in the Campground."

"You got a ride to the Campground?"

"Linc in the white truck didn't give me a ride, but another nice woman did, and she took me right to the Campground. The houses are all different colors."

"It's a beautiful place, isn't it," said Victoria. "Then what happened?"

"Well, she said it was a purple and pink house, so I found the house, and Rocco was lying on the ground. I crept up quietly so as to take him by surprise and put the garrote around his neck, but he was already dead. So I killed him."

"I see," said Victoria, although she wasn't sure she did.

"Ah," said Angelo. "I do see."

Zoe looked up at him.

"Then what did you do?" asked Victoria.

"I came back here to Cannonball Park. I waited for a white truck to pick me up, but it wasn't Linc."

"Lily, there's cream cheese in the icebox, if you'd like some to spread on our graham crackers. Would you please get it? And bring napkins and a knife, please."

Lily got up and left the room.

"From what Lily said, it means she got there between the time he was killed and the time Mrs. Curtain came home and reported the murder," said Victoria. "Do you have any thoughts about what is going on here?"

"Thoughts, yes," said Angelo. "I can tell you, Mrs. Trumbull, I was fully prepared to kill Rocco if that would prevent Lily from doing so. I didn't kill him. I went to the Park and Ride thinking Rocco would go there to pick up his car, waited awhile, then realized he would have to contend with paperwork and fines and transportation before he could pick up the car, so I drove to the Campground to intercept him there. I was also too late. The police were already there."

"Zoe, do you have any light to shed on this?" asked Victoria.

"Only to repeat Dottore Caruso's concern

406

that his daughter not be tried for Rocco's murder."

"It seems clear she didn't kill him, but it's also clear that she was there at the scene shortly after he was killed. It's likely she was the first on the scene."

Lily returned with an armload of napkins, knives, and the two containers of cream cheese Victoria had in the fridge.

"I did hear you say I didn't kill Rocco," said Lily, "but I did. I put the garrote around his neck, the way it's done, and I pulled it tight, the way you're supposed to. He was lying there, dead, so I killed him."

"Did anyone see you when you killed him?" asked Victoria.

"No. I was hoping someone would come by, but no one did. I kept looking and waited for someone to see, but no one got to see that I killed him."

"Shall we celebrate?" Victoria held up her wine glass.

"Definitely," said Angelo.

Zoe agreed.

CHAPTER THIRTY-TWO

After Angelo, Zoe, and Lily left, Victoria went out to the garden. She was coming in, when the phone rang. She hurried to answer, hoping it would be a human and not another robot call. "Mrs. Trumbull, my name is Elmer Rudge. Sergeant Smalley of the state police said you wanted to talk to Red and me."

"I do," said Victoria. "Would you mind coming here to my house? It's a lovely day and we can sit outside."

"Be there as soon as we can get there, but I don't know where you live. We don't have a car."

She gave him directions by bus, and a half hour later he and Red arrived. One had fiery red hair, so it was clear which was which. Elmer was older, taller, and what Victoria called "comfortably built."

"We brought you these," Elmer said, and presented her with a bouquet in a clear plastic sleeve.

"How lovely. Thank you," said Victoria. "You must have known how much I love flowers." She unwrapped them and arranged them in a vase, which she put on the dining room table.

They went outside, where she had set three green resin chairs next to a picnic table beneath the Norway maples. The trees had finished blossoming, and the ground was blanketed with fallen golden flowers. The trees arched over a large grassy area. They weren't yet in full leaf, and the shade was dappled with sun coins, multiple images of the sun projected onto the ground through the pinhole lenses formed by the leaf buds.

"This is beautiful," said Red, looking up into the trees, then down at the golden carpet of blossoms sprinkled with sun coins.

"I thought it would be more pleasant to be outside," said Victoria. "It seems easier to speak freely when you're surrounded by trees."

She'd set a pitcher of lemonade on the table and asked Elmer to pour. They exchanged pleasantries about the weather, their impressions of the Island, skirting the subject for which she'd invited them.

"I'm sorry the wedding fell through and

then tragedy struck," said Victoria, when they'd exhausted all the banalities. "It certainly spoiled your time here. I suppose you had to take vacation time."

"I work at a college, so my schedule is flexible," said Elmer.

"Do you teach?" asked Victoria.

"I work in the geology department, taking care of the rock and mineral collections."

"That must be quite a responsibility."

"I have to make sure students don't mix up labels on the specimens," he said. "After a class is over, I put everything back, make sure every mineral and rock is in its right place."

"You must know enough to teach a course in rock and mineral identification."

"Maybe I could, at that. I for sure could tell students how to identify different kinds of rocks, but minerals are a lot harder. That's a whole field. Mineralogy."

Red was shifting restlessly. He looked up at the branches overhead. Leaned down and picked up a handful of the fallen blossoms. Tossed them into the air and watched them drift down to the ground again. A breeze carried some to the table, where they settled.

"I didn't mean to ignore you, Red," said Victoria. "Did I hear that you work with greyhounds?"

Red sat up straight. "Yes, ma'am. I take care of the kennels at a racetrack. Feed the dogs, play with them." He smiled. "They're really sweet animals, those greyhounds. They love people and they love to sleep when they're not racing. I had to get someone to take care of my dogs while I was here, and I really miss being with them."

"I thought dog tracks were illegal," said Victoria.

"Well, yeah, they are. But people like to bet on the dogs, so there are these illegal dog tracks the cops sort of close their eyes to, and somebody has to take care of the dogs."

"Someone told me — I think it was Penny — that you're involved with finding homes for the greyhounds who no longer run. That's an admirable project."

"The dogs can still run. They love to run. It's their life. They get put away when they can't run as fast as they used to. It makes me sick to think that those beautiful animals would be killed. They call it 'euthanize,' to make it sound like it's okay, but it's murder."

"Red had two decommissioned greyhounds of his own," said Elmer.

Red bent over and picked up another

411

handful of blossoms and threw them from him. The blossoms floated away.

"He can't talk about it. Rocco killed them."

"Oh, dear!" said Victoria.

"Not euthanized — Rocco beat them to death," said Elmer.

"Stop it, Elmer. Shut up!"

"I understand, Red," said Victoria. "They were your family."

Red looked at her, tears in his eyes. "The only reason I came to this . . . this stupid wedding of his is, I decided I would kill him for what he did to my dogs. He doesn't deserve to live, the way he treats animals. And people. He's even nasty to plants. Plants deserve to live more than he does. He doesn't give a damn about anyone but his own greedy, grasping, self-centered, egotistical self." Red took a breath.

He's talking as though Rocco is still alive, thought Victoria. *I wonder if he knows Rocco is dead?* She waited.

Elmer poured lemonade and passed a glass to Victoria and one to Red. Red didn't seem to notice. Victoria thanked him.

"I can tell you now, because it won't happen now," said Red. "My great-grandfather was in the First World War, you know?"

"My husband served in that war," said

Victoria.

"That's the olden days," said Red. "There are history books about that war."

Victoria didn't feel especially ancient. A bit of stiffness here and there. She was glad to sit occasionally. These children. "Tell me about your great-grandfather," she said.

"Somehow he got ahold of a German Luger. That was a gun the Germans had."

"Yes, I know," said Victoria.

Elmer shook his glass so the ice cubes rattled, and drank. Victoria took a sip of her own. Red seemed unaware of the glass next to him.

A rhythmic hammering sounded high up in one of the maples.

"What's that?" said Elmer, startled.

"It's a woodpecker. He's looking for insects in one of the branches," said Victoria.

"That must hurt his head."

"You'd think so," said Victoria. "Apparently not."

Red blurted out, "I bought some bullets for the Luger from the Internet. And I polished up my great-grandfather's gun. And I brought it here so I could shoot Rocco dead. I figured I could get away with it. No one would suspect me." He stopped.

"It sounds as though your plans have

changed," said Victoria.

"Yesterday I was going to kill him. Since I never shot a gun, I went to the beach to practice. Before I could pull the trigger, this cop came by and took my gun."

"Just took it?" asked Victoria, alarmed, her deputy police training alerted. "Without warning you?"

"Well, no. The cop said I should have a permit and the gun needed to be registered, and he'd start the processes for me, and then he put the bullets and my gun in a safe." Red sighed and took a breath. "He said he'd notify me when the permit and registration came through, and return my gun and take me to the gun club and introduce me to the guys and women there, and they'd teach me to shoot."

He noticed the glass of lemonade and drank half of it. He put the glass down. "The cop got my name, date of birth, social security number, phone number, address — everything about me. Even fingerprinted me. He knows more about me than I know about me."

Elmer reached over and refilled Red's glass.

Red picked the glass up and drank again. "I wouldn't be surprised if he knows what size underwear I buy. I'll never be able to steal even a candy bar without the cops coming after me." He turned the glass around and around in the wet spot condensation had made on the picnic table. "Not that I'd ever steal a candy bar."

"Without your gun and with your life history in police hands, you had to put aside your plans, is that right?" said Victoria.

"Someone else will have to take him out. I'm not in the party anymore."

Victoria let a good bit of silence fall after that. The woodpecker moved to another tree, and the hammering began again. A couple of crows landed in the high branches and called to one another and to whatever crows were within listening distance.

She drank her own lemonade. Red finished his, and Elmer refilled it again. Elmer had taken only a few sips of his own.

"I'm interested in your story, Elmer. You'd told me how you're in charge of the geology collections at your college, and I said you should be teaching."

"I'd like to teach. I have an associate of arts degree in earth science I got on the Internet, a two-year degree, but that won't get me anywhere."

"It seems to have gotten you a wonderfully responsible position," said Victoria. "Why don't you get your bachelor's degree?

It shouldn't take you long to finish with your associate's degree behind you."

"Yeah, it's a thought. I get free tuition."

"Do it, then," said Victoria. "You might even get your master's degree, and then you could teach. Free tuition! What an opportunity."

They were quiet for a few minutes, listening to the sounds around them. Cars going by on the Edgartown Road. The town clock struck three. A song sparrow burst into an almost recognizable melody.

Elmer broke their silence. "I guess you want to know about why I'm here, agreeing to come to Rocco's wedding. I hate him every bit as much as Red does. He stole my girl. My first love. We were talking marriage, a house, kids, a garden . . ."

"First love is powerful," said Victoria. "Can you reclaim her?"

Elmer shook his head. "He showed her a life I could never provide that she never imagined existed. Fancy restaurants, parties with lines of cocaine. She learned about that, all right. Shows and meeting the stars backstage. The name Bufano opened doors for her that she went through, and she can't get back. Then he dumped her. Just like that. Now she's a druggie. Sells herself to buy drugs. She doesn't want me, and I don't want the woman she's become. But I'll pay Rocco back for what he did to her. Red told you what his plan was. Well, I'll tell you my plan, and like Red's plan, mine got sidetracked by a nosey housekeeper at the hotel, who happens to have a degree in geology."

Red looked up at that. "You didn't tell me that."

"You didn't ask," said Elmer with a smile.

"You have my full attention," said Victoria. "What was your plan, and how does the geologist housekeeper fit into it?"

Elmer picked up his glass and took another small sip. "I told you about the rock and mineral collection I take care of. Well, the college's collection is one of the best in the state. In the collection are a couple of specimens of this fairly rare mineral called arsenolite."

"An arsenic ore?" asked Victoria.

"It's not common, so it's not considered an ore, but yes, it's a source of arsenic. Its chemical formula is two parts arsenic to three parts oxygen. We keep it in a locked specimen box to keep students from tasting it to see if it really is poisonous. Well, it is. We have a sign on it, warning people not to taste it. I don't think tasting it will kill you. After all, the mineralogy texts say it has an astringent, sweet taste, so someone tasted it. But ingesting even a small amount will definitely kill. An unpleasant death. Stomach pains, vomiting, diarrhea. Arsenic itself doesn't have a taste. That used to be the poison of choice in the past. But it's not easy to get hold of these days. I decided the way to kill Rocco is with arsenic. The symptoms take a couple of days to appear and at first are like a bad case of the flu. By then it's too late. Since I'm in charge of the geology collections, I borrowed one the specimens, one from France that had white crystals. Arsenolite comes as a coating of eight-sided crystals on rock. I planned to knock off and grind up a couple of the crystals, and that's what I did. The mineral is pretty soft, softer than gypsum, so it's easy to make a powder of it. I figured the safest way to get it into Rocco was by putting the ground up arsenolite into a gel capsule and dropping it into his coffee or scotch, where the capsule would dissolve, and he wouldn't even notice it. Anyway, that was my plan."

"I saw your beaker and gel capsules and thought you were into drugs," said Red.

"Me? Drugs? No way am I going to be that stupid," said Elmer. "If I ever get tempted, I'll look at pictures of Madeline then and Madeline now. She was gorgeous, a red-blooded American girl model, shiny black hair, so shiny it had blue highlights when she moved her head. Great big blue eyes, the bluest you've ever seen. Ivory skin, pink lips . . . no makeup. She didn't wear makeup until Rocco . . . Now she's emaciated, scrawny. Hair like straw. Cheeks sunken. Eyes dull. Lips thin. Back bent. She looks like a mummy come back to life, only she's got no life left in her."

"Look, Elmer, you don't need to convince me. I'm not into drugs or gambling. I see all the time what gambling does to people. Saw it in my old man."

"We've strayed from the subject," said Victoria. "What happened to foil your plans?"

"The housekeeper was cleaning my room and saw my apparatus laid out. I hadn't had time to clean it up myself because I heard Red coming and I didn't feel like answering his questions."

"Yeah, I had a lot of questions," said Red.

"I didn't think about the housekeeper. Turns out she's a marine geology intern at Woods Hole. She saw my mortar and pestle, my beaker, the gloves and facemask I'd thrown in the trash that I was going to dispose of myself, and she got all in a tizzy."

"Did she assume it was drugs?" asked Victoria.

"She figured that at first, that it was drugs, but then she decided it had to be something poisonous because a drug dealer wouldn't be that careless with the evidence, and if it was medication, the person wouldn't use gloves and a face mask. She took a sample to the cops and they tested it, and sure enough, arsenic."

"I didn't realize they had a test lab here."

"They don't need a lab. It's a simple kit that takes about fifteen minutes or less to test water samples. Well, when it tested positive for arsenic, the cop told her he had no cause to arrest me, and furthermore she had no right to take anything out of my room, that I was entitled to privacy. But the cat was out of the bag. The cop didn't take me in and fingerprint me, but I was stopped just as effectively as if he had. Someone else can have the pleasure of offing Rocco."

"I don't know whether you've heard," said Victoria. "Someone has."

CHAPTER THIRTY-THREE

Victoria invited Cosimo for drinks later that afternoon. She'd heard him described as looking menacing, with a scar running down the left side of his cheek, contorting his left eye and the left side of his mouth.

When he showed up, she wasn't prepared to find him strikingly handsome despite the scar. Perhaps because of it. Cosimo was tall and slender. A strand of dark hair fell over his forehead. His large dark, almost black eyes, pale skin, large straight nose, and full sensuous mouth made her think of the sculpture of Alexander the Great that had always appealed to her. Well! She felt a twinge of desire.

"I'm delighted to meet you," he said. A low voice, perfectly modulated. He bowed. "For the past two or three days I've heard your name bandied about. When I learned you were a poet, I immediately went to the Bunch of Grapes bookstore and bought several of your poetry books. I hope you will autograph them for me."

"Of course." Victoria smoothed her hair. "It would be my pleasure to sign your books." She was sorry now that she hadn't dressed in something more appropriate than her garden-weary, gray corduroy pants and the loose turtleneck shirt. At least the shirt was clean, and it was printed with tiny pink roses.

She opened the door of the cabinet below the microwave, where she kept her supply of liquor. Most of the bottles dated back several years to the time when Jonathan, her husband, was alive and they'd have people over for drinks.

"Please, help yourself," said Victoria. "And if you don't mind fixing mine, I'd like a very light bourbon and water."

"But of course. I'm an expert mixer of bourbon and water." He retrieved the bourbon, dug deeper into the cabinet, and brought out a bottle of Dewar's. "I'll have a scotch and water. Light on the water."

He poured their drinks while Victoria put together a plate of crackers and cheese, and then they repaired to the parlor. Victoria seated herself in her mouse-colored wing chair, Cosimo in the rocker.

They held up their glasses in a kind of toast.

Cosimo started the conversation. "I understand perfectly why you'd like to talk to me," he said. "You are unofficially connected to the police. If they were to interview me, it would of necessity become part of the record, and that would be something I would like to avoid, if possible. I believe I am free to talk to you, and I believe I can trust you to convey to the police the substance of our discussion without official recognition."

"Absolutely right," said Victoria.

"Where would you like me to start?"

"Before we say anything else, I am so sorry about your brother. I know nothing I say can ease your pain. It must be too great for you to bear at times." She looked away from him. "The senselessness of his death. The agony he went through because of the accident. I'm afraid our conversation is going to bring all that pain back to you."

"Thank you." Cosimo bowed his head. "Please, your first question."

"I'd like to go back to your childhood. You must have been quite young when your mother married Giovanni Bufano."

"I was nine and my brother, Caesar, was six. My father and Giovanni had been close

423

friends, so after my father died, it seemed natural for my mother and Giovanni to get together. His wife too had died. He had two young sons, Rocco, who was thirteen, and Dominic, who was two years younger. Giovanni loved my mother very much, but he was a difficult man to live with. Demanding, obsessive, protective, inflexible, strict — everything needed for a successful businessman, and none of it made for a comfortable, happy family. My mother put up with him, for our sakes, she thought, for ten years. After the accident, she couldn't bear being in the house with Rocco, seeing him every day, so she left him. They never divorced."

"What was Rocco like as an older brother?"

"Not much different from what he is like, or was, as a man. He was cruel. Took pleasure in teasing Caesar, who was only six. He threatened Caesar with awful who knows what, if he tattled. Caesar would cry and run to Mamma, and Giovanni would whip him for being such a crybaby."

"Whip him?"

"Take off his belt and hit Caesar with it. To make him strong."

Victoria shook her head.

"That's the way things were in our families. The belt was how fathers made their children behave." Cosimo took a sip of his scotch. "Even as a child, Rocco seemed to have no sense of other's feelings or even of their existence. It was as though he was the only person in the world. People around him were all make-believe, and they all loved and honored him. He was king of the mountain all the time. He was brought up to be courteous, so he paid lip service to the expectations of his father. But out of his father's sight, he was a snake." He reached for a cracker and topped it with a slice of cheese. "I don't want to disrespect snakes. He could slither out of trouble like a snake. Cold-blooded. Venomous."

"Can you talk about the accident?"

"I can now. Not for years, though. Rocco's father — I never could call Giovanni my father — Rocco's father gave him a car for his twenty-first birthday, an Alfa Romeo convertible." Cosimo closed his eyes. "To celebrate his new car and the fact he'd reached legal drinking age, he went to the local pub and bought drinks for the house. All evening. He came home. Caesar and I were the only ones around, so he invited us to go for a ride in his new car. We were excited. I was seventeen, Caesar was fourteen. And to ride in this beautiful new car.

What teenager could resist. No one fastened seatbelts. We went out for a spin. I don't know where we were. The Hudson River Parkway, I seem to remember. I can remember the wind blowing above my head, trees and other cars tearing by in a blur, and Rocco shouting, 'This is nothing. Wait'll you see how fast she'll go.' And the thrill of the speed. The excitement and terror of going so fast. And that was it. I don't remember the crash. I woke up in the hospital the next day, my face stitched up. Caesar had been in the back seat. He was in a coma for weeks."

"I understand Rocco was unscathed."

"He walked away from the wreck, hailed a taxi, and went home. Went to bed. Never said a word to anyone."

"I can understand why you're bitter about him. And to have the final blow, the irony, to have your brother killed when the killer's target was Rocco."

"I've been careful of my alcohol consumption ever since." Cosimo held up his glass and took a taste of his scotch.

"Do you have any thoughts about who might have killed Caesar?"

"I assume the killer was after Rocco, not Caesar. The two looked quite a bit alike. But Caesar was well liked, while Rocco

426

made enemies. The list would be long. If the killer was after Rocco, he couldn't have known him well, which leaves out most of the people here." He was silent for a moment. "Most of the people here who knew Rocco very likely wanted him dead."

"I suppose we can assume that whoever killed your brother is the same person who killed Rocco."

"Frankly, Mrs. Trumbull, I don't know."

"I made a list of the persons on the Island who knew Rocco and added 'person unknown.' "

"I like the naming of 'person unknown,' " said Cosimo. "Let's hear your list."

"I've included you," she said, looking over at him.

"But of course."

"You, Dominic, and Angelo. Red and Elmer. Lily, Bianca, Zoe, and Penny. Let's go over each one, shall we?"

"Everyone on your list, with the possible exception of Zoe, has expressed a strong intent to kill Rocco. Some we can dismiss as just talk, and those would be Bianca and Penny." He glanced over at Victoria with a smile. "Each one seriously intended to kill him when he jilted her, but in both cases rage with Rocco was short-lived when they learned how impoverished he was. I believe we can rule them out. When they learned the state of his finances, they were content to let someone else do the job."

"I think you're right." Victoria nodded.

"Lily may well be the one who killed Rocco. She was determined to kill him. And she had good reason to do so. He was quite beastly to her. As I guess you heard, she has phenomenal knowledge about killing methods and weapons. More than most PhDs or criminal investigators. Quite incredible."

"I was astonished, just yesterday, by her discourse on weaponry," said Victoria.

"That knowledge coupled with her determination and her mental age is more than worrisome. Angelo and Zoe came here to see that she didn't carry out her intent. At some point I joined them in thinking one of us should be the executioner, to anticipate what we were sure Lily planned." He drank more of his scotch. "Now he's dead. My only hope is that Lily was not the one to kill him. I myself felt and still feel a cold rage against Rocco for what he did to Caesar. I would happily take the blame for ridding the world of him. He had no feeling of remorse whatsoever."

"I can't help but feel sorry for the life he must not have enjoyed."

"He enjoyed life, all right, at the expense

of people he exploited, rich or poor, didn't matter as long as he got what he wanted. And he had the money to take, take, take."

"His father . . . ?"

"Giovanni had no love for his son. You heard, I'm sure, that he disinherited Rocco, disowned him. Rocco was accustomed to his luxuries. He was determined to continue to enjoy them. No matter what. He couldn't believe his father wouldn't pay his bills." He set his glass down. "He simply didn't believe it when Giovanni's battery of lawyers presented him with legal papers that have no loopholes." He took a deep breath. "I'm letting my feelings get in the way of our discussion. Red and Elmer are a puzzle to me. My first encounter with them was at the Tidal Bar, where Rocco was playing the big spender. Red was celebrating his twenty-first birthday, and Elmer was attempting to be funny. Red drank more than he was able to handle. I wanted nothing to do with him and foisted him off on Elmer for the night."

"I talked with both of them earlier today. Both believed they had good reason to do away with Rocco. Both had come prepared to murder him."

Cosimo smiled. "Both such babes. Angelo and I have been brought up by families that believe in righting wrongs in a straight-

429

forward manner. How did they intend to take care of Rocco?"

"One by shooting him, the other by poisoning him."

"They were serious?"

"They thought they were. In both cases the police got involved before either could carry out his plan, so I think we can rule them out."

"Amateurs."

"There's Dominic. I'm not sure what his motive would be."

"In the unlikely event that Giovanni forgave Rocco, it would be the elder son who would inherit the vast Bufano fortune. That would be reason enough. But even more is his feeling for Lily. Dominic has loved Lily since they were children together, loves her still. He despised Rocco for what he did to Lily. He despised him for what he did to Caesar, who, after all, was our brother for ten years."

"I have been told what Rocco did to Lily." Victoria glanced down at her hands. "We've discussed everyone but Angelo."

"Angelo certainly could and would have killed Rocco without compunction. As you may or may not know, Angelo is a professional killer. A hit man. He is never caught. And then there's the person unknown. My belief, since I don't like the idea of any of the people we've mentioned being responsible for Caesar's death, is that person unknown is the most likely. We need to find whoever hired a killer."

"Surely you're not serious."

"Indeed I am. Caesar was killed because he was mistaken for Rocco. I think we can agree on that. None of the people we've discussed would have mistaken my brother for Rocco, even though they bore a close resemblance. My belief is that the hired killer carried out his job, getting the right person in his second attempt. We need to find who hired him."

"What you're describing seems more like something out of a bad novel about mobs. Retribution killings, retaliation, teaching lessons, paid killers . . ."

"Mrs. Trumbull," — Cosimo leaned forward — "you are leading a sheltered life on this idyllic island. In the real world, my world, there are killers and people being killed. Sometimes they are being killed for petty reasons. Because the victim has insulted someone's wife or girlfriend. Because the victim has a gold chain around his neck. Or wears an expensive pair of sneakers. Drugs. For money to buy drugs. Over these last few days you've had the merest glimpse of real life."

"I refuse to believe that's real life," said Victoria. "That's pure evil and is not what life should be like."

Cosimo was quiet for a moment. Then he stood. "Mrs. Trumbull, I salute you." He bowed. "I respect you. I honor you. One of these days you will have made this world a better place for all of us. I know that's true. A world like the one you live in where people can talk about their problems without anger. Where mentally disturbed people like Rocco can be treated, and mentally challenged people like Lily be cherished for what they are."

Victoria felt extremely uncomfortable. "I believe you said you have some of my poetry books. I'll be glad to sign them now, if you'd like."

CHAPTER THIRTY-FOUR

After Cosimo left, Victoria had to get out into the fresh air. It was late afternoon and she was returning from the asparagus bed with a basket full of spears when a silver Bentley came into her drive, went around the circle, and pulled up at her west step. Victoria knew cars, and this one had to be at least thirty years old. The car stopped; a chauffeur got out and opened the right rear door, and an elderly gentleman stepped out. He was probably in his seventies, though she wasn't good at estimating ages. He was tall, bald, except for a fringe of white hair, and quite lean. His clothes looked expensive and new, sporty looking in the way visitors to the Island thought they should dress.

She hurried to where the car had stopped and got there just as the chauffeur opened the left rear door, and helped another elderly gentleman out.

The second man emerged from the car

with a cane. A gold-headed cane with the gold top shaped like the head of a duck. This second man had a mass of fluffy white hair that made him look like photographs of Albert Einstein. He wasn't as tall as the first man, and looked as though he enjoyed his meals. The two stood together, looking up at the high roof with two brick chimneys. The roof had recently been reshingled, and Victoria hoped they noticed.

"May I help you?" she asked the slender man.

"My cousin and I were hoping to meet you," he said. "I assume you are the poet, Victoria Trumbull."

Victoria acknowledged that she was. "Would you care to come in?"

"It would be our pleasure," he said. "My name is Leonardo, and my cousin is Giovanni."

"Please, come in."

Leonardo held the door for her, and Giovanni followed her in.

"May I offer you a glass of wine?" asked Victoria when they entered the kitchen.

"I hope we are not inconveniencing you," said the shorter Giovanni. "You have much work to do. But the wine would be more than agreeable."

"I'll put these in water and wash my

hands," Victoria said.

Leonardo said. "Please, may we help?"

"Open the wine, if you will," said Victoria.

She washed while Leonardo opened a bottle of Concha y Toro Cabernet Sauvignon, and Giovanni leaned on his duck-headed cane. He looked around with interest, at the wide wooden floorboards, the many-paned windows with glass shelves holding plants and colored glass bottles. At the table with a load of an earlier picking of asparagus ready to be prepared for the freezer.

"We are inconveniencing you," said Giovanni.

"Not at all," said Victoria. "I need a break, and I can't think of anything more pleasant than sharing a bottle of wine with two gentlemen. I believe I know who you are."

The wine opened, glasses produced, Victoria ushered them into the parlor. She seated Giovanni in her wing chair, Leonardo in the throne chair, and she sat in the rocker.

"Shall I pour?" asked Leonardo.

"Yes, please."

Giovanni was looking around the room. At the Hessian soldier andirons in the fireplace, the painting of her great-grandfather's ship at anchor, the print of the depressed and drowned-looking woman that hung over the couch.

He looked closely at the picture. "I believe that is a French print that dates from about 1845," he said. "Do you know its history?"

"The picture has hung in that very spot since before I was born," said Victoria. She accepted a glass of the red wine Leonardo had poured and nodded thanks. "My grandmother accompanied my grandfather on a five-year whaling voyage, and that picture hung in their cabin."

Victoria had a feeling that inconsequential conversation would have to precede whatever it was they had come to discuss.

So she mentioned the car. "I've always admired Bentleys, and yours must date from the 1980s. Such perfect condition."

Leonardo said, "You have said what is dear to Giovanni's heart. It is his car. His favorite child."

Giovanni nodded his head. "Thank you, dear lady."

They talked about the car. They tasted the wine. Leonardo held up his glass. "This is very good wine. From Chile?"

"Yes."

They talked about the drive up from New York. The weather. The scent of lilacs in Victoria's garden.

"The beautiful white flowers that are everywhere," said Leonardo. "I am not familiar with them."

Giovanni said, "We have always called those beautiful white flowers 'widow's wreath.' "

Victoria sat up straight. "That's exactly what my grandmother always called them. People keep saying they are bridal wreath, but my grandmother insisted that was wrong."

"Your grandmother was right. We have much in common," said Giovanni, holding up his glass.

From the garden the conversation moved on to Victoria's house. They had noticed the new roof and commented on how well kept-up her house was, considering its great age.

After that, Leonardo cleared his throat and held up his wine glass again, and both Victoria and Giovanni did too. Leonardo sipped his wine and said, "We are here not only because we are enthusiasts of your poetry, but because we have children here. Giovanni's son, Dominic; my daughter, Lily."

"I am delighted to meet both of you. Dominic arrived here and spent a bit of time . . ." She didn't finish, not sure how much to say about Giovanni's son arriving drunken and passed out.

"Please, Mrs. Trumbull," said Giovanni. "I am grateful to you for caring for him in his condition and for seeing that he was taken to the hospital. I am embarrassed by his behavior. I apologize on his behalf."

"Thank you," said Victoria. "When he came yesterday morning, he not only apologized, but I found him to be a charming young man."

Giovanni nodded, looked down, and took a sip of wine.

"I spent a morning with Lily," she said to Leonardo.

"Ah," he said.

"She helped me prepare yesterday's crop of asparagus for the freezer. She's a lovely young woman."

"Thank you."

"She described to me in vivid detail an array of weapons used in the twelfth century."

"My Lily is autistic, I'm sure you realized."

"I believe she is what is known as an autistic savant," said Victoria."

"You should explain, Leonardo, why we are here," said Giovanni. He'd set his glass on the end table and was holding both hands on the gold duck head of his cane.

"Yes. Yes, of course," said Leonardo, turning back to Victoria. "She came here to the Island without my knowledge. She is usually under close supervision at home. She eluded her watchers. I was apprehensive because I feared she had come here on a deadly mission, and I was not wrong."

"I know the situation, Mr. Caruso," said Victoria. "You must be worried beyond what any parent should have to worry about."

He bowed his head.

"We came to you," said Giovanni, "because we were told that you are police and yet not police. We were told we can trust you to convey the subtleties of the situation to the police without creating legal problems."

Victoria acknowledged the compliment. "I'm a police deputy. But whatever is said to me in confidence does not have to be reported back to the police. The police understand Lily's condition. They won't hold her unless there is nothing else they can do."

"Even that is unacceptable," said Leonardo. "Incarceration would be the end of my daughter. She could not tolerate being locked away."

Victoria nodded.

She turned to Giovanni. "My condolences on the death of your son Rocco."

"Mrs. Trumbull, I have no son Rocco. He is long dead as far as I am concerned. Rocco died with the accident that maimed my two stepsons."

"Nevertheless . . ." said Victoria.

Giovanni lifted a hand from the gold duck head. "You must understand this is a family matter. A matter of family honor."

"But . . ." said Victoria.

"There are evil people in this world, born to be evil. The man who was once my son was evil from the time he was a child. I am not sorry to see him removed from the living world. In fact . . ." He paused.

Leonardo continued. "In fact, what we have come to tell you, Mrs. Trumbull, is this. I engaged an assassin to kill Rocco. Giovanni and I discussed this at length. It was not a decision made lightly. The assassin was to do his work before the wedding could take place. We did not want your cousin Penny to marry only to be widowed. Our assassin followed Rocco for several weeks, waiting for the right opportunity. The opportunity came when Rocco visited the Island a week or so before the wedding was scheduled."

"I knew nothing about Rocco's visit," said

Victoria.

"Rocco wanted to assure himself that he was marrying into wealth, so he came here, to your beautifully maintained historic home. Seeing it, he decided his bride came from wealth."

"Far from it," said Victoria, shaking her head.

"It so happened that my stepson Caesar had followed my onetime son, Rocco, to Martha's Vineyard, intending to eliminate him," said Giovanni. "Caesar was a bitter man after the accident. A bitter man. The accident destroyed him. He looked like a man, but he was no longer a man. He followed Rocco to your beautiful house. It was a foggy night. Our hired assassin mistook Caesar for Rocco."

"Oh, my," said Victoria. "Such a tragedy."

"The tragedy is that my stepson Caesar was killed," said Giovanni.

"Please, tell Mrs. Trumbull how it happened," said Giovanni. "It was understandable that Caesar was mistaken for Rocco. Even though they were not related, they looked alike and were often thought brothers."

"There was and is no excuse," said Leonardo. "I take responsibility."

"Mrs. Trumbull, I asked my cousin Leonardo to tell me, for my own peace of mind, where my Caesar died. This is what he told me. Caesar came here, to Martha's Vineyard, with the intention of killing Rocco."

Victoria sat forward. "Caesar came here? To kill Rocco?"

Giovanni turned to Leonardo. "You will have to continue with the story, Leonardo. I can't." He leaned forward and put his head in his hands. "The irony!"

"Yes, the irony," said Leonardo. "Giovanni, here, my cousin, my dear cousin, wished to know specifically where his Caesar died. Caesar was more of a son to him than either Rocco or Dominic. He wished to visit the very spot where he died." He looked up at Victoria. "So we are here."

"What do you mean? asked Victoria.

Giovanni looked up, tears in his eyes. "Tell her, Leonardo."

Leonard sat up straight and took a deep breath. "I hired an assassin to kill Rocco. An honor killing for what he had done to my daughter, Lily. Giovanni understood. The assassin followed Rocco here to Martha's Vineyard and to your beautiful house."

"Rocco?" asked Victoria. "I didn't meet Rocco until the day before yesterday."

"Rocco came to Martha's Vineyard a week or so earlier than was expected," said Leonardo. "We can only assume he wanted to check out the bride's family home to make sure she was what she appeared to be."

"Without your awareness, Mrs. Trumbull," said Giovanni. "That would be Rocco."

"At least, that's what we assume," said Leonardo. "Caesar, intent on his mission to kill Rocco, followed him here, to your home." He paused, and lifted his wine glass to Victoria. "A very lovely old mansion on a considerable property. On Martha's Vineyard, I might add."

He paused, took a sip from his wine glass, set it down on the table, and continued. "My helper, the assassin, came here, following Rocco. From what I have learned since, Caesar too was following Rocco, close on his heels. Like a good hunting dog, a Spinone. I assume he was looking for the right opportunity. To kill."

Victoria looked from Leonardo to Giovanni. There was nothing she could say.

"I have learned this only recently," Leonardo continued, turning to face Victoria. "My helper did not know of Caesar's presence." He paused.

"Go on, please, Leonardo," said Giovanni when Leonardo paused.

"The day, the evening, was foggy. My helper followed Rocco on his visit, unaware

443

of Caesar's presence. Caesar, of course, did not expect danger to himself. Killing Rocco was uppermost in his thoughts."

Victoria gazed in horror at Giovanni. The tale he was telling was unreal to her. A hired assassin was a thing of fiction.

Leonardo shrugged, as though he understood how she felt. "My helper saw a man prowling around the grounds and was convinced it was Rocco. Rocco was also on the prowl, but he was not in the same place as Caesar. When the appropriate time came . . . Well, you can see how it happened."

When Victoria was able to speak after what she'd heard, she said, "Why did the assassin hang Caesar in my cellar? Did he realize he had killed the wrong man?"

"No. He was convinced he'd killed Rocco, and informed me that he had done so."

"My cellar?" Victoria asked again. "Why?"

"He needed to get rid of the body. No one was around. There were no cars in your drive, no lights on in your house that foggy afternoon. He didn't know when you might return."

Giovanni shifted in his chair, took a white linen handkerchief out of his pocket, and wiped his eyes.

"Since your cellar is accessed from the

outside by old-fashioned bulkhead doors, my helper opened one of the doors, went down your stone steps, and saw there was a light that could be turned on down there. He saw your tools, ladders, ropes, drop cloths, and what looked like an unsuccessful attempt at growing mushrooms. A bed of dried manure."

Victoria nodded.

"He also saw there were exposed beams around which a rope could be looped. So he carried the body of Caesar, believing it was Rocco, down into the cellar."

"Rocco was under the impression this was a warning to him. So this was not intended as a warning," said Victoria.

"It was simple expediency. A way to get rid of the body quickly. My helper is not bright enough to think of sending a sophisticated message."

The three sat. Victoria rocked in the rocker. Giovanni sipped his wine. Leonardo reached for the bottle and refilled their glasses. A car went by on the Edgartown Road. The town clock rang the hour. The guinea fowl called their distinctive "go-back, go-back, go-back." A car horn blared. Brakes squealed. The guineas scolded.

Giovanni spoke. "Leonardo, we must trust Mrs. Trumbull with what we know to be the truth. I wish you to tell the rest of the story to her."

Leonardo set the bottle down on the coffee table and leaned back in the chair. "I contacted my helper," said Leonardo. "I informed him that he had taken care of the wrong person. That he must come home at once. Forget his original mission. No more killings. Enough. He was told in no uncertain terms."

"Leonardo's helper knew what awaited him," said Giovanni.

Victoria did not watch television. In fact, she did not own a TV set. Nor did she read books about the Mob. Yet everything she was hearing sounded familiar. And fanciful. This could not be real.

"Yet the helper is single-minded. He had been given a task, and he was determined to carry out that task."

Victoria stopped rocking and sat forward. "So it was your hired assassin who killed Rocco?"

"We believe so," said Giovanni.

"But you're not sure?" said Victoria.

"One can never be sure of anything," said Leonardo. "However, the helper will not make another mistake."

"You killed him?" asked Victoria, horrified.

Leonardo shrugged. "I don't soil my hands with murder, Mrs. Trumbull."

"Justice has been done," said Giovanni. "We hope you can explain to the most excellent sergeant at the police station that Lily did not kill Rocco. He does not need to believe anything she may claim."

"Giovanni and I believe you can explain all this more clearly than we can. He has no need to contact either Giovanni or me."

As soon as the Bentley pulled out of her drive, Victoria called Sergeant Smalley. "John," she said, "I can only explain what I've just learned when you are off duty and can relax over a rather tall glass of bourbon."

Smalley was there within the hour. It was close to midnight.

Victoria related as best she could what Leonardo and Giovanni had told her.

Smalley hadn't touched his drink. "Did Lily kill Rocco? Or did their hired assassin kill him?"

"I don't think we will ever know for certain," said Victoria.

They sat quietly. A car went by on the Edgartown Road. Somewhere a bird made a sleepy sounding call. The town clock chimed.

Smalley lifted his glass to her, and she did

the same.

"I believe this will have to go on the books as case closed."

ABOUT THE AUTHOR

Cynthia Riggs is the author of fourteen books in the Martha's Vineyard mysteries featuring 92-year-old poet, Victoria Trumbull. She was born on Martha's Vineyard and is the eighth generation to live in her family homestead, which she runs as a bed and breakfast catering to poets, writers, and other creative people. She has a degree in geology from Antioch College and an MFA in creative writing from Vermont College. For 20 years she held a US Coast Guard Masters License (100-ton vessels). In May 2013, she married Howard Attebery, who came back into her life after sixty-two years. Howard died in 2017.

The employees of Thorndike Press hope you have enjoyed this Large Print book. All our Thorndike, Wheeler, and Kennebec Large Print titles are designed for easy reading, and all our books are made to last. Other Thorndike Press Large Print books are available at your library, through selected bookstores, or directly from us.

For information about titles, please call:
(800) 223-1244

or visit our website at:
gale.com/thorndike

To share your comments, please write:
Publisher
Thorndike Press
10 Water St., Suite 310
Waterville, ME 04901